Advance Praise for

MOM BRAIN

"Sharp, propulsive, and wildly inventive, Nicole Hackett's latest is *Nine Perfect Strangers* meets *The School for Good Mothers*. A group of women trying to 'fix' their mom brains on a Hawaiian retreat takes dark, unnerving, and deliciously twisty turns. Provocative and whip smart, the book crackles with biting and incisive observations on the complexities of motherhood. I couldn't put it down!"

—Jaclyn Goldis, author of *The Last Time We Saw Her* and *The Chateau*

"Nicole Hackett's *Mom Brain* is twisty and suspenseful, with sharp commentary on modern motherhood set against a lush, escapist backdrop. It's a riveting and eye-opening page-turner that explores the ways parenting can fundamentally impact female identity."

—Audrey Ingram, *USA TODAY* bestselling author of *The Summer We Ran*

"Smart, tense, and deeply human, *Mom Brain* cuts to the heart of what mothers carry. Nicole Hackett writes with empathy and the fearless kind of truth-telling I admire."

—Jessica Guerrieri, award-winning author of *Between the Devil and the Deep Blue Sea* and *Both Can Be True*

"Captivating, smart, and funny, *Mom Brain* is perfect for fans of Liane Moriarty. This wildly imaginative story immerses us in a Hawaiian retreat for struggling mothers—an irresistible setting packed with secrets, mystery, and suspense. Yet this is more than a thrilling, escapist page-turner—it's a compelling exploration of motherhood in modern society, with our fears and triumphs, vulnerabilities and powers. This thought-provoking read defies categorization, offering complex emotions, surprising insights, and a dash of the speculative. I couldn't put this book down!"

—Laura Resau, author of *The Alchemy of Flowers* and *The River Muse*

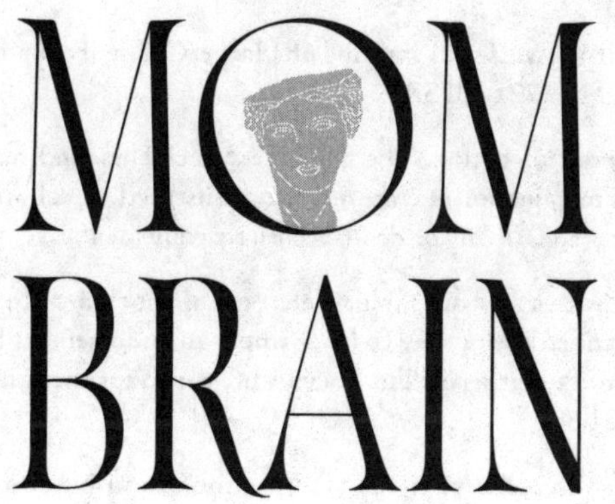

A NOVEL

NICOLE HACKETT

HARPER MUSE

Mom Brain

Published by Harper Muse, an imprint of HarperCollins Focus LLC, 501 Nelson Place, Nashville, TN 37214, USA.

HarperCollins Publishers, Macken House, 39/40 Mayor Street Upper, Dublin 1, D01 C9W8, Ireland (https://www.harpercollins.com)

ISBN 978-1-4003-5034-6 (ePub)
ISBN 978-1-4003-5033-9 (TP)
ISBN 978-1-4003-5035-3 (downloadable audio)

Library of Congress Cataloging-in-Publication Data

CIP data is available upon request.

Art Direction: Halie Cotton
Cover Design: Faceout Studio
Interior Design: Jackie Alvarado

Printed in the United States of America

26 27 28 29 30 LBC 5 4 3 2 1

For women

Mighty is the force of motherhood!

—GEORGE ELIOT

Pacific Ocean

White Hall & Diamond

The Village

Arcadian Bay Café

Shell Room

Cabana

Attendee Villas

Cecilia's Office

Two Dove Hall

Front Office

ARCADIAN BAY RESORT *Oahu*

PART ONE

CHAPTER 1

No one dies on an ordinary Thursday.

This is Georgia's first irrational thought.

And then, in quick succession, the second, third, and fourth:

Asthma attack. Rat poison. Anaphylactic shock.

She just recently saw a video about a toddler who got into rat poison. It was tragic, and worse than that, it was totally avoidable. *Imagine that poor mother,* Georgia thought when she watched it. *Imagine that being your one big mistake.*

"Do the Hildebrandts use rat poison?" she asks.

The Hildebrandts are their neighbors, with whom they are friendly but not particularly close. Will struggles for a moment, confused by the question, and rightly so. Will didn't see the video, and besides, the Hildebrandts don't use rat poison. The Hildebrandts are environmentalists.

"Do they— What?" His eyes don't leave Clover. He's afraid, and he's never afraid. The fear looks almost indecent on his face.

They're standing in their dark bedroom. Georgia is holding their five-year-old, Clover, who breathes in, breathes out. Georgia can feel her little body working; each breath is a strained, unusual whistle. It's such a foreign sound, and this doesn't make sense to Georgia. Never has her daughter felt foreign before. Never, not once. She read once that children's cells remain permanently in their mothers' bodies, another random thought. And then, back to the first one:

It's an ordinary Thursday. No one dies on an ordinary Thursday night.

CHAPTER 2

But even if that were true, it's no longer Thursday. It's actually Friday—one o'clock in the morning—when Georgia speeds into the ER parking lot.

A rumble strip thumps beneath them. "Mommy," says Clover, a question and a reprimand at the same time. At five, Clover no longer believes her mom hangs the moon, but she believes Georgia bears some responsibility for its appearance each night.

"Yes, baby?"

She's talking. That's a good sign. No one dies when they're strong enough to talk.

Clover breathes in, and again, that whistle, that awful, foreign sound. She looks more tired, more *something*, than she should.

Georgia parks badly, jumps from the car. Undoes her daughter's car seat. It isn't Thursday, and it isn't ordinary. In seven hours, Georgia is supposed to be boarding a flight across the ocean. She's going to Hawaii, which feels ridiculous now in the orange halo of the parking lot light.

~

There's a woman at the front desk behind a plexiglass window. She looks at Clover, looks at Georgia. Nods. Types. She tells Georgia to stay there, not to sit down, even though all around them other emergencies wait slumped in their seats.

"Croup," Georgia repeats exactly thirteen minutes later in ER triage. The room smells like antiseptic and Clover's hair, a mix of bubble bath and sweat.

"Inflammation of the airways," the nurse tells her, not for the first time since they've arrived. "It's rarely life-threatening, but still, it's good you brought her in."

Georgia blinks. The way the nurse says it, it all sounds so unremarkable. *Inflammation of the airways.* The last time Georgia bought makeup, the perky salesgirls offered her some product for her "super-inflamed under-eyes."

"The steroid should take care of it," the nurse adds, kindly but distinctly unmoved. This is, for her, just another patient, just another night.

In Georgia's lap, Clover squirms. She didn't like the steroid, a viscous white liquid delivered in a plastic orange syringe, but she took it without complaint. Georgia worries about this sometimes: her daughter's obedience, her rigid regard for directions and rules. But as Will once told her, "She *is* your daughter, you know."

"The steroid. That's . . . Okay." Georgia brings her hand to her forehead, but it's cold in the room, so there's no sweat to wipe. Watching her, the nurse seems to soften.

She says, more gently this time, "She'll be okay, Ms. Evans, although the doctor will probably want to keep you for a little while. Just for an hour or so, to monitor her before you go home."

"Right," says Georgia. "Okay. Yes. Good."

She wants to ask, *How did this happen?* She wants to say, *I still feel scared.* She wants to tell the nurse that she's supposed to go on a trip this very morning, and for reasons she can't articulate, that bears some of the blame somehow.

CHAPTER 3

Clover falls asleep on the drive home, and thanks to the steroid, her breathing is easy and quiet—so quiet, in fact, it's almost like Georgia is alone in the car.

Georgia sits in the car alone sometimes, on those rare occasions she's out somewhere without the girls. She'll turn off the engine and roll down the window and scroll mindlessly on her phone. It's a waste of time, even more when you consider how little time she has to begin with. She doesn't even *like* social media, not really, but she does like how easy it is. She likes the fact that it takes no work and there are no consequences. She likes how little it demands.

Silence. At three o'clock in the morning, on the way home from the ER, a silent car doesn't feel quite so luxurious.

She glances up at the rearview mirror. Clover's head is lolled to the side, her fairy eyelashes soft against her cheeks. Georgia thinks of Will, the breathless way he answered the phone earlier while she and Clover were still in triage, waiting for a room. When she told him the diagnosis, once he registered all was fine, he made a sound like she'd never heard from him before. In all their years together, it was the first time she had witnessed him truly, existentially scared.

She rolls her neck, checks the clock. Clicks on the radio, then turns the volume down so low she can barely hear it. The ER doctor wrote them a prescription for another dose of steroid that they "almost certainly will not need." It now looms beside her on the passenger seat.

It's 3:23 a.m. when they pass the Hildebrandts', and in her head, she says a short apology. It was unfair to suspect them, even as briefly as she did, because of course this wasn't their fault. The Hildebrandts are kind, conscientious people—the type who recycle and donate and vote. They have an electric vehicle and some vague role in the HOA, and the other day, when Georgia crossed paths with Darla Hildebrandt on their driveways, Darla graciously acted like it was any other Tuesday, like she hadn't seen the cop car recently parked in front of Georgia's house.

When she pulls into her own driveway—close enough to the Hildebrandts' that they share a line of boxwoods—the sight doesn't register at first. She sees it, illuminated by her headlights and impossible to miss. And the funny thing is, she understands it to be out of place, although it takes her a beat, two beats, before her mind catches up with what she's seeing.

It takes her that long to be afraid.

Will raps on the window, and Georgia jumps—actually jumps, thumping her chest against the seat belt she's still in. Her husband's face is a shadow outside her window, hard to make out.

She goes to release her seat belt and realizes her hand is shaking; she's surprised she was able to text him with it. She wonders if she's in shock. She's never been in shock before, and the possibility now feels slightly pathetic.

In the back seat, Clover continues to sleep. She has no idea something has happened, and maybe nothing really has.

Georgia unlocks the door, and Will opens it. With the car now off, the headlights dark, the bra hanging on the garage door feels much less threatening. It's just a bra, limp and almost even funny.

(Almost.) The bra is bright red and lacy, and the thought crosses Georgia's mind that someone went out of their way and bought the bra specifically for this purpose. Surely no one just *has* a bra like that.

"I was afraid they might still be out here," Georgia says, apologetic.

Will says gently, "I know."

She stands behind him as he opens the back door and lifts Clover from the car seat. Clover shifts, sighs, but doesn't wake. Georgia follows them up the front walk and into the house. They leave the bra strung from the garage door handle without discussing it.

CHAPTER 4

She hears Will close the door to Clover's bedroom at the exact same time the alarm on her phone goes off. Before bed—before she knew what sort of night they'd be having—she set the three thirty alarm for her eight o'clock flight in the hopes she might do her makeup before leaving. (This was arguably delusional, even then.)

A moment passes, and Will appears in their doorway. His hair stands on end, and she can almost see it: his hand running through it over and over and over again. He did the same thing both times she was in labor, and he does it whenever he's watching an important football game. It makes her feel tender; she wants to comfort him. Alternatively, she wants to crawl under the covers and close her eyes.

She puts her hands on her hips and bows her neck forward, but she doesn't actually feel tired. She suspects this is due to adrenaline, which means that at some point—probably some point very soon—she'll crash. This is unfortunate, as she really doesn't have time to crash.

Will crosses the room and sits down next to her.

"I wonder where she got it," he says.

They should've put a camera on the garage, she thinks. They put one on their front door, but the garage is a blind spot.

She says, "Got what?"

"Croup. Is it contagious?"

She blinks. Will teaches American Literature at an all-boys high school, so he knows quite a bit about quite a lot, although he doesn't know much about biology or medicine or (although she'll never say this) the female body, generally.

"I don't know. But the croup isn't an illness. It's a symptom of an illness. Like—I don't know. A cough. You can get a cough from a million different bugs."

"Ah."

She rests her temple on his shoulder, and he kisses the crown of her head.

"Did they say what the illness is?" he asks her. "What bug she has?"

She closes her eyes. "No. I mean, she has a runny nose. It could just be a cold."

At this, they both go silent. A runny nose. So mundane, it's almost funny. (Almost.)

"I hate that they have our address," she says. She doesn't explain what she means by this.

Will nods grimly, not needing an explanation.

"I know," is all he says.

"I hate that we don't know who's doing it."

He strokes her hair. "I know," he says again.

The first time this happened, the cops asked if she suspected anybody, but of course she didn't. That bra, the first one, was a practical nude color that she could envision coming from a normal underwear drawer. Still, she couldn't picture a single person in her life doing something like that. Not when the people in her life are: Darla Hildebrandt with her yoga butt and Lululemon half-zips. Aaron Hildebrandt in his white crew socks. Her colleagues, all left-leaning and highly educated, who probably wash their bras the way you're supposed to, in one of those little mesh bags.

She says in a whisper, "Maybe I should stay."

He turns to her, and she can't help it; she looks away. She knows this isn't fair to him. She's never once seen in his eyes what she's afraid of seeing, any of the things she's been called since she was revealed as the *Pacific*'s anonymous source: courageous, briefly, but then bitch, slut, and attention whore.

"Is that what you want?" he says, sounding so earnest that this—of all the things that have happened this night—makes her want to cry.

"I don't know. What if it happens again? Clover's breathing, I mean. What if it gets worse?"

"Then we have the medicine."

"But what if it doesn't work?"

"It'll work, Georgia. The doctor wasn't concerned."

"I hate leaving her sick."

"I know you do. And I get it, but she's not that sick, and I'll be here."

To this, Georgia doesn't say anything, mostly because what she wants to say is unfair. Will is a great father—"Danny Tanner–level," as her friend Julie likes to say—and she trusts him totally. But still, he's not the girls' mother. He's not her.

"What should I do?" she says quietly, hoping that maybe by asking the question, she will find the answer becoming clear. Like flipping a coin, that split second before it lands and you realize what you're hoping for. Georgia is notorious for doing this, for everything from what to have for dinner to what show to watch afterward. "Sushi," she'll blurt before Will has even tossed the coin, and somehow, despite how annoying this must be, he never acts annoyed.

But this isn't dinner. This is Georgia, thousands of miles away. Georgia, standing in Clover's doorway earlier that night, unable to move. She could hear the noise, that unsettling whistle, and could see her daughter, a mess of bedsheets and strawberry-blonde hair. It was only a second that Georgia was like this, frozen useless by her fear, but a second is all it takes sometimes.

"I think," Will says finally, thoughtfully, "that you need to do what you think is right. It's totally up to you."

She closes her eyes. This, she knows, is his sincere attempt at an answer, because Will has always suffered from this illusion—an unshakable, unjustified sense that she knows the right thing to do.

"I don't know what to do, though," she says, the tiredness finding her finally. It's a heaviness that starts in her shoulders, extends down her arms and to her legs. Maybe, in a different version of their lives, she could be what Will believes her to be: a woman who knows what to do, and when. In this one, though, she's not that woman. In this one, she's just tired.

CHAPTER 5

In a window seat, next to a pretty woman with a manicure, Georgia sets down her little plastic cup in the top right corner of her tray. The woman beside her ordered a V8 and vodka, and for a second, Georgia considered doing the same. She's never been drunk on a plane before, and while now isn't the ideal time to start, something about the idea felt exciting.

But she didn't. In the end, she just got a club soda, which she fumbled taking from the flight attendant, spilling some on her lap. And then, even more humiliatingly, the pretty woman next to her offered her a napkin, to which Georgia started to cry. "I'm sorry," she said, just as astonished by the tears as the rest of them. "I'm just really tired."

Georgia has made herself as unremarkable as possible since then, doing her best to embody an empty seat, and the woman, surely relieved by this, hasn't said anything else to her. She is now reading an e-reader, which Georgia has not looked at, even though she's curious. She can't remember the last time she read a book other than *Little Critter* or *Amelia Bedelia*. (She meant to buy one for this trip, but she went to Target and cried in the bestseller aisle instead.)

She takes a sip of her club soda and thinks of Clover, of that sound she made only a few hours earlier. That horrible, horrible noise. She wonders if by leaving the way she did, she's creating a lasting childhood wound in her daughter—in both daughters, actually. When she called Will earlier, just before stepping onto the jet bridge, she heard Ruby crying in the background, and the thought struck

Georgia so swiftly, it took her breath away: She was so worried about Clover, she had forgotten to worry about Ruby, their other daughter, now nearly one. And what if something happens? What if there's a plane crash? What if the last memory Ruby has of her mother is Georgia pleading with her at bedtime to go to sleep?

But this is unhelpful. She does not need to be thinking about Ruby, or about plane crashes. She can only imagine her seatmate's horror if she started to cry again.

Instead, she reaches beneath her tray table, finding her laptop bag, from which she pulls a folder. The folder is a heavy matte plastic in a modern but serious shade of millennial pink. She has read its contents before—read them so often, in fact, that with a gun to her head, she might be able to recite them from memory. ("Felony memory challenges are rampant," Will joked when she said this recently.)

On the first page, the font is a simple sans serif in another confident shade of pink. It starts:

> Mothers today are equipped with more tools and information than at any other time in history, and yet, modern motherhood leaves women feeling more drained than ever before. Mothers today are challenged by endless expectations and disproportionate burdens. To put it simply, mothers today are drowning, and despite this, they are one of the least supported groups.

Georgia likes this thought, the idea that some of her predicament is not her fault. She thinks about this paragraph sometimes like a guilty pleasure, like sneaking an ice cream sandwich from the freezer in the middle of the night. But of course, reality inevitably finds her. There's always Clover the next morning, standing accusatorially by the trash can, having found the wrapper in the trash.

And there's the memory of her grandmother, her mom's mom, who more or less raised Georgia after her mom died when she was little. Babcia was a very small, very Catholic Polish immigrant with strong opinions on frozen pierogies, the current pope, and women who complained when they should not. (Which was, in Babcia's mind, most of the time.) (Although it should be noted that Babcia also never had to juggle a law firm's billable hour requirement and the different but equally ludicrous number of kindergarten spirit weeks.)

She continues reading.

> At The Program, we aim to change that. Our philosophy is simple: The best way to support mothers is to give them the tools to support themselves. The Program isn't simply a break from the demands of modern motherhood. We help mothers take back control of their lives with a groundbreaking curriculum based on three main pillars: Relearn, Reflect, and Redefine. Set against the backdrop of the breathtaking island of Oahu, The Program is an immersive weeklong experience that gives mothers the tools to transform their lives and, ultimately, themselves.

It's good marketing. She knows this because when she first read this paragraph, she felt as though it was written specifically for her. No matter the obvious: It's just promotional material. It was probably written by a twentysomething copyeditor still deciding whether she wants to have kids herself. Georgia knows this, and yet it didn't matter when she first read it. She read it, and for just a moment, she let herself believe.

CHAPTER 6

Had it been up to Georgia, she would've gotten a rental car at the airport the way she usually does. In fact, she would've preferred that to the driver The Program offered, the one whose car she's in now. She would've liked to roll down the window, maybe turn on some music. She would've liked the idea that, for however briefly, not a single person in the world knew where she was.

Instead, she's in the back seat, where she doesn't roll down the window. She crosses, then uncrosses her legs, nervously taps her foot. It's a very nice car. The seats are black perforated leather that smells exactly the way you would expect black perforated leather to smell. The driver is wearing a matching black polo, and when Georgia first saw it, she felt the illogical urge to apologize. (It's too hot to be wearing something so dark, although this is obviously not her fault.)

On Georgia's lap, her phone doesn't have service, which isn't a shock. They're climbing what she knows to be the footprint of an extinct volcano, and it does indeed look prehistoric. The trees are fluorescent and leafy, and the ground is carpeted with plush green moss. The road winds into a pocket of mist trapped between ridges, so much more breathtaking than even the most beautiful pictures online.

This isn't what she first imagined from Hawaii. Before everything, before The Program was even a thought in her mind, she'd had a shockingly uneducated grasp of the islands. She'd imagined postcards, mostly: white sand beaches, fruity little drinks with paper umbrellas. She'd imagined Polynesian men juggling fire for a drunk resort crowd. It's embarrassing now, in the back seat of this nice black sedan, looking out at the vast brilliance of the island, how easily she fits into the role of tourist.

As the car ascends farther, her ears start to pop, and she feels something that's either very big or nothing at all. She thinks of the folder tucked into the bag beside her and the woman with the manicure on the plane. Just before they landed, feeling jittery, Georgia couldn't help herself: She asked the woman if she was there on vacation, because Georgia has an annoying tendency to talk when she's nervous. The woman was gracious and said something in response, although Georgia was so anxious she didn't hear what it was.

The Program is hosted by the Arcadian Bay Resort, a "vivifying" (per the website) luxury resort on the eastern side of the island. It's not clear from the website whether the resort is open to the public when it's not being used by The Program, which is something she would have figured out already in a different circumstance. She's usually a meticulous researcher—"rabid," as Will jokes—but things just happened so fast. There were no spots open in The Program, but her employer (Bird and Chen LLP, one of the largest law firms in the capital) made it happen, and Georgia was in no place to question, much less to research.

The driver makes a sudden turn, and Georgia grips the handle above the window. She has a friend from work, Julie, who calls it the "oh shit" handle, which is funny mostly because Julie doesn't normally curse.

The driver glances at the rearview mirror, but he's wearing sunglasses, so it's hard to make eye contact. She smiles anyway, as if to say, *All good back here!*

They're now descending a steep hill to the Arcadian Bay Resort, which is tucked along a bay that is, confusingly, not actually called Arcadian Bay. Based on the website, it seems that all the rooms have a view of the water, and as much as Georgia hates the water normally, even she agrees this is nice.

As they approach the resort, she peers over the driver's shoulder. She can see the bay in the distance, a shimmery expanse of cerulean water. Beyond it, the extinct volcano rises into the clouds.

Beautiful, she thinks.

She thinks of Clover struggling to breathe.

They come to a stop on the far side of a circular driveway. Her driver, moving briskly, opens her door while she's still gathering her bag. When she steps out, her feet crunch over a bed of tiny pink seashells.

In the middle of the driveway, on a circle of grass, is a Greek-looking sculpture: a woman, totally naked, with a soft, healthy stomach and round, sumptuous breasts. She has a crack in one arm, and the other is pointed at Georgia. Her eyes are empty, but somehow despite this, she still looks mad.

CHAPTER 7

The statue, as it turns out, is of the goddess Aphrodite. That's what the mousy girl tells Georgia as she leads her across the resort campus a few minutes later. She's wearing a light pink polo shirt with a logo on the breast pocket ("ARCADIAN BAY RESORT" wrapped around a conch shell). They're moving quickly as the girl narrates the campus, explaining that Cecilia Clements had the statue shipped from "like, actually Greece, I think." And then, in a single breath, "And down there, you'll see the villas. Each one has a view of the bay, which was super important to Cecilia when they were designing everything."

Georgia has heard a lot about Cecilia Clements, but she's never met her personally. Cecilia is the septuagenarian owner and founder of a rapidly growing DC-based organization called SHE, a client at the law firm where Georgia works. It is through this connection that Georgia is here, a favor to the firm, though not quite to Georgia specifically. Georgia hasn't done work for SHE herself (she works on patents mainly, whereas SHE seems to work primarily with trade secrets), but she walks past its headquarters sometimes on her way to lunch.

The villas are at the very bottom of the hill, lining the mouth of the bay. The staircase to them is narrow and precariously steep.

"You're in, like, one of the nicest suites available," the girl says chattily. She's bouncing happily, unlike Georgia, who has one hand on the railing, the other clutched to her waist.

"Each villa is a duplex, and I'm so sorry, but I forgot to see who you're sharing with. But anyway, I'm sure you'll meet her at Opening Dinner tonight."

They reach the bottom of the steps.

Opening Dinner was on the itinerary Georgia got in the mail a few weeks earlier, accompanied by a packing list. She is now, in fact, prepared for two formal dinners—one the first night, one the last. (She also packed a third, just in case.) The rest of the packing list was much vaguer with various cryptic suggestions: *something to lounge in, something to move in.*

"Something to move in?" Georgia said to Will when she read this. "Do you think we're going to be *working out?*" The thought panicked her, which is ironic given everything else that was going on at the time. Then again, it's possible Georgia was worried about the surprise exercise not because she doesn't exercise (she doesn't), but because it illustrated something else: the fact that she had no idea what to expect.

The partner at her law firm, the one who works with Cecilia and secured Georgia her spot for the week, is one of those equally terrifying and mystifying people who *like* to exercise. Her name is Dana, and when she told Georgia about The Program, Georgia spotted a sleek black Fitbit around her wrist. "Take up space," she said to Georgia at that meeting, with a sort of sincerity that made Georgia blush. "This is still your narrative. Don't give them that."

Once in her villa, she calls Will like he asked her to, even though for him, it's the middle of the night.

"Gi," he says sleepily on the first ring. In her head, she does some quick math: six hours ahead, so close to midnight. She should have let him sleep.

"Hey," she says. "Made it."

"Good. That's— Hold on."

There's a rustle, and Georgia leans against the railing in front of her. She's on her villa's patio, the farthest out she can be without disconnecting from the Wi-Fi. (She still doesn't have service.) Around her, daylight is melting into a deep, syrupy orange, and she feels an ache looking out at the beginnings of a beautiful sunset. She can't quite name the feeling, but it's something familiar. Regret, possibly.

"Sorry," he says finally, his voice stronger. "Okay, so how are you? How was the flight?"

"Flight was fine. I'm—fine." She thinks of the woman with the manicure, her e-reader in its nice leather case. Georgia wants to imagine her in a fabulous resort somewhere, maybe having a fruity little drink. "Tired. How's it going there? Clover okay?"

"Clover's fine. Well, pissed she couldn't go to school this morning."

"Predictable."

"She is definitely your daughter."

This isn't an accusation, and she knows that. But still.

"Yeah. Well." Her thought floats off. She thinks of her phone, the most recent anonymous message: *You don't deserve to be a mom.* Will tells her to ignore the messages, and she does try. She really does.

"So," Will says after a moment. "How's Hawaii?"

She circles her toe on the floorboard. The villa is on stilts, although the tide is currently so low that beneath her she sees only black sand and smelly seaweed clumps.

"You know, I can feel the meltdown getting sucked out of me already."

Silence.

This was a joke, but it's not funny. In her law firm's defense, they specifically *didn't* use the word *meltdown* in any of their messaging.

The word came after the announcement, on Reddit threads and social media posts. Officially, she suffered a "mental health crisis," the type that a week in Hawaii should fix right up.

"Gi—" Will starts, but she cuts him off.

"Sorry," she says. "That wasn't funny."

And she thinks: *I hate this*. She hates that she's here without him, describing something to him that he, in a different version of their lives, might've experienced himself. They almost chose Hawaii for their honeymoon, and maybe *that's* where they went wrong. A butterfly flapping its wings in China and all the rest. Maybe there's a world out there where they are here together, on vacation, enjoying the romantic sunset. Tomorrow, they could pack a lunch, make a day of it. Come back after and have sex in the shower, which she usually finds slippery and stressful, but she wouldn't, not as this version of herself.

"But it's . . ." She closes her eyes, breathes in a giant whiff of seaweed. "Nice. It's very nice."

"Nice," Will repeats, and she feels the ache again, this time more intensely.

"Yes. 'DC woman discovers that Hawaii is pretty.' Alert the media at once."

He chuckles, but it sounds hollow, and then it stops.

CHAPTER 8

The partner at Georgia's firm, the one who presumably came up with the solution of sending Georgia to The Program, pronounces her name *Dan-uh*, not *Day-na*, which Will thinks is pretentious. Will, who doesn't normally have mean thoughts like this. "What's wrong with the normal pronunciation?" he said, which was unfair to Dana, because *Dan-uh* is a normal pronunciation. Still, Georgia appreciated the effort it took for Will to be this petty on her behalf.

"This is still your narrative," Dana told Georgia that day in her office, which was possibly a nice and normal thing to say in that situation, although it was just as possibly the type of thing you say only if you are, in fact, pretentious. Maybe the narrative really does still belong to Georgia, but the narrative feels like a luxury at this point. The more pressing problem, the one she cares about, is what actually happens next.

And that isn't up to her at all.

The problem is that no one can agree on what should happen next, because no one can agree on what exactly she deserves. Will thinks she deserves grace, and of course he does. (Besides being her husband, he's a very compassionate man.) Her law firm thinks she deserves a chance to correct the situation. (The Program, they say, is a good start.) The internet is split; most think she deserves justice, although that's either a kindness or a threat, depending on who you ask. Her friends don't know what to think.

In her villa bedroom, getting ready for dinner later that evening, she stands in front of the full-length mirror and tries to see herself the way Will does. Will, who thinks she's beautiful, which is generous if not totally untrue. She's "big-boned," to put it diplomatically, with a flattish chest and biggish nose. Thinnish lips, largish pores. Not ugly, maybe even pretty in the right light with the right makeup, but not beautiful, and certainly not beautiful enough for her wrongs to be ignored. Not when the wrongs are as big as hers.

Even before they published the article in the *Pacific,* they expected it to be big. There were talks of the "zeitgeist," which Georgia agreed was exciting even if she didn't know what the current zeitgeist was. Women's empowerment? Lactational freedom? #MeToo? This was the sort of information she once would've known, when she'd had the extravagance of extra brain space. At one point in her life, the whole thing would've consumed her: this legion of women speaking out, all their stories different, but in some ways—in the important ways—exactly the same. Unwanted sexual advances. Pay cuts after pregnancies. And Georgia's: an invasion of the most private of spaces—her firm's room for nursing mothers. Of course it would be big! Everyone would pay attention. *Georgia* should have been paying attention, but she wasn't.

Instead, when the article came out, hand, foot, and mouth disease was running rampant through day care, and Ruby—with blisters in the back of her mouth, an alarming but not unheard-of symptom—was refusing to eat. And so Georgia was dealing with that, and also with her basement, which was suddenly collecting water, and a billable hour requirement that seemed to hover perpetually outside her reach. She gave her interview for the article, but that was the extent of her involvement, because Georgia, it turns out, was too busy for zeitgeists.

She started really paying attention only when her name came out as one of the anonymous sources for the article, but by that point, the damage was done. By then it was much too late.

She tucks a piece of hair behind her ear, then untucks it, but it doesn't matter. Like always, she can't see herself the way Will does. And yet, she can't see what the internet does either. Her law firm called her story a "misrepresentation of events" in its official statement, but to the internet, it's much simpler. To the internet, Georgia is a liar.

She gives up finally and turns from the mirror. She moves to her villa's little kitchenette, where on the sleek little table, her welcome basket sits. The girl from earlier—her name is Leila, Georgia has since figured out—was emphatic about the welcome basket when she gave Georgia her keys. She told Georgia excitedly that the dried pineapple was made right here on the island, and Georgia thanked her with matching energy, not having the heart to tell her that pineapple makes her tongue itch.

Based on the map in her welcome basket, it should take her less than five minutes to get to dinner, but she gives herself ten minutes just in case.

The air is thick and salty, and in the glow of sunset, everything takes on a flattering tinge of pink. In this light, it's easier to imagine she is just like any of the other women on the island—beautifully, sympathetically stressed out. One week at The Program costs just over ten grand, and because of this, Georgia has a certain (perhaps unfair) expectation of whom she's going to meet: college-educated, progressive suburban women with white Range Rovers and two point five kids all named Dax. They'll do Pilates and drink their vegetables and have a bit too much Riesling at their monthly bunco nights, and sure, maybe they'll be in crisis, but it will be a tidy, solvable issue bearing no resemblance to Georgia's catastrophic events.

Dinner is under a cabana at the edge of the bay with sand along the perimeter and a thatched palm roof. There are two tiki torches at the front, between which stands a tall, smiling woman with widely spaced teeth.

"Aloha," says the woman as Georgia nears. She is very white with a halo of reddish flyaways framing her face.

"Aloha," Georgia replies, feeling immediately stupid. She clears her throat. The tiki torches smell like citronella, the scent of summer, and she feels a pang of nostalgia for some alternate version of her life.

"You must be Georgia Evans," says the woman. "I'm Izzy, operations assistant here at The Program." She doesn't stop smiling even as she's speaking, and there's something very campy about this. Actually, there's something corny about her in general—possibly the way she stands, her feet set wide in an athletic stance. Or maybe it's the vague cheapness of her printed polyester dress. Her hair is pulled back into an inelegant ponytail, and she's not wearing any makeup. Georgia isn't sure why, but she decides she likes her at once.

"Yes. That's me. I'm— Yes."

The woman smiles, and Georgia wonders if this kind, cheerful corniness is what the whole week will be like. From the promotional material, she was expecting something else—something scarier, although perhaps that was just her being paranoid. She knows, objectively, that not everyone is a threat.

"Super," says Izzy, sounding genuinely excited. "Well, looks like you're in Pod Three. Let me take you back."

CHAPTER 9

There are four women in Pod Three, not counting Georgia: two blondes named Dede and Alice, a Black woman named Simone, and Logan, a gaunt woman with blue-green hair.

"We'll be starting soon," Izzy tells them with Georgia still standing next to her. "In the meantime, y'all can get acquainted with our icebreaker activity."

The woman directly to Georgia's left—Dede, one of the blondes—leans her head back and closes her eyes exasperatedly. This reaction startles Georgia, not necessarily because of what it is (this is exactly how she feels about icebreaker activities, actually), but more so because of the freedom with which she does it.

Izzy smiles down at Dede, looking totally undeterred by this response.

"Why don't you take the lead, Dede?" she says. "Have some fun with it." She holds out a small stack of what look like pink note cards. Dede sighs loudly, but she pushes herself forward and takes the deck.

"It's giving freshman orientation," she grumbles, to which Izzy responds with a cheerful chuckle. Georgia doesn't know what to make of any of this.

Izzy leaves them with Georgia still standing awkwardly half behind Dede. Dede looks up at her and frowns. Dede is very small and very, very thin. Georgia slides quickly into the seat beside her, feeling the heat of her stare.

"So your name's Georgia?" she says, her tone somewhat accusatory.

Georgia nods. "Yes. And you're—Dede?"

Dede ignores this. She is full-on examining Georgia now, the skin on her forehead fighting valiantly against an inquiring wrinkle. She is quite pretty, actually, although there's something a bit child-like about her as well.

"*Geor-gia*," she says again, this time like she's sounding it out. She pulls her mouth to the side in exaggerated thought. "You know what? I actually love it. Very vintage chic."

"Oh." Georgia doesn't know what to say to this, mostly because she isn't sure whether it's a compliment or an insult. "Thanks, I guess. My dad's mom was named Georgia Jean."

At this, Dede gives an unexpected hoot.

"Georgia Jean! Ohmygod. I *love* that. It sounds like a country song."

This time, Georgia doesn't even try for a response.

"My name's also a family name. Deidre. It comes from, like—I don't know. A great-great-great-aunt or something like that."

Georgia nods. "Oh. That's nice."

"Yeah," she says, before turning abruptly to the blue-haired woman across the table. "Logan, are you named after somebody? I *love* asexual names."

Logan—whose stringy, blue-green hair hangs to her shoulders—starts to flush. She also seems at a loss for what to say, to which Georgia feels very sympathetic.

Next to Logan, the other blonde, Alice, says unkindly, "I think you mean unisex?" There's nothing about Alice's face that's obviously off—she has all the correctly shaped features in all the correct spots—but for some reason, the cumulative effect isn't quite right. She somehow looks more like a sketch of a human than the actual human herself.

Dede gives a good-natured shrug, which causes Alice to suck on her teeth.

"Whatever," Dede says. "So should we do this or what?" She gives the note cards a flippant wave, to which no one responds. She plucks up the first card and squints at it for a moment before tossing it aside.

"It says to share your greatest fear," she says, sounding deeply bored. "I mean, this isn't even like, *creative*."

It's not creative, but Georgia doesn't mind. It's better than some icebreaker games she has played, where she's expected to come up with a hypothetical TED Talk title on the spot.

"So I'm from LA," Dede says, now sitting up straighter. "And we have fires there like, *all the time*. Anyway, when I was little, there was this awful one. Like, historically, historically bad. It came all the way to my neighborhood, where my aunt also lived. She was my *favorite aunt*, by the way, although obviously I don't wish fire on anyone. Anyway, she had this beautiful house that was all terracotta and white stucco with this adorable little courtyard, but then the fire came, and it burned the whole thing down." She shakes her head as though disgusted. "So that's mine. Fire."

For a moment, none of them say anything.

Then Logan says worriedly, "Was your aunt all right?"

Dede puckers her lips.

"Well, she lived, if that's what you mean. But her house burned down, so she wasn't like, great."

Logan doesn't seem chastised by this. She responds with a serious nod.

"But she moved to Rhode Island after that," Dede adds. "And I mean, no offense to Rhode Island, but she's the only person from my family who doesn't live in California. Like, literally, the singular person. And I don't know, does that seem right to you? Rhode *Island?* It's not even a real island, did you know that? And I'm sorry, but it's like, if you're going to be an island, then *be an island*, you know what I mean?"

Logan continues nodding through all of this, her expression studious. No one else seems sure how to respond. Georgia is both disappointed and thankful her friend Julie is not here, because this is the sort of thing Julie would laugh at, and when Julie starts laughing, Georgia usually does as well.

Dede, seemingly unaware of the silence around her, tosses the rest of the cards onto the table.

"This is *so* morbid, though," she says. "Like, right? Why couldn't we start with our favorite pets or something?"

This seems to reinvigorate Alice, who says dryly, "This isn't Girl Scout camp."

If this were directed to Georgia, she would feel like an idiot. Dede, though, just scoffs.

"You know, I heard Cecilia is a *bitch*," she says with a wicked smile. "My husband works with a guy whose wife just came a few months ago, and he says Cecilia's a *total* nazi."

At this, Georgia winces, although Dede doesn't seem to notice. She lets this hang in the air for a moment before she adds cheerfully, "But whatever she's doing, it apparently works."

"I bet he wouldn't call Cecilia a bitch if she were a man," says Alice.

"Well, yeah," says Dede. "Who would call a man a bitch?"

Across the table, the Black woman, Simone, snorts. Alice's eyes shoot to her before drilling back into Dede.

"What I mean is that the same qualities that are celebrated in men make a woman a bitch."

(This isn't totally true. What makes Alice a bitch would make a man a dick.)

"And besides," Alice adds, nostrils flaring, "why does it matter? As long as she delivers, she can be as bitchy as she wants."

"You sound like my husband," Dede says, wrinkling her nose. "He's like, 'Money? Who cares about money as long as you come back like Joey's wife?'"

No one, not even Alice, has anything to say to this.

CHAPTER 10

No one announces Cecilia Clements's arrival, because there's no need. In the center of the cabana, not saying a word, she seems to appear from nowhere, and at once all the women around her grow quiet.

There are four tables total under the cabana, three filled with what appear to be attendees, presumably three pods. At the fourth sit staff, including Izzy, although that's not where Cecilia came from. And indeed, with her matching linen pant set and delicate gold bangles around her thin wrists, it's hard to imagine her in any way associated with Izzy, who has, at some point, acquired a silk lei.

"Welcome," says Cecilia in a thick and velvety voice. "My name is Cecilia Clements, and this is your first night at The Program."

She isn't using a microphone, which Georgia suspects is on purpose; the address feels informal, almost intimate. Still, Georgia has to lean forward to hear over the soft sound of the tide outside the cabana, the chorus of noisy bugs from the bushes and trees. She gets the effect, but she would appreciate something a bit more practical.

"I know we're tired," says Cecilia. "Our journeys here have been long and strenuous. We are weary travelers, and on this road, more work lies ahead."

Next to Georgia, Dede makes a clucking sound, and privately, Georgia agrees: It is a bit *much*. Then again, what did they expect? It costs five figures to be here, and besides, Cecilia's not wrong.

Georgia *is* a weary traveler, and maybe it's nice to have someone make this feel poetic instead of just sad.

"And we will work," says Cecilia, these words cutting decisively through the background noise. "This week may be one of the most challenging of our lives. But just as important as our struggles is our rest." She raises her arms here in a way that reminds Georgia of Jesus Christ on the cross, which is unusual, as Georgia has never been especially religious. There's a brief pause, quiet but not quite silent, before Cecilia continues. "And so, in this space of restoration, I want you to feel responsible tonight for one thing and one thing only. Tonight," she says, "your only duty is to enjoy yourselves."

The buffet is a spectacle. There's more food with more garnish than Georgia had even at her wedding: heaps of fresh fruit and colorful sushi and nutty-smelling rice. Servers in prim white shirts wait at attention behind the platters, filling up women's plates. Georgia is behind Dede, and when they reach the smoked pig—whole, with intact eyeballs—Dede audibly retches. (She's a vegetarian, as she loudly announces.)

Georgia isn't a huge drinker, but she gets a drink anyway. It's lavender with an edible flower floating at the surface. She feels guilty about this; she knows that somewhere across the ocean, in a city that now feels worlds away, Will is sleeping with the baby monitor by his ear, each whimper, each cough, his alone to bear.

Back at their table, Alice has sectioned her plate into precise portions. Dede is swaying in her seat to the song overhead, something tropical. She looks completely at ease, and watching her, Georgia wonders what brought her here to this island—what brought any of them here, what long and strenuous road they've been on. She has the unnerving thought that she might even tell them why she's here, before considering the possibility that her drink is stronger than it tastes.

CHAPTER 11

Georgia had a friend—well, a friend of a friend, really—who once, in college, called her "anal." He wasn't being mean, at least not intentionally. He said it with one breath, and with his next, he ordered a burrito. And it was this—the banality of it, his excruciating matter-of-factness—that was so mortifying. They were in line at a fast-food Mexican restaurant, and Georgia had just ordered a salad, which wasn't *why* he'd called her anal, although the salad felt humiliating after that.

When Cecilia Clements appears back in the center of the cabana near the end of dinner, Georgia is drunk, which she understands to be highly inappropriate given the circumstance. And yet, despite this, or maybe because if it, she feels exhilarated. She thinks of the friend of a friend and wishes he were here to see her now, drunk in a situation she shouldn't be. Not so anal, is it?

"Ladies," says Cecilia, swimming slightly in Georgia's vision. She pauses for a moment even though all the women under the cabana have gone quiet.

"I want to first thank our culinary team. We are, as always, grateful for the creativity and joy of their nourishment."

Cecilia turns to the waitstaff, a line of only women with arms folded behind their backs. Cecilia bows, her hands pressed together at her chest. Georgia almost starts clapping but is just sober enough to stop herself.

The moment feels longer than it needs to be. Across the cabana, Izzy sits with the other staff members, looking attentive. At Georgia's table, Dede finishes her third drink with a single gulp, then works to fish out the flower. (She gave the flower from her second drink to Logan, who had never before experienced an edible flower, so Dede was insistent that she "at least take a bite.")

"Now," says Cecilia, looking back to her congregation, while Georgia takes another sip of her drink, non-anally. "A lot of our work this week will be conducted in our small groups—our pods, if you will. However, as we move through our time here on the island, I think it is important to remember that we are, ultimately, a unified coalition. We are only so strong as we are united."

"Oh my *god,*" Dede mutters, somewhat but not totally to herself. Having retrieved the flower, she tosses it in front of Logan, who looks down at it alarmedly.

"As we set out on this pursuit of healing and progress," Cecilia continues, evidently not hearing Dede across the cabana, "our first task is to break free from the shackles of isolation and anonymity. With this in mind, I would like for us to take this opportunity tonight to introduce ourselves to our fellow travelers."

"Lord," says Simone quietly, as next to her, Logan twirls a piece of bluish hair nervously around her finger. Next to her plate sit one and a half partially eaten hibiscus flowers.

"It's normal to be hesitant," says Cecilia, her expression tender. "To push oneself out of one's comfort zone is to elicit an array of uncomfortable feelings. What is crucial is that we embrace these feelings rather than fight them, for this is where true change occurs. And change *will* occur, if you are open to it. This is my promise here to you."

A few of the other women nod along with this. Logan picks up the newest flower and takes a hesitant bite.

Cecilia says, "So who here is ready to embrace the discomfort? Who will open themselves up to the challenge of going first?"

When Georgia was pregnant with Clover, her friend—the friend of the one who called her anal, actually—was also pregnant, a few months ahead of her. The friend, unlike Georgia, planned for an unmedicated birth. "I want to push myself," she told Georgia with a sort of sincerity that Georgia found equal parts annoying and admirable. The friend went through with it too, at a birthing center with essential oils and a curated playlist. Georgia, a few months later, accepted all the drugs she could get.

"I will," Georgia says, raising her hand. She looks up at it with a strange sense of detachment, like it's not hers, or at least not under her control. She remembers now why she doesn't drink. She likes to be in control, and this, her raised hand, is the exact opposite.

"*Excellent*," says Cecilia in a way that makes Georgia feel simultaneously terrified and pleased with herself. She purposefully avoids the eyes of the other women under the cabana as she stands up.

"Georgia Evans," Cecilia announces as Georgia makes her way forward, coming to a stop close enough to see Cecilia's white, nearly translucent flyaway hairs. "Georgia hails to us from DC, near SHE headquarters, in fact. Georgia, we're so very glad to have you with us. Why don't you tell us a little about yourself?"

Georgia is surprised, but not in an unpleasant way, that Cecilia knows who she is. Cecilia is much taller than Georgia expected. She's even taller than Georgia, who shot up to an embarrassing five foot ten her sophomore year in high school. And yet, whereas Georgia has always had a thick "linebacker" stature (per an uncle who didn't understand that this was a devastating thing to hear as a fifteen-year-old girl), Cecilia is as lean and willowy as a ballerina.

"Er," Georgia says, doing her best to sound sober. "Well, I'm Georgia. I'm a lawyer. I do IP—intellectual property—law in DC."

Silence, and maybe rightly so. Hearing it out loud, she recognizes this to be very boring. She tries to think of something more interesting about herself but cannot come up with a single interesting fact.

"Wonderful," says Cecilia, sounding genuine. She makes a motion with her hand, and from the staff table, one of the women stands up. She hurries toward them, holding what appears to be a small pink towel.

Cecilia nods briskly as the woman hands her the piece of fabric. The woman bows slightly, her eyes on the ground.

"Georgia," says Cecilia. (It's terry cloth, Georgia can see now—a terry cloth washcloth.) "You look radiant this evening."

At this, Georgia just nods, unsure what to say.

Cecilia says, "Please, would you wash your face for us?"

There's a beat, and it probably feels longer than it actually is, but in it, Georgia performs a series of quick calculations to determine whether she's actually asleep. Her dreams have always felt exceptionally realistic, and maybe this is one of them—a version of the naked dream, perhaps. The dream where she shows up to an important work function in her underwear. But no, here stands Cecilia, and over there, Izzy in her silk lei. The chill of the slight breeze, the tingle of salty air on her neck, all of it very real.

"Erm. Sorry?"

"A meaningful bond can never be achieved if we maintain our barriers. And as women, we are so skilled at shielding ourselves—hiding our bare face, as one example." She holds out the washcloth. It's folded into a perfect square. "Now, Georgia, I am asking you to remove your shield. I am asking you to wash your face and feel the strength of your raw self."

Georgia is wearing makeup. Of course she is. It's not much—a thin layer of foundation, some color on her cheeks—but still, the thought of removing it here, in front of these women, is distressing. Her blotchy, airplane-dried skin, the sick yellow beneath her eyes that won't go away no matter how much sleep she gets: These are not things she shares with most people, let alone with complete strangers like this.

"Um." She takes the washcloth and looks around. None of the other women are moving. Dede, who was previously leaning back with her arms crossed in front of her, has now pushed herself forward. Her eyes move between Cecilia and Georgia interestedly.

And what else is there to do but obey? So she does. She closes her eyes and brings the cloth to her face. It's warm. It's . . . *nice*. She starts on her right cheek, moving in slow circles. She thinks of the friend of a friend in line for a burrito and wonders if he was right.

She hands Cecilia back the cloth. The breeze from the bay feels cooler now against her damp skin. She expects to feel embarrassed and is surprised when she does not.

"Excellent," says Cecilia. "Thank you, Georgia. There is such beauty in your bravery."

Georgia just nods again, feeling a lot of things at once.

"Now," says Cecilia, handing the cloth to the silent staff member who has again appeared beside her, "here in this space of beauty and vulnerability is where true connection occurs. Georgia, I want you to tell your sister travelers one thing that might surprise them about yourself."

When Georgia will replay this moment later, she will stop the memory here, on this spot in particular, and try to recall what was going through her head. *What* exactly she was thinking when she looked Cecilia straight in the eye and said, "Well, I'm slightly allergic to pineapple, but I ate the bag of dried pineapple in my welcome bag anyway."

Cecilia looks at her for a moment, expressionless. A beat turns to two. And then, abruptly, she throws her head back and laughs.

"Excellent," she says. "Oh yes."

And then it's over. Georgia returns to her seat, and another woman comes to the front. She, too, washes off her makeup, and Cecilia was right: There is indeed something beautiful about it. Like a baptism, Georgia thinks drunkenly. Cecilia is gentle and encouraging, although she doesn't laugh again like she did at Georgia's answer.

When they finally finish, it's time for dessert. A line of white-shirted servers wait, ready with cups of sherbet and plates of pie. Georgia gets a piece of key lime, which she's never tried before because she doesn't usually like citrus. She's pleased, but not surprised exactly, to discover that she likes it after all.

CHAPTER 12

At four the next morning, Georgia wakes abruptly from a deep sleep. She blinks for a second, getting her bearings, then checks the clock and is disappointed by the time. Of course she was aware of the time difference before she came, but she naively thought it wouldn't affect her. As though she is so uniquely tired that the normal rules of jet lag wouldn't apply.

She checks her phone. As usual, she doesn't have service, and in her room, the Wi-Fi is slow. Giving up, she closes her eyes and goes over every single thing that happened the previous night.

The memory is vivid in some spots but blurry in others. Were it not for her dull headache, she might've thought it was all a dream. But no, it was real. It was as real as the other scrubbed faces of Pod Three. Alice's bare face looked older without her makeup. Dede's, the exact opposite. Logan and Simone weren't wearing much to begin with, so they looked more or less the same. And did any of this surprise her? Not really. The women are actually, unsurprisingly, more or less exactly as they appear. Dede owns a barre studio. Based on Logan's answer, it seems she might've had some trouble with the law. (Her greatest fear is "crazy people with guns," to which the rest of the pod just nodded silently.) Simone is a tenured professor whose dissertation was on gender intersectionality in the third-wave feminism movement. She's here as part of a new mental health initiative. ("They had me pick a program," she told the audience after washing her face, "and I figured, Hawaii's not the worst place to be.")

At four thirty, Georgia rises from bed and pads across the villa. She picks at the welcome basket, wishing she had more of the dried pineapple. She then checks the itinerary, opens the fridge and closes it again. Finally, she wanders out to the patio, where the slightest, haziest light of dawn traces the ridge of the mountain across the bay.

At 6:23 a.m., the phone in her villa rings, which she hears through her screen door. She jumps up, mostly out of surprise, and reaches it by the end of the second ring.

"Hello." It occurs to her only after she has answered to wonder who it is.

"Georgia, good morning. It's Cecilia."

"Cecilia." Georgia feels dumb suddenly, like this is the first time she's experienced a phone. *Hello* feels like the wrong thing to say. *Hi* is somehow worse.

"Good—good morning."

"I hope I didn't wake you."

"Oh no, not at all. I was just . . ." She looks around, like the answer she needs might be there. The truth is, she was just crying—not hard, nothing *breakdowny*. Just a few tired, self-indulgent tears.

"Excellent. Well, I wanted to invite you to breakfast this morning, if you'll humor me."

Georgia scratches her chin. She should feel flattered, and maybe she is. It's hard to tell.

"Breakfast. Yes, okay. That— I'd like that."

"Beautiful. Seven o'clock in my office, then."

CHAPTER 13

It's either the morning sun or her expensive-looking blouse that makes Cecilia look radiant on her office patio later that morning. Or maybe Cecilia just glows.

"Oolong?" she offers Georgia, who has just sat down. Georgia nods. Cecilia's office is high on the hill, overlooking the bay and its tidy line of villas below.

Cecilia pours two cups from an elegant teapot, and, watching her, Georgia thinks of the last time she had oolong: in college, from a can, alongside an oversalted bowl of takeout ramen. She usually looks back on this time in her life fondly—broke and sleep-deprived but ultimately hopeful—although looking at Cecilia now, takeout ramen hardly feels like something to be proud of.

"I apologize again for the change in schedule," says Cecilia, handing her a cup. "You were probably looking forward to breakfast with your pod."

She wasn't, actually, but this feels rude to say.

"No," she says. "I mean, yes, I'm sure it would've been nice. But this . . ."

She motions to the table: a serving platter of mango, a handle tray of flaky croissants. Cecilia smiles, not unkindly, but it isn't exactly friendly either. It looks more amused. Georgia reaches for the mango and uses the tiny silver tongs to pull out a slice.

"I was so glad we were able to make space for you this week," Cecilia says. "Your law firm has been such a source of wisdom over the years, and reciprocating that is my great honor."

Georgia nods. It makes sense, she supposes, why Cecilia seems to know her personally. Georgia is, after all, in a pretty unique situation. When she told Julie about The Program, Julie's eyes were wide. "And that's it?" she said. "Just a week at this program, and it's all put to bed?" She didn't mean to sound blasé, but it landed that way regardless. *Just a week at this program.* It's one of the few times Georgia has let herself get angry with her friend.

"I'm excited to get started," Georgia says, and without meaning to, she thinks of the first bra, the one on her front door. Underneath, in chalk, one word: LIAR.

Cecilia beams. Georgia takes a sip of the oolong. It tastes nothing like the canned drinks she had in college. She takes a slice of bacon next, which Cecilia watches with an expression that makes Georgia self-conscious. It's like she's a child who's done something unexpectedly well.

"I don't normally invite my students here, to my office," Cecilia says finally. "This veranda is a work-free sanctuary, and I take that separation very seriously."

Georgia nods. *Her* students. It feels possessive.

"I think that's good," she says. "Really—healthy."

Cecilia frowns, and Georgia's immediate impulse is to correct herself, although she doesn't know what mistake she made. Instead, she takes a sip of her drink, as in the distance, a bird swoops from the sky and disappears into the sea-green bay. Georgia doesn't see it emerge.

"I've read up on you, Georgia," Cecilia says after a moment, picking up her teacup. "As charitable as we can be here, we are also quite scrupulous."

Georgia swallows. Despite the tea, her mouth now feels dry.

Cecilia takes a sip of her drink, her eyes not straying from Georgia's over the cup's edge.

"You've been treated very poorly," she says, her voice betraying nothing, "and some say it's warranted. But I've always prided myself on being a good judge of character, and I feel quite confident that what we're doing here is a first step in righting a grievous wrong."

The words are so light and so elegant that it takes Georgia a moment to register their meaning. She imagines Cecilia scrolling through an internet's worth of comments and seeing all the worst things that can be said about a person: *Bitch. Liar. Cunt. Whore.* Cecilia's judgment is not nearly the first, as there is no shortage of judgments in the online world. No, what separates Cecilia here is her kindness.

"That's— Thank you," Georgia manages, feeling unexpectedly emotional. "I really appreciate that."

CHAPTER 14

There's a statue at the entrance of the resort's "Two Dove Hall," as it's called, that is a stylistic counterpart to the Aphrodite statue out front.

Georgia is late—she had to run back to her villa after breakfast to grab a notebook—but she nonetheless stops to study the statue. Like Aphrodite, the doves are empty-eyed. They're facing one another, their beaks almost but not quite kissing, and as Georgia nears it, she notices the inscription at the base: EQUALITY IS DIVINITY. She's not sure what to make of this.

She hurries into the auditorium just as the lights are starting to dim. She finds a seat at the end of the first aisle she comes to, next to Dede. Dede raises her eyebrows but doesn't say anything. They're here for their first event of the day, an "edification mod," per the itinerary. (Georgia also doesn't know what to make of this.)

"Good morning, ladies!"

Cecilia has appeared on the stage up front, which is dark save for the circle of light on her. She looks different from how she did at breakfast—not *not* elegant exactly, although with her hands raised like they are, and with a little microphone clipped to her neckline, she has the definite air of someone at a pep rally.

"I hope we're all feeling energized," she says, as beside Georgia, Dede slides lower in her seat. If she's like Georgia, she might have a headache from the lavender drinks yesterday, and with no drugs allowed at the resort—ibuprofen included—there are few options for relief.

"I am always feeling extra inspired after Opening Dinner," says Cecilia. "We're here, we're settled, and now it's time to begin."

Georgia thinks randomly, unpleasantly, of the bra back home, which Will has since thrown in the garbage bin. He told her that this morning, and also that the cops are "looking into it," although they have no leads yet.

"As you know," Cecilia continues, "the first segment of our journey is titled Relearn. Notice the verbiage we use here—*re*learn. As women, we have been imbibed with so much information about motherhood, but rarely do we consider where this information comes from. It is our belief here at The Program that truth is the foundation for meaningful change, and to learn the truth, we must be willing to approach it with clear eyes and honest hearts."

As she speaks, a large screen descends slowly from the ceiling behind her. And then, without warning, the auditorium goes dark. A chill tickles the base of Georgia's neck, and she can feel the women around her shifting in their seats.

It's only like this for a moment, however, before the screen flickers, glowing black. The image is unidentifiable at first, until it zooms out enough to reveal a beady black eye. A little bit farther, and the beady black eye takes its place beside a twitching pink nose and long, translucent whiskers. Farther still, and a rat's unnerving little fingers bring a cracker to its little mouth.

"This is a mother."

The narrator's cold opening booms through the auditorium from no one place in particular. Beside Georgia, Dede shudders.

"Meet Rat Mother Number Five," he says. He has a pleasing British accent that provides a sense of scholarliness to the video. It's male, baritone, and authoritative, perfectly cast for a documentary.

"Rat Mother Number Five has recently welcomed a brood of

ten pups. This was her first pregnancy, and her first exploration into motherhood is today."

The camera zooms out farther to reveal the four glass walls of Rat Mother Number Five's terrarium. Except for the pulpy material covering the floor, the cage appears completely empty. Georgia looks around for Cecilia, but she has disappeared.

"Rat Mother Number Five has spent her entire life in captivity," says the narrator. "In her world, Rat Mother Number Five is never starved for anything. In fact, Rat Mother Number Five has learned to call for food with a dedicated food lever, which she is free to use at her whim."

The camera's lens brings a small lever into focus, barely visible in the corner of the glass cage. It's beside a chute that travels up the side of the wall, disappearing from view.

"Today, however, Rat Mother Number Five's lever has been reconfigured."

On-screen, Rat Mother Number Five raises her nose to the air and sniffs, her little whiskers trembling. She surveys for a moment, then scampers toward the lever. With efficiency, she bops the tiny pedal with her foot.

There's a collective gasp throughout the auditorium as, on-screen, a tiny pink rat pup comes shooting into view, like a very small, very wrinkled alien being shot through a waterslide. Rat Mother Number Five trills and hurries to the squirming intruder.

"Instead of food," says the narrator, "the lever in Rat Mother Number Five's cage has been reprogrammed to deliver newborn pups."

The women in the auditorium watch with fascination as on-screen, Rat Number Mother Five examines the newly deposited baby.

"But this isn't Rat Mother Number Five's pup," the narrator tells them. "Rat Mother Number Five has been delivered a stranger, as she is acutely aware. Rats, like most mammals, are able to recognize their offspring by smell, sight, and touch."

Something unsavory gnaws at Georgia's stomach as Rat Mother Number Five continues to sniff the stranger. It's an ugly little thing, like a newly hatched chick with angry, raw skin. Rat Mother Number Five nudges it, then scuttles away, back to the lever. She presses, and another pup slides into view.

"Virgin females," the narrator continues, "that is, female rats who have never been pregnant, lose interest in the lever soon after they've discovered the reprogramming. That, or they choose not to differentiate between the pups and the food they're accustomed to."

At this, Georgia swallows uncomfortably.

"Mother rats, however, exhibit quite peculiar behavior. Indeed, mother rats are rarely disappointed by the switch. To the contrary, brain analyses show that rat mothers find the incoming pups just as satisfying as their virgin counterparts find food."

On-screen, Rat Mother Number Five stomps on the lever a third time, sending a third rat pup careening into the cage. The narrator remains quiet as she pounds the lever again and again and again, until finally the pups are unable to clear the mouth of the chute, clogging the tube with frantic, squeaking bodies.

The screen goes black so that when the narrator speaks again, his words rain down on the dark auditorium like the voice of God.

"What we have learned from mothers like Rat Mother Number Five is that—like any addiction—motherhood is a psychological condition. When Rat Mother Number Five is sacrificed, researchers will find distinct proteins and morphological changes in her brain that are exclusive to motherhood, but which resemble the changes that are most often associated with addiction. In other words, a mother's brain is, in its most basic essence, that of an addict."

It takes Georgia a moment to digest what the narrator is telling them. *Sacrifice.* So they will be killing Rat Mother Number Five. Georgia chews the inside of her cheek, keenly aware of Dede beside her, who refused to even look at the roasted pig last night.

The screen flashes back on, this time showing a rat alone in the frame, surrounded by blank white space.

"Meet Rat Mother Number Two," the narrator says, a distinct shift in his tone—less descriptive, now almost loving. "Rat Mother Number Two is the mother to seven new pups. She gave birth two days ago."

There's something unnerving about Rat Mother Number Two. Unlike Rat Mother Number Five, Number Two isn't preoccupied by anything around her. She stares straight into the camera, like she can see through it to the throng of curious women on the other side.

The shot pans out to reveal more of Number Two's surroundings, which include, somewhat distressingly, a handful of rat pups crammed into what appears to be a clear plastic drinking cup. They crawl over one another to scratch fruitlessly at the cup's walls. Between Number Two and her cupful of pups, a black mat extends from one side of the screen to the other, showing no signs of an edge.

"The electrical grid separating the mother from her offspring is adjustable," says the narrator. "With the turn of a knob, researchers are able to control the voltage it emits."

It's clear now that Number Two isn't looking at the camera but rather at the crowded cup of pups. She stands at the very edge of the electric grid, as close as she can be without touching it. It strikes Georgia that Number Two understands what the grid does, a thought that makes her feel a little bit sick.

The entire auditorium seems to be holding their breath as they watch Number Two consider the electrical mat. Georgia imagines herself on the edge of it, looking out at Clover and Ruby, trapped and frightened. She knows at once, with absolute certainty, that she would find a way to them. She would do whatever it took.

It's for this reason that she doesn't gasp when Number Two steps onto the grid, unlike Dede, who takes a sharp intake of breath. Onscreen, Number Two also lets out a small, strangled yelp before taking another step. Then another. Eventually, she makes it across the mat with ragged, shuddering breaths, but the shot cuts out a split second before her reunion with the pups.

Instead, a new scene appears with Number Two back at her starting spot. The women in the auditorium watch as again, Rat Mother Number Two contemplates the mat separating her from her chirping newborns.

"With each run," the narrator explains above them, "power to the mat is increased."

This time, Rat Mother Number Two sets a hesitant paw on the mat. She lets out an eerily humanlike squeal, but still, she again scurries across it. And again, the screen cuts off just before she makes contact.

"Researchers sought to determine the mother's threshold for physical trauma," says the narrator. "They wanted to understand the point at which she would place her own survival above the needs of her pups."

Number Two cries more loudly the third time, and Georgia silently wills her to stay put, to refuse her role in the researchers' game. And yet, for a third time, she makes it across the mat, and for a third time, the screen robs the audience of reunion between mother and children.

On the fourth run, Number Two hesitates longer, her eyes darting from one edge of the screen to the other, calculating. Georgia feels her stomach churn, recognizing the expression as one not too different from how she has felt herself.

Again, no payoff. The video cuts off just before Number Two reaches her young, and again, the mother starts from the first side.

It goes on like this with each cry becoming shriller, each run across the mat less efficient as the rat mother totters and zigzags, delirious with pain. "Stop it," Dede whispers, but the whisper is lost in Number Two's screams.

And then, finally, it does stop. The rat mother's final cry is weak, more of a breath than an actual shriek. She makes it halfway across the mat before she staggers, then collapses, her legs continuing to twitch even as her eyes close.

The screen goes black. Dede is now picking aggressively at a hangnail on her thumb, a faint but penetrating *scratch scratch scratch*.

"Mothers," the narrator says finally, speaking into the blackness, "undergo countless profound changes throughout their journey into parenthood, but perhaps none is as confounding as their willingness to disregard themselves when it comes to their children. It's antithetical to the most basic rules of evolution as we understand them, a puzzle to which only mothers hold the key. And what we've learned, thanks in part to mothers such as Rat Mother Number Two, is that a mother's mind is as predictable as it is complex." A pause, perhaps for theatrical effect, before he tells them, "A mom brain is simply the neurological hardwiring for self-sacrifice."

CHAPTER 15

They have an hour between their final edification mod and dinner, and an hour, if she were motivated, would be plenty of time to take a shower and do her hair. And yet, rather than being in the bathroom, getting ready, Georgia finds herself lying on the couch, trying to figure out what about the videos earlier that day felt so wrong.

It wasn't the rats necessarily; she doesn't have a strict moral opposition to animal research. She can't, not while working with as many scientists as she does. It's impossible not to have, if not approval of, at least a healthy respect for how the sausage is made. Still, she feels as though she witnessed something excessive today—not cruel exactly, but gratuitous.

Dede stomped out of the final mod when it was over, because Dede does have a strict moral opposition to animal research. Izzy, the operations assistant, was with them at the time, and she watched Dede go with a strained expression, like she was unsure of what to do. Georgia felt bad for Izzy then; it wasn't her fault. Maybe it wasn't anyone's fault. Maybe it only felt gratuitous because Georgia rarely experiences the actual realities of science.

She closes her eyes and leans her head back. She thinks of Rat Mother Number Two and how human she sounded when she screamed.

She sits back up and pulls out her phone. She thinks about calling Will but remembers the time difference. He texted her earlier with a picture of the girls eating dinner: a messy, delicious grin on each little face. Ruby's was painted with mashed sweet potato. Clover had Chick-fil-A, one of the few things she'll reliably eat. (At their last well-child visit, the pediatrician suggested that Georgia instead offer a variety of fruits and vegetables, making her wonder if he'd ever actually met a child himself.)

She types Cecilia's name into the internet search bar. The screen goes white, working hard. She has exactly zero service anywhere at the resort, and while there's Wi-Fi, it hardly works.

She wonders if Cecilia Clements is a psychopath.

The thought hits her with such stunning randomness, she lets out a little laugh. Then she sobers and examines the possibility. Animal research is one thing—an uncomfortable thing, but a sane thing. A normal thing for a scientist. But why *show* it like that? "It's all for the shock value," Alice said importantly after the first mod, and because it was Alice who said it, Georgia thought it was one of the dumbest things she'd ever heard. Now, though, she considers the annoying possibility that Alice was right.

Her phone tings with a message. The Wi-Fi can at least do this.

She sees Julie's name and feels immediately more tired. She considers skipping dinner. Would she get in trouble? She isn't in school. It's not like she's cutting class.

She opens the message.

I know you're probably busy, but give me a call when you can. I might've figured something out.

Georgia reads the message again, then a third time, all but hearing Julie's voice in her head. Julie is the type of person you expect to be one thing but, in the end, is the exact opposite. The first time Georgia saw her friend in court, cross-examining a hostile witness, it was like Georgia was seeing her for the first time.

She scrolls back up through their chain of messages. From a week ago:

We might have a civil case.

Georgia's reply:

It's just a bra tho. No one damaged anything.

Julie responded only:

Mental distress.

It's so silly, in a way that's unbearably serious. Sue someone for her hurt feelings. Sue someone for emotional injury. Georgia read once that heartbreak activates the same part of the brain as physical pain, and something about this, although sad, was also extremely satisfying. "See?" she said to an invisible audience. "It really does hurt!"

She thinks again of Rat Mother Number Two, her eyes lifeless even as her foot continued to twitch. So much of it was disturbing, not least of all because Georgia understood. She watched the rat mother scurry and fall, shock herself over and over and over again, and thought, *Yes. Yes, that's* exactly *how it feels sometimes, isn't it?*

CHAPTER 16

"It's messed up," Dede says later that evening, stabbing a piece of broccolini with her fork. "I mean, what the hell, right?"

They're in the Arcadian Bay Café around a circular table where their servers have just delivered their main course. Georgia is sitting next to Dede again, who doesn't look like she's showered since that afternoon. This makes Georgia feel slightly better about the fact that she spent the last hour sitting on the couch.

"I thought it was extremely informative," says Alice, who does look like she showered. Her hair is perfectly straight, which is irritating only because Georgia's hair, especially in this humidity, is not. ("Voluminous," as her kind hairdresser might put it. Once, tipsy on vacation, Will compared her to Doc Brown.)

"Yeah, well, they could've just *told* us all that stuff without like, showing it like that," Dede says grumpily. Her hair—while not straight—is piled in a way that looks chicly untidy, something that Georgia has never been able to achieve herself. "It was totally inappropriate, if you ask me."

Dede pushes her vegetables around her plate, reminding Georgia of Clover. She feels immediately tender at the thought.

Alice says tightly, "Would you rather they do those sorts of tests on humans?"

"I'd rather they not do them at all, actually."

Logan says quietly, "You know, they used to do drug trials on monkeys."

Dede shoots Logan an uncertain look, as though unsure

whether Logan is on her side or not. Logan doesn't notice. She's looking down at her plate, which is already clean. She's wearing a faded T-shirt with the Lucky Charms leprechaun on it, although it's so worn and she's so thin, her collarbones are visible through it. She also seemed affected by the videos, although unlike Dede, she spent most of the day with her face knotted in a worried frown.

Georgia moves a stalk of broccolini from one side of her plate to the other. She doesn't feel hungry. In fact, she has a slight stomachache. It's hard to say if this is because of the travel, the lingering hangover, or the text from Julie on her phone, still unanswered.

"Cecilia seems like a big fake to me," Dede says after a moment. "I mean, does she even have like, credentials?"

"She has a doctorate in neuroscience," Alice says at once.

"So she's a doctor?"

"A doctorate. A PhD."

Dede sniffs. "You know, my brother-in-law has a PhD, and he can't even figure out how to post an Instagram story."

This is met with silence. Alice stares at Dede with a bewildered expression. Dede pops her last bite of broccolini into her mouth with chutzpah.

"You know what I think?" Dede continues, a shift in her demeanor. The turn in conversation seems to have brightened her spirits. "What I think is that they're going to use *us* as rats."

To this, Alice responds with an unkind snort. Logan's eyes widen. Simone's face is the only one at the table Georgia can't read. It's the same expression she wore all day while watching the videos—attentive but otherwise inscrutable.

"Use us as rats for *what* exactly?" Alice says. Alice also has a five-year-old, apparently. Georgia wonders if the girl knows the words to "Baby Shark" like other kids, or if they listen strictly to Chopin.

"Experiments," Dede says darkly. "*Tests*."

"You're not serious," Alice says. It's hard to tell whether she finds the idea exasperating or if she just feels that way about Dede generally.

"I am." Dede is energized. "Why wouldn't I be?"

"Because it's ridiculous."

"Is it though? I mean, think about it. Weird videos. An isolated island. And you can't tell me Cecilia doesn't give *major* cult leader energy."

"This isn't TV."

"Crazier things have happened." Dede looks grimly around the table. "The government has done secret experiments on people before."

"She's not the government," Alice snaps. "And no, actually, they haven't."

"You don't know that."

Alice rolls her eyes and looks around for support. Georgia's eyes fall to her plate. Even if she doesn't agree with Dede, she doesn't want to pile on.

A beat passes before Simone says evenly, "Well, the Tuskegee Experiment did happen."

The sound of her voice seems to startle everyone. It's low, but it has the effect of a shout. Alice looks especially surprised. Her eyes narrow, sizing Simone up.

"So, what?" Alice says. "Are you saying you agree with Dede?"

"No." Simone's voice is cool. "I'm saying people in power are capable of doing bad things."

"Oh, for God's sake." Alice pushes herself back. Standing, she's only a head taller than Georgia in her seat. "Does it ever occur to you all that maybe *you're* part of the problem?"

The question feels rhetorical, but even if it isn't, Alice marches off before any of them can come up with a response.

CHAPTER 17

The next day begins their first of several "practical exercises," per the itinerary in Georgia's welcome basket. When Georgia read this the night before, she had to give herself a stern pep talk. She has been called many things in her life, and "practical" is indeed one of them, but it's usually in the sense that she buys mostly neutrals and avoids stilettos. She is not practical in a way that would be helpful in a survival-type situation. She is not someone who can use a compass or tie a good knot.

She is, however, practical enough to wear a sweatshirt, and on the beach this morning, she is grateful for this bit of foresight. It's much cooler by the ocean than it is by the bay, and she can tell by the way that Dede is standing that she's cold. (Georgia suspects that Dede—wearing a macramé cover-up over an electric-blue bikini—has never been described as *practical* in any sense of the word.)

"Beautiful, isn't it?" says Izzy, who drove them to the beach earlier in a Program van, greeting them with a sort of buoyancy that wasn't returned. Most of the women seemed tired, although Dede's reaction was openly hostile. She still has not forgiven Izzy for the rat video, it seems.

No one answers Izzy now, although most of the women at least turn in the direction Izzy is pointing. The sun is still below the horizon, creating a haze against the jagged rocks that rise from the water. It is indeed beautiful, although there's something eerie about it too—fairytale-ish in a way, like the rocks are hunched giants.

"It's freezing," Dede says flatly, the only one who hasn't turned toward the sunrise. She stands with her arms folded across her chest, an accusatory expression on her face, as though this—the weather—is also Izzy's fault.

"It is a bit chilly," Izzy agrees, summoning an admirable level of hospitality. "You know what?" She kneels down in front of the large tub she brought from the van. It's opaque white plastic and probably too big for one person to carry alone (although when Logan offered to help her, Izzy was adamant that she was fine).

"Here we are," Izzy says brightly, pulling from the tub a pink sweatshirt. "This should help, I think."

She holds the sweatshirt out to Dede, who looks at it with a wrinkled nose. Beside her, Logan shifts her weight. Logan is wearing a fluorescent orange rain jacket and limp canvas joggers. She's the only one in the group who doesn't look tired.

Dede ends up taking the sweatshirt, which she jams huffily over her head. None of this seems to faze Izzy, who gives off the cheerful air of a camp counselor in her oversized straw hat and sunscreen on her nose.

"Cecilia should be here in a moment," she says, checking the phone she keeps strapped to the waistband of her shorts. "Why don't we get our equipment sorted while we wait?"

The equipment—a collection of headsets—is also pink. From what Georgia can tell, none of the headsets are labeled, although Izzy hands them out in some sort of inscrutable order anyway. They're heavier than they look, and Georgia feels nervous holding hers, the way she feels nervous holding other people's babies. (She loves babies, but she doesn't want to be responsible if one breaks.)

"Please," says Izzy, polite still, but with a new firmness in her voice, "hold off on exploring the equipment for now." She isn't addressing Dede directly, although Dede is the only one to whom the instruction applies. She has turned the headset over and is poking at something at the bottom.

"Are these VR headsets?" says Alice, who is also wearing a sweatshirt—a crisp navy crew neck with COLUMBIA across the chest. Today, her blonde hair is tied into a small, slick nub of a ponytail at the base of her neck.

"Yes," says Izzy. "But Cecilia will explain more when she arrives."

Alice licks her teeth under her lips. Georgia gets the impression that she doesn't like waiting, for answers or for people.

Cecilia arrives just as the sun is cresting the horizon. She's wearing a flowy chiffon set that seems suddenly like the exact right thing to be wearing in a situation like this.

"Good morning, ladies," she says, her voice cutting clear through the humid morning. She seems to glide over the sand rather than traverse it, so unlike Georgia, who tripped over a half-buried piece of driftwood on the way from the van.

The only one who responds is Logan, who brings her hand to her forehead in a soldier's salute. This seems to momentarily distract Dede from her sullenness. She gives Logan a flabbergasted look.

Cecilia smiles broadly. She has a way of looking at the women that Georgia doesn't like, although it's hard to put her finger on exactly why. It's tender, but perhaps too much so—borderline condescending.

"I must admit," Cecilia says, taking a step forward so she eclipses Izzy, "I have a soft spot for the first day of practical exercises. I view this as an inflection point in our time together. Here, on this beach, is where we commit."

Simone sniffs. Cecilia's eyes find her, and for a second, it seems as though she's annoyed. The expression is gone so quickly, however, Georgia isn't sure if she misread it.

"Ms. St. Clair," Cecilia says. If she's annoyed, there's no hint of it in her voice. "I suspect you're eager to get to work this morning."

The air feels brittle suddenly, and Georgia wonders if she read Cecilia's expression right after all. And yet, Simone doesn't look admonished. She lifts her eyebrows slightly in a way that channels a distinct lack of deference.

Cecilia smiles, looking amused.

"If you'll step forward, Ms. St. Clair, we can jump right in."

Simone steps forward wordlessly. She's wearing socks and athletic shoes, the only one in the group not in sandals. Georgia felt bad about this earlier, embarrassed by the mistake on Simone's behalf. Now, though, she wonders if Simone knew her shoes were wrong for the occasion, and if that—the wrongness—was the point.

Cecilia says, "You're wondering, I'm sure, what it is you're holding."

Simone raises the headset, again without saying anything.

Cecilia says, "Any guesses?"

It strikes Georgia here that what she's witnessing is actually a power struggle, an unspoken game of chicken. Will Cecilia get Simone to speak, or won't she? No sooner does she think this, though, than Simone says evenly, "No idea."

Cecilia nods, looking satisfied. She turns toward the rest of the group.

"What you're holding is the cornerstone of The Program—our patented tools of immersive virtual reality."

At this, Dede's head whips toward Georgia, the patent attorney of the group. Her eyes narrow in betrayal, and Georgia wants to defend herself. She had nothing to do with this! But she stays silent.

Cecilia says, "You'll recall that with your applications for The Program, we requested three-minute videos of each of your family members."

Georgia does recall. In fact, Will was highly skeptical of this requirement. "Is this a moms' retreat," he said, "or are you auditioning for *The Voice?*"

Cecilia says lightly, "I think the reason for this request will soon become clear."

Georgia shivers. Cecilia seems to be speaking to her directly, as though she has somehow seen into Georgia's mind and witnessed Will's disrespect.

"Ms. St. Clair," Cecilia says, turning back to Simone. Simone looks her in the eye.

"You can call me Simone," she says.

Cecilia nods cheerily. "Would you please put on your headset?"

A moment, just a brief pause, before Simone lifts it. She places it on her head, and it seems to fit perfectly without adjustments. The headset is bulky, hiding most of her face above her mouth.

Everyone seems to inhale then, waiting. Even the breeze, clean and salty, comes to a halt, the ocean's breath, like theirs, bated. Simone moves her head one way then the other, tracing the edge of the water, although it's not clear if she's looking at the water or at something else.

And then, unexpectedly, she reaches out, her hand moving in front of her. She waves it, cutting the air in soft, then choppier, motions before lowering it back to her side.

"Damn," she breathes.

CHAPTER 18

Georgia has never used VR before. One of her colleagues—a younger guy who, to HR's horror, occasionally comes to the office in loafers without socks—has a headset. He plays golf on it, apparently, which he likes to bring up to whoever will listen. Georgia has been cornered by him only once before, near the coffee machine, trapped by the slow drip of her vanilla latte. "They still can't get the humans right," he said, sounding jolly, "but the grass." He winked with the OK gesture, which felt vaguely inappropriate, although Georgia couldn't tell you why.

That's what Georgia expected from VR: mostly realistic grass with less realistic humans. And that made sense, given what she's seen from Pixar movies. They seem to have a problem with humans as well. It's shocking, then, when Georgia pulls her headset down over her eyes and sees by her knees an entirely realistic Clover.

Like Simone, Georgia reaches out, and like Simone, she finds nothing. Her hand swipes through air, but in Georgia's headset, it slices Clover's head. Clover frowns, disapproving of her mom's behavior, and the expression is so lifelike, so *her daughter*, that Georgia rips the headset off at once.

Around her, the other women are battling something similar. Logan's mouth is agape as her arms flap frantically around. Alice moves more twitchily, like someone trying to catch a fly. Simone is standing with her arms limp beside her, staring straight ahead into the ocean, and Dede's headset is in the sand beside her, where she apparently flung it off.

"Please," Cecilia says calmly to Dede. "Be gentle with the equipment."

Izzy hurries over to Dede's headset. She scoops it up and holds it out for Dede, who snatches it back without taking her eyes from Cecilia.

"What *is* this?" she demands. "What are these things?"

"As I said," Cecilia explains gently, "these are The Program's proprietary virtual reality headsets."

"But *why?*"

Alice has taken off her headset now too, as has Simone. The only one still wearing hers is Logan, who has wandered away from the group, toward the water. Izzy trots after her as Cecilia assesses Dede, who—under Cecilia's stare—seems to falter. She crosses her arms, but her indignation looks less convincing than it did before.

Cecilia turns from her finally, addressing the group as a whole.

"We've shared with you the first pillar of The Program: Relearn. Part of this relearning includes a more conventional approach to education, as we saw yesterday. Learning, though, is not merely an exercise in observation. True relearning requires harmony between all systems of the body, both mental and physical."

Across the beach, Izzy is guiding Logan back to the group. Logan has taken off the headset and is wearing a dazed expression.

"So to answer your question," Cecilia says, nodding toward Dede, although her eyes continue to travel from woman to woman, "we're using these headsets today because navigable *experiences* are foundational to success in The Program."

Her expression changes here; she seems almost teary. No one in the group says anything. The slight breeze has resumed, and it snakes up Georgia's neck, making the peach fuzz hairs stand on end. She thinks of Will suddenly, longingly, simultaneously wishing he were here and glad he is not. He is too nice to say what he thinks most of the time, but he can't always hide it on his face, and she both does and does not want to know what his face would look like now.

"Georgia," Cecilia says abruptly, turning to face her. Georgia has the same sense she had earlier, that somehow, Cecilia is privy to her thoughts. She arranges her expression into what she hopes conveys polite attentiveness.

Cecilia smiles.

"Would you like to start us off?"

CHAPTER 19

The second time she sees Clover in the headset is as strange as the first. The rest of the beach looks the same: pink-hued sand, sparkling clear water. It's like she's looking through a window with the exception of her daughter, who shouldn't be there.

This time, though, Clover is not standing by her side. Clover is now crouched thirty feet down the shore, near the water. Her back is to Georgia as she examines something in front of her, and Georgia marvels again at how realistic the hologram is, how even the curve of Clover's slight shoulders is accurate. She is filled with an immediate and intense need for her actual daughter, for the smell of Clover's shampoo, the baby-smooth skin of her cheeks.

For a moment, she doesn't do anything, unsure what she's supposed to do. If it were her actual daughter on the beach, there would be no question. Clover still can't swim—not well, anyway—so if this were actually Clover, Georgia would hurry down the beach and position herself between her daughter and the ocean. At the pool last summer, this was the source of a minor fight between her and Will, who accused her of helicoptering. "You act like she needs to be at arm's length at all times," he said, as though this was not a perfectly reasonable thing for Georgia to expect from a small, inefficient swimmer.

"Mommy, look!"

Georgia's eyes are drawn to the hologram, who is holding up what appears to be plastic six-pack rings. Trash. Georgia isn't sure if the pile of trash is real or if it's part of the device's projection, but it's immediately clear that it is not something for a child—even a holographic one—to be playing with.

"Clover, put that down please," she says, starting toward her. She can't help but think about Rat Mother Number Two, how instinctive mothering can be sometimes.

"Look, Mommy! Look at this!" Clover holds up something else in triumph. Georgia squints. Is that a . . . syringe? She feels a flutter of anxiety, an ingrained response that hasn't caught up with the actual situation—that this image of her daughter isn't the real thing.

"Clover, put that down!"

She has not even finished the command before another sound catches her attention. This one is as familiar to Georgia as her own heartbeat.

She whirls around. Farther down the beach in the opposite direction, Ruby sits at the shoreline. Like the real infant, holographic Ruby totters slightly, still mastering the ability to sit on her own. A wave breaks just offshore, and as the water rushes toward the baby, she claps in delight.

All at once, Georgia feels whisked upward by a strange, out-of-body sensation, as though she is watching herself from overhead. She sees herself frozen, like she was that night in Clover's doorway, hearing her breathing. And now, halfway between both of her beautiful daughters, she is so equally pulled by each of them that she is unable to move either way.

But then there's a snap of recognition and she regains her faculties. "Put that down now!" she shouts at Clover in the most commanding voice she can muster, one that would leave the real Clover whimpering and Georgia awash in guilt. She hates yelling at Clover because Clover takes it so personally, but sometimes there is no other option. She can only go to one of her daughters. The other's safety comes down to a yell.

She starts toward Ruby.

Except.

Except Ruby isn't there.

The panic rises to the base of Georgia's throat, as real to her as the ground beneath her, even if the holographic Ruby is not. She lost Clover once, very briefly, at the grocery store last fall. Clover was standing there next to Georgia as she compared two avocados, and then, in an instant, she was gone. It all happened so fast. Faster than fast! A second! A breath! Before that, she had never believed mothers who said that. "I turned my head for just a second!" they would say, and Georgia would feel so very sympathetic but also, privately, not convinced. Really? Just a second? Maybe it *felt* like just a second, but catastrophes do not happen so fast. And yet, she really had turned her head for just that second, and it really did happen just like that.

An employee found Clover only a few minutes later, oblivious to her mother's panic, holding a bag of corn chips.

She feels that same sense of lightheadedness now, flying down the beach. She's afraid of water—terrified of it. Her greatest fear, as she told the group at Opening Dinner, although she was wrong. She realizes now there are things she fears so much more than that.

CHAPTER 20

When it's over, Izzy packs the headsets back into the white plastic tub. The sun has climbed halfway up the sky now, high enough that Georgia no longer needs her sweatshirt, although she hasn't taken it off. The thought crosses her mind to offer to help Izzy, although it floats away just as easily. Instead, she stands and watches without a word.

Cecilia left a few minutes ago. She told the women, "Good work today," to which all of them stared back in silence. It's hard to see how Cecilia was being honest, how any of them performed in a way that meets even the most generous interpretation of the word *good*.

Georgia isn't the only one who lost a child; all of them did, all in seemingly different ways. When it was Logan's turn, she started digging, her daughter apparently buried. Alice started running into the trees. Even Simone, so immovable normally, made it knee-deep into the ocean before Izzy pulled her back. When Dede went, she ripped the headset off and slammed it into the sand a second time. "This is bullshit," she said, and perhaps out of pity, Cecilia didn't scold her about the fragile equipment that time.

"Cecilia is meeting with the other pods this morning," Izzy says once she has clipped the lid of the tub back in place. Despite the sunscreen and despite the hat, the bridge of her nose is turning pink. "After that, we'll meet as a large group to discuss."

No one has anything to say to this. Perhaps the other women, like Georgia, feel as though they've been unexpectedly slapped. It's hard to see what the point of these humiliating exercises was—unless, of course, the humiliation was the point.

Back at the resort, they have a free block of time until after lunch, when all the pods are to meet in Two Dove Hall again. Izzy says this with an energy that this time Georgia finds annoying. She can feel that her mood has shifted since they left the beach, moving from a sort of stunned disorientation to irritation. If it is The Program's goal to make the women feel as though they're incompetent mothers, there's really no need. Georgia could have done this on her own for free.

Because Alice is in the unit adjoining Georgia's, it would make sense for them to walk back together. Alice, though, hurries from the van without giving Georgia the opportunity to join her. (Georgia isn't disappointed by this.)

Alone, she makes her way back to her villa the long way, snaking along the coastline of the bay. She types out a text message to Will but doesn't have service to send it. It's a little past four at home, and Will has probably just picked Clover up from kindergarten. The thought makes her feel extremely vulnerable—Clover in her booster, her backpack tucked carefully between her feet. Georgia was so wildly anxious about Clover's first day of kindergarten, which is apparently the worst thing she could've been. According to the parenting experts, she was *supposed* to be channeling confidence, and ironically, this—how little confidence she had in her confidence—only made her feel more anxious.

As she climbs the stairs to her villa, her phone tings, connecting to the Wi-Fi. She looks down, thinking her message to Will went through on its own. Instead, it's Julie, a message time-stamped earlier, when Georgia didn't have service.

Call me?

Julie has a bad habit of phrasing things that aren't questions like they are. Georgia has mentioned this only once, right after the *Pacific* article leak. This was the worst version of Georgia, the unkindest, and Julie—apparently understanding this—simply bowed her head.

Georgia meets her own eyes in the mirror above the dining table, where her welcome basket sits thoroughly picked through. She's not wearing any makeup, and yet, miraculously, she doesn't look that tired. It strikes her that despite her doubts, The Program has gotten this one thing right, at least.

She considers ignoring Julie's message, but she doesn't. She dials, and Julie answers at once.

"How's it going?" she says, sounding nervous.

"It's good," Georgia says, mostly to be kind.

Julie stays quiet, and it feels deliberate, like she's expecting Georgia to say more. But Georgia doesn't have more to say. She's still working out what she feels about The Program herself.

And yet, because Georgia is Georgia, she says, "It's a little different from what I imagined, I guess."

"Yeah? How so?"

"It's . . ." But Georgia can't find the words. She's standing in the middle of the villa that is sticky with humidity, that's uniformly (but tastefully) beige, and she truly cannot tell if all this is nice or horrible or somewhere in between.

"I don't know. I guess I don't know what I expected."

Julie makes a sound of acknowledgment, and Georgia tries to picture her. She's probably still at the office, which she won't leave before six. Julie has a good office with a big sunny window and a long mahogany desk, and she keeps it all impeccable—diplomas professionally framed on the wall behind her computer, little containers for her extra staples and binder clips. She has a son who's only a few months younger than Ruby, and she stores her breast pump in a leather tote bag under her desk. When Georgia's name first started circling the internet, when Julie first heard about it, she had just been in the firm's nursing room herself. She came to Georgia's office still holding the tote bag, and when she realized this, she moved the bag a little bit away from her body, as though separating herself from something obscene.

"Well," Julie says now, sounding not much different from how she did that day in Georgia's office. "I called because I think we have a case—if that's what you want, obviously."

Georgia closes her eyes, trying to decide whether this is indeed what she wants. She has friends who feel very strongly about this word—*wants*—primarily because they believe theirs, as mothers, have become irrelevant. Georgia, though, has not experienced this in her life. Actually, Georgia's wants are in the forefront, but they're the big, sweeping wants that are hard to see when you're up too close. She wants her daughters to be happy. She wants them to be safe. She wants them to look back on their childhood fondly when they're older—or at least she doesn't want them to bring up their childhood to a therapist later in life.

She wants these things, and for these grand wants, her littler wants are often pushed to the side. An uninterrupted night of sleep. An uninterrupted conversation with Will. The freedom of popping into a store without the ludicrous ten-step process that is Clover buckling and unbuckling her own booster seat. Those wants *have* become irrelevant, but she traded them willingly, and for this reason, she cannot complain.

Does she *want* to go through a lawsuit? That isn't the right question, at least not the way Julie means it.

"Do you think it will help?" Georgia says, knowing as she asks that it's a pointless question. There is no way for Julie to know.

Julie is quiet on the other end of the line, because that's what she's like. She thinks carefully before she speaks, weighing each thought, each word. Maybe it's the result of being an attorney, or maybe that's why she became one. Georgia considered herself to be this way too, once, before she proved this theory about herself incorrect.

"It could," Julie says finally, softly. Georgia can hear the faint lap of the bay against the shore outside her villa, and for some reason, the sound is grating.

"Just like The Program could help," she says, not intending to be mean exactly, although that's the way it comes out regardless.

"Georgia," Julie starts, but Georgia cuts her off.

"I'm sorry. That was— Sorry. I appreciate you doing this, Jules, but I don't think so. It's just—it's too much. I'm too tired. I just . . . can't."

Julie says she understands, and Georgia wonders if she actually does. She wonders if Julie expected this from Georgia, if this is the sort of woman she now is. Tired. Defeated. She doesn't think this is the way she's always been, although she's unsure if this is because she changed or because she never actually knew herself.

CHAPTER 21

Georgia decides to go for a walk before the next group meeting. Will, when he called her, was in the throes of dinnertime and could barely get a word out over Clover and Ruby. He promised to call later, once the girls were in bed, and when he hung up, Georgia's room felt doubly quiet.

Outside her villa, she follows the pebbly path to a fork in the trail. She decides to take the route toward the water, which blinks in the sun that's now perfectly overhead.

The path leads her to a line of kayaks. A vine, escaped from somewhere, climbs up the rack and weaves itself between two boats, suggesting that they don't get much use. And for the better, in Georgia's opinion. She has been in a kayak only once in her life, during a summer camp in middle school, with an unusually mean girl who capitalized on Georgia's fear of water by sloshing the boat back and forth randomly with a wicked laugh.

She heads toward the boats and is only a step away when she jumps.

"Oh!" she says, more of a breath than a word. She thought she was alone on the beach, and the sight of another person catches her by surprise.

"Sorry," she says to Dede, who's sitting with her back to the kayaks, her head resting against them. "I didn't see you there."

"I noticed," Dede says without inflection. She doesn't lift her head. She still seems sullen, although Georgia has not yet worked out whether this is because of The Program or if Dede is simply the sort of person who is always this way.

Georgia takes a step back. She doesn't know if she should say something before she leaves or if she can simply slip away. Dede is wearing a pair of oversized sunglasses, and it's unclear whether her eyes are even open.

She is turning to leave when Dede says abruptly, "Are all husbands total pricks, or is it just mine?"

Georgia stops. Dede is sitting in the exact same position, and for a moment, Georgia second-guesses whether Dede is actually talking to her. But then Dede leans forward. Her hair is still pushed up in the back where it was pressed into the kayak, and looking more closely, Georgia can just see her eyes through the sunglasses. She's glaring at Georgia, suggesting that this was indeed a question for her.

"Er," says Georgia, uncomfortable. She doesn't want to say what she thinks: No, not all husbands are pricks. Hers isn't.

"Brooks can be such a dickwad sometimes," Dede says in Georgia's hesitation. Georgia nods, less sure now what to say than before. Dede pushes herself up sharply and marches toward the water, and for a brief moment, it looks as though she's about to walk straight into the bay. Instead, she winds her arm back and chucks a rock. It lands a little ways out with a small plop.

"How the heck are you supposed to skip rocks?" she says angrily, although this time the question feels rhetorical. She stares out after the rock for a moment until the water settles. She then turns back to Georgia.

"Why are you here?" she demands, her tone accusative.

"Um." Georgia looks around. "I don't know. I just wanted to take a walk, I guess."

"Not *here* here. I mean, why are you at The Program?"

"Oh." Georgia rubs her shoulder. This is not a conversation she really wants to be having.

"Brooks wanted me to come," Dede says, barely pausing for Georgia's answer. "He said me being sad all the time is *exhausting*."

She reaches down, picks up another rock, and flings it into the water after the first. She doesn't seem to be trying particularly hard to get them to skip.

"I'm sorry," Georgia says hesitantly. "That sounds unfair."

"It's infuriating, is what it is. I'm not even sad either. Not really. I'm just . . ."

The sentence floats off. Only her side profile is visible, but from it, Georgia can see her scowl. And Georgia agrees: She doesn't look sad at all.

"It's just disappointing, is all," Dede says at last with a sniff. "It's just disappointing when you do everything right and you still feel like crap."

She turns and seems to examine Georgia for a moment. Georgia fights the urge to wrap her arms around herself, to protect herself from being analyzed.

"I was perfect postpartum," Dede says, her voice growing hard. "I lost all the baby weight immediately—like, I was back at the studio after six weeks. Everyone thought I was crazy, but my doctor was like, well, if you feel good enough to do it, then it's fine. And I just wanted to be back to normal, you know?"

Georgia nods, knowing in some ways but not in others. When she was six weeks postpartum with Ruby, she counted moving the Pack 'n Play from one room to the other as exercise.

"And I've always done what they said," Dede continues. "Always, everything right. I lost the weight and went back to work and yada yada yada. But it's been years now, and everything is still different. *I'm* different. Not sad, just . . . it's just not what I expected, is all."

She looks at Georgia, clearly awaiting some type of feedback, although Georgia doesn't know what she can offer, what Dede needs.

"Nothing can prepare you for what it's really like," Georgia says finally, gently, the best she can come up with.

Dede makes an unkind snort. She reaches down and plucks up another rock from around her feet, which she again chucks into the water. Georgia is pretty sure she has to throw it sideways if she wants it to skip, although she doesn't say this.

"What's funny is that Brooks is *exactly* the same as he always was. Nothing changed for him. He didn't ever have to do like, a million stupid core exercises just to fix his abs."

Georgia nods. Her abs have also changed since having children, although she has not done a million stupid core exercises to fix them.

Dede says, "Do you ever wonder why they don't have a Program for the dads?"

Georgia shakes her head. She doesn't have to think about this one. "No," she says, "I don't."

CHAPTER 22

After lunch, in Two Dove Hall, Georgia's pod sits in the same proximity, although not necessarily together. Alice is in the row in front of Dede and Simone, separated from Logan by three empty seats. Dede and Simone are directly next to each other, although they might as well be on opposite ends of the room. Dede is slumped low in her seat with her sunglasses still on. Simone's face is, as always, unreadable.

When Georgia arrives, she hesitates for a moment, then chooses the seat next to Simone. Simone glances up, and Georgia smiles weakly, which Simone returns with a dip of her chin. The other women in the room are busy with chatter; it seems that the other two pods do not share the same dynamic as theirs.

Georgia settles into her seat. In front of her, Logan is picking at green nail polish that is mostly gone. Alice glares at this, which Logan eventually notices. She stuffs her hands between her legs and looks up at the ceiling interestedly.

And then, like it did yesterday, the auditorium goes dark. This time, though, the effect is not quite as theatrical, perhaps because the women are expecting it.

Cecilia appears onstage, backlit and luminous. She has changed since their exercise on the beach, out of her chiffon and into a gubernatorial suit.

"Ladies," she says, her voice somehow both tranquil and authoritative. The auditorium is now quiet, but Cecilia waits a moment anyway.

"Ladies," she says finally, this time with a slightly different inflection. She smiles, and it seems real. Georgia thinks of her on the beach, how she clapped her hands together after their final run, apparently satisfied.

"First and foremost, congratulations. You made it through your first day of practical exercises, which is an achievement. You are in the depths of your journey, and while we have not yet arrived, it is important to acknowledge the progress we've made so far." As she speaks, the screen that showed the rat videos yesterday starts to lower from the ceiling behind her. When it reaches the floor, she smiles out at them and says, "And now, let us take the next step forward."

The screen illuminates abruptly. For a second, it's bright white, but it quickly changes. With an unpleasant jolt of recognition, Georgia sees Clover on the beach.

The air in the auditorium seems thinner suddenly. Georgia can feel her cheeks starting to burn. She braces for the other women in the room to look at her, sympathetic or curious, although no one does. It strikes Georgia then that no one in the auditorium knows who Clover is but her.

Cecilia takes a step to the side, into the shadows. On-screen, Clover is paused, crouched by the water. And it's a wonder how lifelike the image is. The color of her hair, the spray of freckles across her shoulders. Things Georgia didn't realize she'd memorized until she recognizes them here.

"Georgia Evans," Cecilia says, her voice somewhat disembodied in the darkness. Georgia tenses. Dede leans forward to look at her over Simone's lap, although Georgia studiously avoids eye contact.

"Georgia, where are you?"

Georgia doesn't know what to do. Should she stand? Raise her hand? The auditorium is so dark, it's possible Cecilia wouldn't see her anyway. She'll have to *say* something, she realizes with the same paralysis she feels in public bathrooms when someone knocks. What does a normal person say in that scenario? Because she always says something stupid, like *Hello there*, or *No thanks!*

She raises her hand, and thankfully, Cecilia sees her. She nods in approval.

"Ah. Yes. Everyone, you will recall Georgia from Opening Dinner, our first volunteer. It seems fitting, then, that she shall lead our expedition today."

Georgia nods dumbly in the dark. Dede is still looking at her, and Georgia feels an odd sense of responsibility to do something more, although she's not sure what.

"The headsets," Cecilia says, striding across the stage, "are equipped with a recording feature. What you see here, on-screen, is exactly what Georgia saw on the beach this morning."

It seems, thankfully, that Georgia's involvement is now over. She lets out a breath and loosens her clenched fists on her lap. Dede, still watching her, seems to find her performance unimpressive. She thumps back into her seat.

"Georgia's daughter," says Cecilia, now on the opposite side of the stage, "is five years old and is, as you will soon see, in a somewhat precarious situation. Let's watch."

No sooner does she say this than the holographic Clover on-screen is set into motion. It's somewhat disorienting, a memory formerly inside her head, displayed for the rest of the women to look at. Georgia read once that no one's memories can be trusted, as memories by nature are simply a reconstruction of events rather than a true record. Every reconstruction, the memory changes—details added, others smudged over. It's why Will sometimes insists she didn't tell him about book fairs or meet-the-teachers when, without a shadow of a doubt, she absolutely did. In these moments,

Georgia longs for this, an objective replay they can consult, although in these imaginary scenarios, the replays are always vindication. It never occurred to her that she might see something she would rather not, parts of her to which she was previously blissfully blind.

Her voice, for example, how screechy she sounds as she cries for Clover to put down the needle. The frantic head movements, more like a golden retriever than the steady version of herself she likes to imagine. The sound she makes when she realizes Ruby has vanished. She could go the rest of her life and never want to hear that sound again.

On-screen, everything pauses. In the sand, there's a slight indentation where Ruby's plump little thighs were and now are not. Georgia can feel the same sense of panic she felt then, by the ocean. It's all so real, even though it's anything but.

When Cecilia speaks again, her voice is gentle.

"An emotional experience, no doubt. And one to which we, as mothers, can all surely relate."

Georgia's breathing feels ragged. It's worse than she thought it was—worse, even, than her first experience of it. It's slower this time, a methodical twist of a knife.

"But what I ask," Cecilia says, bowing her head slightly, "is that we remove our emotional lens for a moment. With gratitude, let us set it aside temporarily and analyze this experience through the lens of objectivity."

Silence. The way Cecilia says it, it's as though she's asking them to actually do something, although no one in the crowd seems sure of what.

And then Cecilia smiles, a look that's almost hungry.

"Looking at this objectively, as uninvolved observers, I want us to consider what went wrong here. In the cascade of events we just witnessed, is it possible to identify a point of inflection?"

And yes, Georgia thinks. Yes, isn't this the question? Is this not what keeps her up at night? Even in her sleep, it's like her mind is searching, analyzing and reanalyzing the fabric of her life for one crimp in the material, the point when she could have turned it all around. If only she had a replay like this one, maybe it would all be clear.

Cecilia cocks her head, waiting for an answer. Georgia spots Izzy near the front, turned in her seat. She, too, looks expectant, but based on the quiet audience, she is clearly expecting too much.

Finally, Cecilia says, "It's often difficult, on first try, especially when the answer is so embedded in our understanding of motherhood."

She turns toward the screen, which starts moving again, this time in reverse: an empty shoreline, the view whipping back toward Clover. There's a gull Georgia didn't notice before, skating backward through the sky.

The video stops.

"Here," Cecilia says. "This moment."

Georgia squints. She feels her heart racing, the way she usually does when she's the center of attention, although this feels less familiar.

"What do we notice about this moment?" Cecilia says.

Georgia tries to identify how she's feeling. Anxious? Panicked?

The video starts again, the view whipping back the other way. The horrible screech, the bounce of Georgia bounding down the sand. It stops, reverses, stops again. Plays, but this time muted, in slow motion.

"Hesitation," says Cecilia, a narrator to Georgia's frenzy. She lifts her arm and the video stops, pausing the view on cotton candy clouds and jewel-toned water. "An instant of hesitation before choosing which child to go to."

Georgia's heart is beating in her ears now, but through the thrumming sensation breaks recognition. Yes, she did hesitate—only briefly, for no more than an instant, although an instant is all it takes sometimes. An instant when Georgia was looking at Clover, an instant when the ocean swallowed her youngest daughter, her baby girl. It seems so clear now, in the back of this dark auditorium, an outsider to the situation, but in it, it felt very different. In it, there was Ruby, clearly in more urgent danger, but there was also Clover, five years old, with the soul of an old woman. One dimple on her left cheek. A baby tooth missing where she knocked it on a stool. As a mother, Georgia should not have hesitated, should have recognized the bigger danger, but as a mother, she also didn't have a choice.

"It's understandable," Cecilia says to the now-captive audience. "It's more than understandable—it's biological. Georgia registered the danger in the garbage, and in the split second she turned from her youngest, she was no doubt running through the litany of risks that accompanied her ultimate decision."

Georgia blinks, her eyes surprisingly stinging. It's as though Cecilia has opened her up, pulled out the tangle, and said, *Yes. Yes, I see this, and it makes sense.* Because Cecilia is right: In that moment, caught between her two daughters, she was performing a complex set of calculations. They were fast, only a second, but time is different for a mother. As mothers, seconds are all they have.

When Cecilia speaks again, her voice is tender.

"We learned yesterday about the neurological changes that accompany motherhood, and while that information is valuable, it can also be difficult to understand what that means in practical terms. It can be difficult to visualize its effects in our lives. Here, though, in this video, we have an intricate portrait."

She motions to the screen, and it does look like a painting. Paused, silent, it's beautiful.

"*This*," Cecilia says, "is mom brain. This is decision-making clouded by our biological sensitization to our children. So attuned are we to each and every minute stimulus, we are unable to see the larger picture. The objective realities so obvious to us in this auditorium are lost in the brain of a mom."

CHAPTER 23

Will calls her after the large group meeting, when Georgia is getting ready for dinner.

"Hey," he says, sounding tired. And of course he is. Dinner in normal times is exhausting. Alone, it's a marathon. They've argued before—good-naturedly sometimes, other times less so—about whether dinnertime or bedtime is the hardest part of the day. He says dinnertime, although Georgia can think of few things more soul-sucking than a child standing in her doorway, hollering into the hall that she's not tired.

"How are you?" says Georgia. She's in the bathroom of her villa, in front of a vessel sink that's shaped like a giant pink seashell.

"Good. Fine." He exhales. "Tired."

"Is it too late? I can call back tomorrow."

"It's not too late."

She wonders if he's lying, and then if he's mad. So far, despite everything, she has never seen him get angry, at least not at her. He is, in this respect, a marvel of a human.

"So," she says, "I take it they required the whole circus today?"

Will laughs, but it sounds half-hearted, even though it's his joke. "I feel like a dancing monkey," he has said before, which is both funny and extremely unfunny for being so true. The books, the songs, the stories—it's an increasingly ridiculous set of stunts they must perform each night before Clover agrees to go to sleep.

"Pretty much. Well, and Ruby is sick now."

Georgia meets her eyes in the mirror.

"Sick? What's wrong with her? The same thing Clover had? Is Clover feeling better?"

"Not sure, not sure, and yes."

"What are her symptoms?"

"Fussy, mostly. Some snot. Nothing huge."

"Does she have a fever?"

"I don't think so."

"You didn't take her temperature?"

"It's fine, Georgia. She isn't warm."

For the first time, he sounds snappy, and Georgia's immediate impulse is to snap right back. Almost instantly, though, she feels guilty. She has no right given the circumstance.

"Sorry," she says, turning from the mirror and toward the bedroom. "It's just—I worry."

"I know you do, Gi. I know. But please, don't."

And just like that, the fight in his voice is gone. She lowers herself onto the edge of the bed that she made that morning, even though she's sure housekeeping would have done it for her if she'd left it a mess.

"She's okay, then? Just a little snotty?"

"Just a little snotty."

"Okay."

And she says it a second time, in her head. *Okay.* Everything is okay. She thinks of the video from earlier—her panic, the jerky way it manifested on-screen. That wasn't an anomaly; here she is now, doing the exact same thing.

CHAPTER 24

The next morning, while Cecilia is conducting meetings with some of the other attendees, Georgia's pod is treated to a pontoon ride.

To be clear, *treat* here is Izzy's word. It's not the one Georgia would've used, not the event she would've planned, but not wanting to be difficult, she straps on her life vest and smiles weakly at the pontoon captain, a large local with long, impressive curls. He dips his chin in response but doesn't smile.

When the motor starts up, as the seat beneath her starts to rumble, Georgia grips the pole closest to her. Across the boat, she catches a look from Simone, who gives her a tiny but encouraging nod. Georgia tries to smile back, although she suspects it appears more like a grimace. She tells herself to breathe.

The boat is slow-moving. It chugs through the cove, crawling past the resort, and even once they're out on the bay, it barely creates a wake in the water. Dede, not under the boat's cover, stretches back on the bench and lifts her face to the sun, and Georgia wonders what life would be like to be her.

The water is bluish where they are, but farther out it turns green. The sky overhead is clear, a sparkling contrast to the clouds that look trapped by the volcanic ridges in the distance. When Georgia braves a peek over the edge of the pontoon, she spots a school of yellow fish zigzagging playfully in the water, and she considers the fact that none of this is objectively scary. So why does it feel that way to her?

The boat's motor is loud enough that it's hard to hear anything on board, although Georgia assumes that none of them would be saying much even if they could. Logan, one arm over the back of her seat, is examining the water with a determined expression, as though contemplating a puzzle in her head. Dede looks like she's fallen asleep, and Alice is trying to keep the front of her caftan from flapping open in the wind.

When the boat starts slowing, Georgia grips the pole again, bracing for disaster. Once, in her early twenties, with more free time for self-reflection, she did try to get to the root of her phobia. As far as she can tell, it's some ambiguous mix of genetics and seeing the movie *Titanic* at too young an age.

The motor sputters off, and Izzy, protected today by a nearly opaque layer of sunscreen, stands up. She has to hold on to her seat to keep from falling over.

"Ladies," she says, sounding buoyant, "we have a treat for you today." She grabs the seat edge and lifts it. Underneath, stored beneath the chapped plastic, is what appears to be snorkeling equipment.

"Snorkeling!" she says merrily.

Once, in a creative writing class in college, Georgia's professor started the semester with an icebreaker game. It was the second semester of her senior year, and Georgia had mistakenly assumed she was safe from this sort of torture. She found it especially unfair given the class she had signed up for. (She had not, for example, signed up for public speaking.)

The icebreaker required them, unoriginally, excruciatingly, to title their imaginary autobiographies. When the professor announced it, the girl next to Georgia audibly groaned.

The answers were what you would expect from a group of nerdy writing students: *The Girl with the Apple Laptop. Fool Fighter. A Mostly Uneventful Series of Days.* The girl next to Georgia, the one who groaned, called hers *Just Here for the Credits.*

After much agonizing, Georgia came up with *In Pursuit.* She was quite proud of it actually, but when she told her roommate about it later, her roommate frowned. "I don't get it," she said, but when Georgia asked her what she thought Georgia's title should be, she just shrugged. "I dunno. *Go Along to Get Along,* maybe?"

This answer continues to haunt Georgia even now. In fact, it was one of the first things she told Will when they met, even though it had been years since the class. "Just so you know what you're getting yourself into," she said, which he met with a confused laugh. He didn't understand why it was such a bad thing, and Georgia didn't try to explain it—why this being her primary feature was so terminally sad.

Georgia thinks of this now, watching Izzy hand Dede a mask and a snorkel. They've stopped at a reef that is full of sea life, according to Izzy. Apparently, just beneath the boat is a bale of sea turtles.

Georgia again thinks of her college roommate, whom she'd met in an introduction to poli-sci class when they were freshmen, and whom Georgia still follows passively on Facebook today. In college, the roommate wanted to be a politician—Congress, specifically, although she never made it. She currently lives in New Jersey, married to the guy she was dating in college, and sells makeup through an MLM.

"Simone," says Izzy. "You're next."

Simone and Georgia are the last ones; Logan has just received her mask with an expression that is equally excited and terrified. Without meaning to, Georgia meets Simone's eyes across the boat.

Simone frowns slightly, as though noticing something, although Georgia doesn't know what.

Simone turns to Izzy and says, "I'm good."

Izzy cocks her head. "You're . . . good?"

"Yeah. I've seen too many shark movies."

Dede snickers. Izzy seems unsure what to do with this, and indeed, Simone has not left much room to argue. Alice, who was the first to get her gear, makes a small sound of impatience.

Finally, giving up apparently, Izzy turns to Georgia.

"Well, Georgia, you're up then."

Georgia finds Simone's eyes again. Simone lifts her chin just slightly. It's impossible to tell whether this means something or if Georgia just wants it to.

She says to Izzy, "Actually, I'm good too, I think."

CHAPTER 25

Dede is the first one into the water. She's followed by Alice, then Logan, who pauses warily on the boat ladder. She's wearing board shorts and an oversized T-shirt instead of a swimsuit, and with the snorkel mask, she gives off the impression of someone who has raided a garage sale.

"You got it," Dede says encouragingly. She's treading water with seemingly no effort. Even the mask looks somehow natural on her.

Logan glances back at Izzy, then with a big inhale, she lets go of the ladder. She lands in the water with a graceless plop, to which Dede cheers. It strikes Georgia then that although it feels otherwise, she really knows very little about these women at all.

Izzy is the last one in. She pauses on the ladder and gives Simone and Georgia a meaningful look. The seriousness is dampened slightly by the curls that stick perpendicularly out around her mask and the solid white layer of sunscreen across her forehead.

"The turtles act like you're not even there," she says, as if she's trying to say something else. Georgia nods, not knowing what else to do. Izzy sighs, then lowers herself into the bay with the others.

From the water, the women's voices are slightly garbled. There's a splash, and they set off. Georgia does feel a sense of regret that she's not going with them, although the idea of being with them also feels totally out of the question. She recently had a panic attack in the penguin exhibit at the aquarium, not even *in* water, just in a glass tunnel beneath it. While Clover was clapping excitedly, enamored with the little black-and-white bodies zipping and splashing, Georgia was doing her best not to pass out.

"I'm terrified of water," she says to Simone, mostly because she has the annoying need to talk when she's nervous. "I think I said that the first day. It's almost like a phobia, actually."

"Yeah," Simone says, which Georgia doesn't understand as an answer. Simone has leaned back so her face is in the sunlight, her long braids dangling over the side, looking totally at ease. If it's possible for people to have opposites, Georgia thinks, Simone is hers.

"So your university sent you here?" she says, this time because she actually is curious.

Simone doesn't open her eyes. "Mm-hmm."

"And they paid for it?"

"They did."

"That's nice."

Simone doesn't respond.

Georgia looks at her hands. She goes a successful thirty seconds before she says, "Have they sent other people here before? Other moms from your school, I mean?"

At this, Simone looks up. The boat is swaying slightly in the bay's gentle current, which Georgia is doing her best to ignore.

"One woman, last year."

"And did she like it? Did she . . . I don't know. Find it useful?"

There's an accidental urgency in Georgia's voice, and when she realizes this, her cheeks burn with embarrassment. Simone owes her nothing, least of all answers to questions Georgia can't even bring herself to ask outright.

But Simone doesn't look annoyed. She looks vaguely interested, albeit also uninvested, the way Georgia probably looks when people are arguing in public.

"I don't know," she says finally. "She took a sabbatical afterward. Went on some trip. So either it didn't work, or it did exactly what it was supposed to."

"A sabbatical?"

"Yup. Apparently this place 'opened her eyes.'"

"Opened her eyes to what? Where did she go?"

Here, something in Simone's expression shifts. It's not unkind, but it's more critical than before.

"I don't know. We weren't close."

Georgia chews on the inside of her cheek. A sabbatical. A friend of hers took a sabbatical a few years prior. She documented it all on Facebook—pictures of her atop an elephant, looking sanctimonious at Victoria Falls. "What, does she think she's Julia Roberts?" Georgia said to Will one night, feeling petty. (The pettiness made her feel a little bit better, but not much.)

CHAPTER 26

Later that afternoon, after the boat ride, Cecilia calls the women from Georgia's pod to her office for individual meetings. The pink polo girl, Leila, finds Georgia in her villa when it's her turn. She knocks even though the screen door is open, even though Georgia is visible through the doorway, on the couch.

Leila is less chatty this time as she leads Georgia up the narrow staircase toward Cecilia's office. She doesn't pause until they reach the top, where she turns to Georgia with a professional expression. Her lips are plump and shiny with lip gloss, and as she takes in Georgia's appearance, a look of concern passes over her face. Georgia gives what she hopes to be a reassuring expression, although Leila doesn't look especially reassured. She turns and swipes her key fob at Cecilia's door.

Cecilia's office is as magnificent as Georgia remembers it. Afternoon sun pours in through the front of the room, illuminating the desk and shelves. Cecilia isn't here, although Georgia is still too out of breath from the climb to ask where she is.

Leila shows her where to sit while she waits, a white tufted chair in the corner.

Georgia isn't sure why she's so surprised when Leila leaves her there. It seems, strangely, like a lot of responsibility, Georgia in this beautiful office alone. She crosses her legs and tries not to scrutinize her surroundings, not wanting to be nosy. She glances at the shelves, where there are no pictures, only a sparse stack of white-spined books with black block letters. On the desk in front of her sits one of the pink headsets. She gazes at it for a moment before looking politely at her nails.

When Cecilia arrives, she comes in through the back of the office from the patio. Today she's wearing a long blue dress with a magnificent matching blue cape. It reminds Georgia of a painting her grandmother had in her bedroom, a portrait of the Virgin Mary with an oddly adultlike baby Jesus on her knee.

"Georgia," Cecilia says, sweeping toward her. For a moment, it seems as though she might give Georgia a hug, and Georgia panics, not knowing how to react. Thankfully, Cecilia just reaches over her for something on the bookshelf by her head.

"Lovely to see you," she says, moving to her desk. She turns, and in the direct sunlight, she almost sparkles. "I trust you're finding everything satisfactory so far?"

Georgia nods, mostly out of habit, but also because *satisfactory*, she feels, is a fair assessment.

Cecilia appears pleased. The thing she's holding, the thing she plucked from behind Georgia, is a small white remote.

"You're making wonderful progress with our curriculum," Cecilia says, which Georgia finds surprising. She thinks of how disappointedly Izzy looked at her on the boat earlier that afternoon.

"That's . . ." Georgia searches for the word. Not finding it, she says, "Thank you. That's nice to hear."

Cecilia doesn't smile at this, but something about her eyes looks amused. Georgia's gaze travels over Cecilia's shoulder, to the books just behind her head: *Maternal Influence. Neuroscience in the Feminist Era. Motherly Rage.*

"Well," says Cecilia, bringing her hands together, the remote clasped between them. "I like to have these meetings before we get too far into our work. To measure our progress, I find it essential to commemorate where we started—a reference point for our journey, if you will."

Georgia nods as Cecilia raises the remote. Around them, window shades start to descend. When they stop, the room is totally dark.

And then a screen illuminates. It's small, in the corner of the room opposite Georgia. Georgia wonders how she didn't notice it before. It shines on Cecilia's face from the side, giving her features a harsh, slanted appearance. Like this, she doesn't look quite as majestic as she did before.

The screen is white for a moment, then black. And then, against that, a brilliant glowing butterfly.

No, not a butterfly. A brain.

"Your brain," Cecilia tells her, and Georgia feels immediately embarrassed, like her own naked body has been cast on the screen.

"Not a literal image. A representation constructed from the data collected by your headset."

Georgia feels something unsavory in her stomach.

"Data?" she says.

"Data procured from the electromagnetic pulses generated by your brain before and during your practical exercises yesterday."

Georgia touches her head, but Cecilia doesn't pause for further questions. She presses the remote again, and on-screen the butterfly pulses—squirming, writhing.

"Interesting, isn't it?" says Cecilia. She's looking at Georgia, not at the screen, which Georgia registers, although she can barely pull her eyes away from it herself. It seems to be alive, and she supposes it is. She's suddenly struck with an intense wave of vertigo, causing her to clasp the arms of her chair.

On-screen, the white butterfly is marred by a sudden splotch of red.

"The amygdala," Cecilia says lightly. "The part of the brain activated during times of stress."

The splotch turns to two—two angry red eyes in the middle of the twisting white and gray. Georgia feels transfixed by the image.

"A totally normal response," Cecilia says, causing Georgia to finally meet her eyes. "We see this in nearly every attendee, in some capacity. Surprise. Outrage." She raises an eyebrow. "Fear?"

Georgia's eyes move back to the screen, where her own fear pulses red, impossible to deny. She *was* afraid, actually. She was afraid before the exercise even began. She was afraid because the headsets were foreign and unexpected, but also because in that moment she had such a grand capacity to fail.

Cecilia is quiet now, her expression attentive as she gazes at the screen. Georgia wonders if this is what the other mothers' brains looked like, if theirs were also red with fear.

Between the two red splotches another forms, this one blue. It's small at first, although it seems to be pulsing outward, the color deepening with each beat.

"The hypothalamus," says Cecilia. "Specifically, the area called the medial preoptic area, or the MPOA. Or, as it's sometimes referred to, the maternal circuit."

The three dots are arranged in such a way that they almost look human, like a face. It's unsettling but also weirdly beautiful.

"Did you know that researchers are able to distinguish a mother's brain from a non-mother's brain just by looking at them?" says Cecilia. "Just by looking at images like this?"

Georgia shakes her head, although she doesn't find it all that surprising.

"I didn't."

"Some changes to a mother's brain are obvious. For example, mothers' brains show notable shrinkage in gray matter, the part of the brain activated during decision-making."

Georgia nods, knowing this to be true. Shortly after Ruby was born, Georgia took it upon herself to find a good family dentist—an easy task, objectively, although at four months postpartum, it felt insurmountable. The list of options was long and paralyzing, so the task that should have taken thirty minutes ended up taking her weeks.

"Other changes involve certain neurotransmitters," Cecilia continues, "especially oxytocin. In most people, oxytocin is the hormone that reduces fear and pain, but it has also been linked with maternal behavior. Interestingly, researchers have been able to manipulate oxytocin and oxytocin receptors in animal models to mimic maternal behavior in animals who have never given birth."

The colors on-screen are moving in synchrony now, and it reminds Georgia of a sort of dance. It's unfathomable that this is her brain—that she's *looking* at it—but at the same time, it seems familiar too.

Cecilia says, "At The Program, we are particularly interested in the maternal circuit, which we believe to be the primary driver of maternal behavior. In fact, we have been able to successfully associate activity in this area of the brain with some key maternal instincts."

For a moment, neither of them says anything as they both watch the screen. Georgia has always wondered if mothering is learned, and if so, what that says about her, and about her own mother and her grandmother and all the women who came before them. The thought is either comforting or horrifying, depending on her mood, although she was wrong to think of it this way. Because that's not the way motherhood works, is it? She can see it here: all her victories, all her faults, just electrical impulses in the end.

"This is a beautiful response," Cecilia says finally, her eyes finding Georgia. "Exceptional. I'm expecting great things from you based on what I see here today."

CHAPTER 27

The next day, Izzy again collects the women of Georgia's pod in the same white Program van from the day at the beach. It seems that snorkeling has reinvigorated Dede, who doesn't go so far as to greet Izzy as she climbs into the vehicle, but who at least finds a seat without an audible huff. Even Logan, who has a vaguely sick look about her normally, looks healthier. Her cheeks seem fuller when she smiles at Georgia, and the bridge of her nose is pink from the sun.

The women are quiet as they pull out of the resort parking lot. Over the radio, music plays faintly, something in Spanish. Izzy hums to it as though the song is familiar. In front of Georgia, Alice, too, looks different, perhaps because she has not forced her hair back into submission. It hangs loose around her cheeks with a slight wave to it, and Georgia almost feels compelled to tap her on the shoulder and tell her how pretty it looks this way.

It's clear almost immediately that they're not heading to the beach again. At a fork in the road just outside the resort, Izzy takes a left where she previously took a right. The itinerary for today reads only "practical exercise" with no suggestion of where (or really, what) the exercise will be.

A little while into the drive, Dede cranes her neck to look over Izzy's shoulder.

"We're going to a mountain?" she says suspiciously.

The women turn collectively to their windows. Georgia, who is wearing sandals, because the itinerary didn't suggest she shouldn't wear sandals, feels her stomach drop.

"It's called a tuff ring," says Izzy, "a low-standing volcano that forms a crater."

This doesn't do much to soothe Georgia's nerves. Beside her, Logan also looks anxious, although she, at least, is wearing a pair of sneakers.

Dede says, "Tuff ring. Sounds made-up."

At this, Izzy remains diplomatically quiet.

As the van climbs, Georgia searches for a distinguishing feature, something that makes the incline a tuff ring and not a mountain. She can't find it, although she holds on to the one silver lining that on a mountain, at least, they're not near the water.

Except, they are near the water. Close enough to see it, at least.

Izzy parks the van and leads the women down a short paved trail to a building that wasn't visible from the road. It's stark white with a tall, solid door that's surrounded by a frame of twisty kiawe trees. Izzy swipes her key fob and leads them through a hallway that opens to a vast room with a grand cathedral ceiling and an entire wall of glass. Visible through the glass, in the far distance, is a mammoth crater, at the center of which is an embayment—electric blue with a map of coral visible just beneath the surface.

"Y'all can find a seat," says Izzy, who doesn't have the tub of headsets from the first practical exercise. Today, she's holding only a clipboard and a tote bag.

The women draw away from the window reluctantly. It is, though terrifying, a mesmerizing view. It is only then that Georgia registers how oddly the room around them is furnished.

The chairs are scattered in no clear pattern, and the chairs themselves also seem haphazard. Closest to Georgia is a midnight-blue wingback. Near Simone, an emerald-green chaise. Dede plops down into a magenta club chair with topaz furniture buttons. The cumulative effect is distinctly eclectic, a sharp contrast to the building's sterile exterior.

"Cecilia will be meeting us momentarily," says Izzy, "but we can get our materials sorted now." She contemplates the tote bag she's holding, but then, abruptly, she looks up as though she's forgotten something. "Everyone comfortable? Y'all happy with your seats?"

Georgia accidentally makes eye contact with Logan, who has sunk deep into a fluffy yellow egg chair. She shrugs, as though Georgia is the one who asked the question. No one else responds.

"Okay, well, if I can get y'all anything, please let me know."

It's such a departure from their first exercise, which felt like a test for them to pass. Here, it's like they're Izzy's guests. Georgia wonders if this is intentional. Perhaps the goal is to tear them down before building them back up.

Izzy returns to her tote bag, from which she pulls a stack of pink folders. She flips open the first one and considers it for a second, then hands it to Logan, who is closest to her. Logan hesitates before taking it, moving with the careful slowness of someone handling a bomb. Izzy strides over to Dede and hands her the next one.

Georgia's is last. It's not clear if they're allowed to open the folders, although Dede has, and Izzy—now busy writing something on her clipboard—seems unbothered by this. Georgia decides it's probably okay to look at hers as well.

At first, she doesn't know what she's looking at: a formal-looking piece of paper with some handwritten text and some that is typed. She starts to read, but even then it takes her a moment to realize it's *her* handwriting on the page. When she does, it's with a little start, like seeing yourself unexpectedly in a photo, the momentary disbelief that *that's* how you look.

But it is indeed her own handwriting: scanned, reprinted, but clearly hers. It's a photocopy of her application for The Program, which she filled out at her kitchen table only a few weeks ago after they'd put the girls to bed. It was a night shortly after the first bra incident, right after they'd gotten the video doorbell for the front door, which they hoped would catch the assailant in the act if they ever came back. (What they caught, mainly, was squirrels.) Georgia sat at the table for a long time that night, putting her pen to the paper, then lifting it back up. Normally a form like this would be easy for her. A form is usually where Georgia thrives! But not this one. This one stumped her. The first question alone felt impossible.

What do you hope to get out of your experience at The Program?

She couldn't decide which was worse: a lie or the truth.

CHAPTER 28

When Cecilia finally arrives, she is dressed more formally than Georgia has seen her so far. Her hair is pulled back tightly from her face, and she's wearing a fantastic blue power suit with shoulder pads that makes Georgia wonder if maybe she could pull off shoulder pads. She stands in the middle of the room with Izzy in one of the chairs beside her, and has just asked the women to open up their folders, unaware—or perhaps ignoring the fact—that most of them already have.

"While your applications were not long," she is saying now, her voice just as mellow as usual, an interesting contrast with the suit, "they provide crucial insights for us here at The Program. They are, if you will, our first windows into your minds."

Georgia looks down at her folder, a strange feeling overtaking her—betrayal, almost, as though the folder has done something she didn't think it would do. She thinks of a literal window, her *own* windows back home, how she imagined the bra culprit's face appearing there some nights. "Do you think they might be . . . stalking us?" Georgia said to the police after the first bra incident, the idea so ludicrous, she was embarrassed to voice it out loud. Worse still was the way the officer responded, like this was a reasonable thing to worry about.

"Dede," Cecilia says, the abruptness of her voice catching them all—including Dede, by the looks of it—by surprise. Dede has tossed her folder to the ground by her feet, and when she looks up at Cecilia, her face goes through the visible stages of startled to defiant to determinedly bored.

"Dede, did you have any difficulties with your application when you were filling it out?"

Cecilia's eyes don't stray from Dede's face when she asks this. She has apparently made the decision to ignore the fact that Dede's folder lies irreverently on the ground.

"Not really," Dede says flatly, picking at a nail. "It was a pretty normal questionnaire."

"Ah." Cecilia doesn't appear moved by Dede's rudeness. In fact, she looks like this is the exact answer she was hoping for. "But the application wasn't just a questionnaire."

"Aren't all applications like, famously questionnaires?"

Next to Georgia, Simone lets out a small snort. From deep within her yellow egg chair, Logan looks alarmed.

Cecilia just smiles. She looks Dede up and down for a moment, as though considering how to answer this. Then, without saying anything, she turns to Georgia.

"And what about you, Georgia? Any trouble with yours?"

Georgia feels the eyes of the other women on her, and her cheeks start to warm. The absurd thought crosses her mind to answer this question honestly. *Much trouble actually. Trouble all the way down.*

"I don't think so," she says.

Cecilia cocks her head. It's as though she knows Georgia is lying, and perhaps she does know. Georgia is a historically bad liar, after all.

"I mean, it wasn't easy," she adds, which is still probably a lie, but at least a little closer to the truth. "Some of the questions were . . . tough."

Tough. Why did she say that? She doesn't like that word. She has a long personal history of hating that word, in fact. *Tough.* She was so *tough* when her mom died. That's what people said, usually with a look of satisfaction, as though that explained everything. As though this horrible thing was possibly a bit less horrible because Georgia was so tough.

"Tough," Cecilia repeats, sounding curious. "Could you explain what you mean by that?"

But Georgia cannot explain what she means by that. She cannot explain why she did what she did, or how she ended up here as a result. There were no spots open at The Program, and yet here she sits, and she cannot explain why that happened to the last person in the world who deserves good luck.

"Well," she starts, but then stops. She looks down at her application, to the first question. *What do you hope to get out of your experience at The Program?* The truth is, she was hoping for nothing, because she no longer felt she deserved the luxury of hope.

"It's just been a really tough few months," she says at last, surprising herself by using the word again. If her answer surprises Cecilia, however, she doesn't show it.

"Yes," she says gently. "Of course. And would you like to share with the group what made these last few months so tough?"

The room now is totally quiet. Even Logan, who has been struggling valiantly against the fluffy chair, goes still. Georgia grips the folder in front of her. Her body seems to be buzzing, and she recognizes the feeling from the first night on the island, although this time it's sharper. This time, she won't be able to blame the alcohol.

"Well," she says, keeping her eyes determinedly on Cecilia, "I'm sure you all have heard about that article in the *Pacific*. With the moms? They interviewed a bunch of victims of sexual abuse." She sneaks a glance at the other women—Dede, leaning forward with intrigue; Logan, barely visible now from deep within her chair.

"And they interviewed me too," she continues. "Anonymously, of course. It was supposed to be anonymous, anyway, but someone online figured out who I was probably talking about, and once they figured that out, my law firm figured out who I was. And they accused me of lying, and then *that* got out, and I . . ."

She stops, feeling slightly dazed. She's so close to saying it, she realizes, which is scary. Scarier is the fact that she *wants* to tell them. She wants them to see who she really is and what she has done. She thinks of her grandmother, her little Polish Babcia, so devoutly Catholic and thus so convinced of her sins. Growing up, Georgia thought this was depressing, that someone like Babcia—who didn't sin, not really, not the way most people do—still thought of herself this way. It was almost as if she *liked* the label, liked to revel in the inherent badness of being human. It's only now that Georgia wonders if what she actually liked was the freedom from being good.

"And I did," she says, her voice accidentally louder and harder than it was before. It seems to echo though the silent room, and to Georgia's ear, it sounds like a stranger. "I did lie," she tells them. "I said I was sexually assaulted in my law firm's nursing room, but I wasn't, and when that came out, it obviously created a big mess. So I'm here to . . . fix that mess, I guess."

For a moment, no one says anything. Georgia wonders if this is how Babcia felt in confession, whether it was at all satisfying to truly shock the priest.

"Thank you, Georgia," Cecilia says finally, breaking the silence, and for the first time, she doesn't sound sure of herself. She is looking at Georgia with a new and unexpected expression, something like genuine surprise. "We appreciate your honesty."

Georgia nods, a strange feeling overtaking her. For a moment, she has the horrible thought that she's going to cry, but she doesn't. That's not what this feeling is. So what is this feeling? Her heart is beating quickly, thrumming in her ears, and she wonders if she has ever felt more alive.

"All of us here have come in search of something," Cecilia says finally, turning from Georgia to address the group, "whether we have allowed ourselves to be honest about what that is or not. And this is our greatest challenge, because to be honest—with others, but more importantly, with ourselves—is not easy. It is a skill, and like any skill, it takes practice."

Here, she nods to Izzy, who jumps into action. From the tote, she pulls out a bag.

"Practice," Cecilia says, "can be difficult, especially when a skill is new. It is for this reason that we employ the use of certain tools to help us take those first critical steps."

She takes the bag from Izzy and holds it up for the women, although no one in the room seems to know what they're looking at.

"Does anyone here have experience with psilocybin?" Cecilia asks.

CHAPTER 29

Silence.

And then Dede says abruptly, "Are you talking about magic mushrooms?"

Cecilia nods, her expression pleasant. "Colloquially referred to as magic mushrooms, yes."

Dede laughs, a single, disbelieving guffaw. Alice is wearing a peculiar expression, a furious and unsuccessful attempt to appear unaffected. Even Georgia, nerves still whirring from her confession, feels her mind go still.

"The research on psilocybin psychotherapy is relatively new," says Cecilia, "but compelling. Here at The Program, we have used it to great effect. It is a tool by which we have achieved some of our most remarkable breakthroughs so far."

It is not what she's saying that is so disorienting (although perhaps it should be). What Georgia finds the most bizarre is the complete matter-of-fact way Cecilia is saying it.

Psilocybin. *Mushrooms.* What does she know about mushrooms? It's a party drug, right? Not an actual problem? But *is* that right? She doesn't actually know. How would she know? And why on earth would Cecilia have magic mushrooms here?

"You're suggesting that we trip on mushrooms right now?" Alice says, asking the question for all of them. Her voice is higher than usual and notably strained.

"Yes," Cecilia says simply.

Alice gawks. Dede lets out another laugh.

"I mean, this can't be legal, can it? Or safe?" Alice's voice has turned panicked, which she seems to sense with embarrassment. She sits up straighter and pulls her shoulders back, which doesn't help.

"It is legal, and I assure you, it is very safe."

"Legal for everybody?" Logan says, struggling against her chair again, fighting to stay afloat. "Even people who have . . . less than perfect histories with the law?"

"Yes," Cecilia says gently. "Perfectly legal."

Dede's hand shoots up, although she doesn't wait for Cecilia to acknowledge it before she speaks.

"Do our husbands know about this?"

Georgia winces. Cecilia bows her head.

"We respect your privacy," she says. "So, no, nothing that happens here will be disclosed to anyone without your consent. And please be reminded that this is totally voluntary. If you would like to opt out of this portion of our curriculum, it is completely and totally your prerogative."

Dede grimaces. Georgia feels a jolt of something. Excitement? Fear? She imagines the frenzy of fireworks she would probably see in her brain if she could look at it now. She isn't against drugs, not necessarily. She dated a boy early in college who was, as he referred to himself, an "intuitive pothead." (She's pretty sure, now, that he made that up.) Georgia smoked with him a handful of times in various house party basements, and while she didn't like it exactly, she didn't *not* like it either.

How do you take mushrooms? Just eat them? Do you chew? Are they washed? In college, to her horror, she witnessed a roommate eat a pack of white mushrooms from the store without rinsing them off first.

"Psilocybin," Cecilia says, filling their silence, "has been used throughout history in religious and spiritual contexts. It gives us the opportunity to perceive our surroundings through a different lens—a different state of consciousness, if you will."

From the tote bag, she pulls out one of the smaller bags, and from that she produces what appear to be little pink capsules. For some reason, this—the pinkness of them—strikes Georgia as both ridiculous and very real.

"There is virtually no risk of physical dependence," Cecilia tells them. "And the effects generally last no more than eight hours. During that time, you will be able to open up thought processes that may have been difficult to access otherwise."

She strides over to Logan, who seems to have accepted her fate inside the chair. Cecilia takes Logan's pink folder and holds it up with one hand, the psilocybin still raised in the other.

"As we embark on the next phase of our journey," she says, "we reflect on the contents of the folders before you. In these folders are the stories you've told yourselves about your lives, stories about what brought you here and what you're hoping to find. And perhaps some of these stories reflect the truth. But today, here, I want us to dig deeper. I want us to look at ourselves honestly and unflinchingly. I want us to look without being afraid of what we might see."

CHAPTER 30

Taking psilocybin, it turns out, is easy. It's as easy as swallowing a pill.

And yet, as soon as Georgia does it, she's overcome with a full-bodied sense of panic. It's the undoableness of it, she realizes, the understanding that wherever she's heading now, there's no turning back.

As quickly as this feeling comes over her, however, it fades. She searches for Simone's eyes across the room—Simone, wearing her usual inscrutable expression, which Georgia now finds comforting. She barely knows Simone, but she trusts her judgment, and here she is, just like everyone else.

Georgia leans her head back and closes her eyes. Waits. She pictures herself in an airport, waiting for her flight. She likes airports. She likes how they're between destinations, between phases, somehow between time. She likes that in an airport the playing field is briefly even. No matter how poor or rich, happy or sad, healthy or broken, everyone at the airport is at the mercy of the airlines and must endure the same Hudson News snacks.

Someone—Cecilia or Izzy—has turned on music, something faint and noninvasive. Georgia opens her eyes and blinks for a second, like a newborn baby seeing the world for the first time. Across the room, Dede's magenta chair glitters. In it, Dede sits with her head back, the way she did on the pontoon, her face to the sun. Like the chair, Dede also sparkles, which is both remarkable and totally unremarkable, in some hard-to-explain way.

Dede feels Georgia looking. She lifts her head and meets Georgia's eyes with a dreamy grin. And Georgia realizes something suddenly: *Life* is an airport. In the end, they're all the same—holding up their arms in full-body scanners, trying to charge their phones. Doing their best with what they have, waiting for their flights to take off.

Her gaze falls naturally, inevitably, to the folder in front of her. The folder is closed, and yet somehow, she can see the application beneath the cover. Or maybe she can hear it, or feel it. She has the faraway notion that her senses are a bit jumbled, although this does not strike her as a problem. In fact, she wonders why she ever bothered separating her senses in the first place.

She holds up the folder and looks at it. She speaks to it like it can hear.

"You weren't trying to hurt me," she says.

"I wasn't," says Julie, who has taken the place of the folder in her hand.

Georgia stares, then starts to laugh at this strange handheld version of her friend. At first, it's a little laugh, but then the laugh snowballs into a full-bellied shake. She laughs and laughs and laughs, then all at once she stops.

Julie is life-sized now. She's standing in front of Georgia with a little half smile on her face. In her arms is her little baby, Heath. Heath, such a happy little elf, only a few weeks younger than Ruby. Ruby is not like Heath. Ruby is a spitfire. That's Will's word, and when he says it, Georgia—the opposite of a spitfire, definitionally—is filled with such pride.

"Mommy," says Julie, although Julie is no longer Julie, but Clover. Clover! Georgia's first baby, although she's a baby no more. Maybe Clover was never a baby. She's also different from Heath, but in a different way from Ruby. Clover was born serious, unimpressed. "I feel like she's just humoring us," Georgia said once to Will when

Clover was little. "Like, here she is, being a toddler against her will."

"Clover, baby," Georgia says, confused now about why her daughter is here. Confused about why Clover is holding a baby—baby Heath. But no, that's not baby Heath. That's a different baby, one she knows. Somehow, unexpectedly, Clover is holding the baby version of herself.

And that's when she realizes: There are more babies. Many babies! In her lap, a newborn. A wobbly toddler by her feet. A two-year-old with a tooth missing from falling off a stool. And not just that: There are more Clovers. A teenaged Clover. A Clover in her twenties. All people Georgia has never seen but whom she has known her whole life.

"Clover," Georgia whispers to the woman in front of her, with Clover's same big brown eyes. The woman smiles back at her mildly, mutely. From behind her, the teenaged Clover waves. Every version of her daughter, all here together. Georgia feels a new feeling, but also an ancient feeling, what it is to be a mother: all at once overjoyed and devastatingly sad.

And that's when it hits her: It's always like this, isn't it? Clovers and Rubies, Rubies and Clovers, everywhere all the time. Not the centers of her world; the foundation of it. The truth and reason on which all decisions are made.

And that's why she's here, she realizes.

It all makes sense to her, finally.

CHAPTER 31

They stay in the big room for a while, even after their trips are over, until the daytime sun turns low and orange in the sky. The drive back to the resort after that is quiet, but it's a more comfortable quiet than on the way there. The mood is almost sleepy, that happily exhausted feeling Georgia imagines people get after exercise.

When they get to the front office, Izzy turns around in her seat. She gives them all a strange look, like she finds them funny. Georgia wonders if they are being funny. She used to find her intuitive pothead boyfriend funny in the beginning, until he just became annoying.

"Y'all did a great job today," Izzy says, sounding earnest. "Dinner tonight will be sent to your rooms. Take this time to yourselves to really reflect on your experience. Tomorrow, we'll meet back up as a group."

As they're walking back to their villas, Dede says to no one in particular, "That wasn't what I was expecting." The others all murmur in agreement. Georgia notices that the pink evening light makes Dede's skin look even brighter than usual. Truly vibrant. She then wonders if it's actually the pink light or just the mushroom powder. (Before they left the big white room earlier, Cecilia told them to expect the "afterglow" period, which she described as a state of relaxation and bliss.)

"Well," Dede says when they reach their villas. They all pause here for a moment, looking at one another, although no one seems to know what to say. "See you tomorrow, I guess," she says finally, and they all nod, deciding this is enough.

Georgia's dinner is already waiting for her back in her room, a thick tuna steak with sesame seeds on the outside. She lifts the steel plate cover and looks at it for a moment, marveling at the pinkness of the fish, the electric green of the wasabi. The corner of the plate is decorated with a cheery purple flower, and she thinks of their first night on the island, those edible flowers that Logan kept eating. She's overcome suddenly with a swell of affection toward the women in her pod—toward all the mothers on the island, actually. All the mothers in the world.

She texts Will before she calls him, to make sure he's still up. When she does call, he sounds wide awake. "I was about to get in bed," he tells her when she questions this. "Just as soon as I get off the couch."

And she can imagine this, imagine him, blue light from the television making shadows on his face. He stays up later when she's not there, because, in his words, "There's no responsibility." (He doesn't seem to realize the implication of this: that the responsibility in this case is her.)

"Long night?" she says, missing him suddenly. Missing their home. She wonders if she should stay up later with him more often, the way all the influencers say she should. More quality time with their partners! More quality time with their kids! More protein and sex and collagen and nonfiction reading and swishing oil around in your mouth at bedtime because that's somehow supposed to be good for your health.

"A little," Will says—Will, who never worries about these things, mostly because Will isn't a worrier, but also because no one tells him to worry about these things. If Will caught her swishing oil in her mouth, he'd think she'd gone insane.

"Clover was in a mood," he says, "and Ruby's still not feeling well—still not over that bug."

Georgia hears this and immediately braces herself for the worry. *What are her symptoms?* she would usually ask him. *Have you called the doctor? What have you given her so far?* But while the questions do cross her mind now, they don't feel as urgent. They're light and wispy, and then they just float off, unasked.

"Ugh. I hate to hear that," she says. "I'm sorry."

"We're fine. Don't worry."

But she's not worried, she realizes amazedly.

There's a beat of silence before Will says, "So how are you doing? How's it going out there?" He sounds unsure of something, and she wonders if he noticed her lack of questions, her lack of worry. If he knows something's up without being told.

"I'm good," she says. "I'm . . ."

She looks down at the tuna in front of her with all its hundreds of tiny seeds. It strikes her then that she's only one person in a very big world of people, and that all the worries that seem so big to her are—in the grand scheme of things—really quite small.

She wonders, then, if she might still be a tiny bit high.

"You're never going to believe this," she says, deciding it's better to tell him now than later, "but today—just a little while ago, actually—we did psilocybin."

Hearing the words, she can't decide if they sound very serious or extremely unserious. A joke that's not all that funny. She wonders if Will will think she's kidding. *She* might think she was kidding, if she didn't know better.

"Psilocybin?" he says after a very long pause. "Like, mushrooms?"

"Yes. But we didn't use them in like, the drug way."

"In what way did you use them?"

"In the medical way. It was all very clinical."

Will doesn't say anything for a moment, and she considers the possibility that he might get mad. He's not the sort of husband to get mad about things like this. Georgia has a friend from college whose husband checks her credit card statements, which she told Georgia with a tone of cheerful exasperation, like this was just one of those quirky little things husbands do. But Will doesn't. Their bank accidentally started sending him text updates on all her charges, and not only did he not read them, but he found them highly irritating and asked the bank to stop.

"Well," Will says finally, in a voice that reveals nothing, "that's a little shocking."

He doesn't sound mad, Georgia notes. He sounds, for the most part, tired.

"It was. When she announced it, we all about fell out of our chairs."

"When who announced it?"

"Cecilia. The Program head or whatever."

"Ah."

"But apparently they use mushrooms a lot for therapy. And, you know, I think I've heard of that before. They use it to help people be more open to . . . things."

"Open to *things?*"

"Like treatments."

"And is that why you used them?"

Georgia starts to answer, but then she stops herself. *Is* that why they used them? In a way, she supposes so, but she's not totally sure either, mostly because she's not totally sure what treatment it would be opening her to.

"I don't know," she says finally, truthfully. "I mean, we were supposed to reflect on why we're here, but I guess I don't know . . . the point of that."

There's another beat of silence. Then Will sounds a little stiff when he says, "I see." And this is understandable. This ambiguity is not exactly reassuring, as he is sacrificing a lot for her to be here. Working at the high school is quite the scheduling challenge when single-parenting a kindergartner, not to mention the fact that Ruby is sick. Combine that with the fact that someone keeps putting bras on their various door handles, and she can see how it would become very overwhelming, very fast.

She remembers, then, the many Clovers she saw in her trip, and how this should've felt overwhelming, although it did not. It felt completely obvious, actually. She saw all those Clovers and understood immediately what it meant.

She says without segue, "Do you ever think I—I don't know. That I'm blinded sometimes? Like, do you ever think I'm *too* focused on the girls?"

This time, there's a definite edge to Will's voice when he answers. "Too focused on the girls? Is that what they're telling you?"

"No." (Although more realistically, yes.)

Will sighs, and she can see that this conversation is not going anywhere productive.

"Well, no, Georgia," he says tiredly. "I've actually never thought that once in my life."

CHAPTER 32

"You want us to do what now?"

It's the morning after their psilocybin trips, and the women of Pod Three have just gotten out of the van, which is parked along the side of a dead-end road that doesn't seem to have any designated parking spots. Simone stands with her hands on her hips as Izzy gives her a "hospitality smile" (as Dede calls it). From the smile, it's clear Izzy doesn't know whether Simone's question was an actual request for clarification, or something else.

"The first little portion of the trail is a bit tricky," Izzy says, landing midway between answering the question and ignoring it. "But I promise y'all, the majority of the climb is a walk."

They're together for another practical exercise, although this time they're not at the beach or the white building from the day before. Earlier that morning, Izzy drove them along the coastline until, just as the sun broke free from the horizon, they turned and started climbing a steep residential road up the side of a hill. The houses here have the understated, slightly run-down look of expensive places that are trying to look inexpensive, or perhaps the other way around. Between the two houses where they now stand is a trailhead that, if Izzy had not pointed it out as a trailhead, Georgia never would have identified as such.

"A walk," says Simone in a tone that is somehow both skeptical and totally devoid of emotion. It is clear that she, like Georgia, does not trust what Izzy considers a "walk." To Georgia, a walk is the two blocks from her office to the metro, long enough to change out of her work heels and into her slides, but not so long that she couldn't do it in heels in a rush. She suspects, though, that Izzy has a different definition of the word, perhaps one closer to Alice's, who is wearing a serious-looking pair of running shoes.

"Ya'll will be fine," says Izzy. "Don't worry."

But Simone doesn't actually look worried. She looks mostly uninterested in the rope in Izzy's hand, which they're apparently going to use on the "first little portion" of the allegedly walkable trail.

"Who wants to go first?" Izzy says brightly. She gives them a hopeful expression that no one returns. Georgia notices that the peaceful feeling from yesterday has started to wane.

"I mean . . ." says Dede, stepping forward. She's wearing a set of light blue workout tights and a matching cropped tank. Her butt is perky, as is her gravity-defying ponytail.

Izzy gives her an affectionate smile, which Dede ignores.

"Once you're out of the trees," Izzy says as Dede takes the rope from her, "you'll see the path open up. We're going to the second pillbox. Don't worry, you can't miss it."

Dede doesn't say anything to this. She rolls her shoulders, assessing the trail before her. Only the first few yards are visible before it disappears into the scraggly trees and bushes, although those first few yards shoot straight up. It's steep, and it's narrow, and Georgia cannot imagine a person climbing it.

And yet, Dede does. She flips her ponytail over her shoulder and takes a strong step forward. She ascends the incline so easily, so gracefully, that Georgia wonders if maybe she can do it after all.

Dede disappears into the foliage, leaving behind her the quivering excess rope. She doesn't call back to assure the women she's okay, although there are no sounds to suggest she's not okay either.

Izzy plucks the end of the rope from the ground and turns back to the rest of the women.

"Who's next?"

Georgia exchanges a look with Logan, whose eyes are wide. Simone's hands are still on her hips, her eyebrows raised. Alice sniffs loudly and takes a step forward.

"Excellent!" Izzy's enthusiasm appears sincere. "Up you go, then."

Alice takes the rope and, unlike Dede, doesn't hesitate. She marches toward the base of the trail, looking determined. She hoists herself up, although she's not as agile as Dede. Her foot slips, and she responds with an enraged little growl. She recovers quickly, and while she doesn't make it look quite as easy as Dede did, she pulls herself up into the trees as well.

"Oh-kay," says Izzy, like it's two words. She turns to the remaining three women. "Not so bad, is it?"

A few years ago, shortly after Clover was born, Will trained to run in a 5K at the school where he works. Will was, before this, not a runner. In fact, it was one of the ways in which he and Georgia were most similar—not unathletic necessarily, but they weren't the sort of people to use hotel fitness rooms either. Georgia remembers the training not specifically because she remembers Will running, but because she remembers crying about it once. She wasn't sure if she was crying because she was jealous or because she felt betrayed by him, as though their mediocre athleticism was in fact a marital commitment. In hindsight, she was probably crying because she was newly postpartum with Clover, and the hormones made very normal things unbearable. (She, for example, cried multiple times over a certain diaper commercial.) Still, in that moment, it felt devastating: Will moving forward while she felt, in so many ways, like she was stuck.

"I'll go," she says, surprising herself. This isn't like her, but that's a good thing. That is, as far as she can tell, the entire point.

CHAPTER 33

It becomes clear approximately twelve steps up the hill that Georgia has made a grave mistake. The trail is slightly less steep beneath the trees, although just barely, and her arms are shaking with exhaustion already. She can no longer see Izzy or the other women behind her, and Alice and Dede are climbing fast enough that they're not visible either. If she lets go, she will fall, and probably no one will notice until she reaches the ground.

What was she thinking? She imagines Will getting a call from Cecilia later. *So sorry! What a disaster! Your wife has fallen down a hill and died*. People at her funeral will shake their heads and wonder what she *thought* was going to happen. What business did she think she had, climbing a hill this steep?

She takes another step. Her arms tremble and her quads burn. Why didn't she exercise more in her life? It didn't have to be a 5K! It didn't even have to be for aesthetics! She should have trained for functionality so she could climb a hill like this.

But that's not fair to her past self. After all, why in the world would she have to climb a hill like this? In what scenario, apart from one where she's gone completely insane, would she be involved in this kind of activity?

It's getting hotter and hotter the higher the sun climbs, although maybe it's because of the exertion and her growing panic. She *has* gone completely insane, she thinks. That's why they tell you not to do drugs! Because it leads to impaired decision-making! The imaginary people at her imaginary funeral shake their heads. *She really brought this upon herself*, they think.

She heaves again, emitting a full-bodied grunt, and just like that, she's out of the trees.

~

The ground beneath her levels dramatically, so much so that her hand, the one holding the rope, falls limply to her side. Ahead of her, a long stretch of trail is visible. It zigs and zags up the hill, cutting through an expanse of tangled, ankle-high grass that is green in places but mostly brown. The trail presumably crests somewhere in the distance, although it's far enough away that Georgia can't tell where.

The rope, it turns out, is tied to a tree in a regular-looking knot, which might've given her pause if she'd known that at the bottom. (She had expected something a little more regulated.)

She drops it and takes stock of the situation. Alice and Dede are visible halfway up the hill, Dede ahead, although Alice seems to be taking ground. Georgia looks back, but she cannot see anyone on the trail behind her. She is, for all practical purposes, alone.

She notices then that the afterglow period is quickly fading. If the light she felt last night was a candle, that candle has now burned down completely, leaving only the last flickering gasp of the waxless wick. She does not feel optimistic about the hike before her. It doesn't even feel particularly realistic. It's true that the trail seems much less steep here than it did in the trees, but it's still steep, and it has come to Georgia's attention that she is spectacularly out of shape.

And yet, if not up, the only other way is back down, which

seems even less realistic, given the slope. That, or she can remain right here until . . . what? None of the other women look strong enough to carry her, not even Dede, who has the toned but ultimately lean limbs of a celebrity. How would they move her if she can't do it? Helicopter? She imagines them strapping her up the way they strapped up that cow during that one wildfire, which she watched on the news. It seemed funny at the time, the cow dangling in the air as the helicopter whisked it to safety, but it feels much less funny now. There was nothing *funny* about the indignity of that cow's rescue!

Well.

Well, that leaves her with only one option, which is up.

CHAPTER 34

It's not only her quads firing off now. Her calves and even her shins screech in protest as she makes her way along the trail. Either she's not going to make it off this island or she's going to come back in unbelievable shape. She wonders if maybe *this* is The Program's secret. How stressed out can you be if you're seriously fit?

The trail moves back and forth across the face of the hill, at times veering a bit closer to the edge than feels safe. She's high enough now that the roofs of the neighborhood they drove through are no more than building blocks far below, the white sand beach only a ribbon along the coast. The spindly palm trees are miniaturized, although the ocean is, even from here, terrifyingly big. The water nearest land is fluorescent, but it gets deeper blue the farther out you look.

She continues to climb until, finally, she reaches a structure. It's made completely of concrete, with solid walls on three sides and an open space across the fourth, a lookout over the steep edge of the hill. Every visible surface of the concrete is covered in graffiti, shockingly synthetic against the sunburnt grass around it.

The first pillbox, Georgia thinks. It has to be. Using her hand as a visor, she scans the trail ahead of her, and sure enough, she finds an identical structure not far away.

The fact that Cecilia is already at the second pillbox when Georgia arrives is surprising in a way that feels unpleasant. It's not clear how she got up here, although context suggests that she, too, must have climbed. But when? The group started not long after sunrise, which means Cecilia must have started much earlier. Georgia tries to imagine her hiking the dark trail alone, which is unsettling.

Today, Cecilia is wearing a pair of large oval sunglasses and black overalls with practical-looking pockets. It is the most casual she's seen Cecilia so far, which only increases Georgia's uneasiness, like seeing someone important in their pajamas. Alice and Dede are standing in opposite corners of the pillbox, deliberately not looking at each other and, perhaps just as deliberately, not looking tired. Georgia, though, doesn't have the luxury of pretending. She leans over with her hands on her waist, despite having the vague notion that she shouldn't be leaning over. (Something about blood flow, she thinks.)

"Wonderful view, isn't it?" says Cecilia pleasantly, speaking to Georgia with the casual ease of two people meeting up for coffee. Georgia attempts a sound of agreement, although it comes out instead as a gasp. At this, Dede gives her a look of secondhand embarrassment.

The air seems thinner here than it did at the bottom. A single bird trills somewhere in the distance.

"'Apapane," Cecilia says rather cryptically, until Georgia realizes she's talking about the bird. Able to breathe again, she stands up straighter and looks around for the 'apapane, which she can't find. She sees Simone, Logan, and Izzy in the distance, making their way slowly upward.

When they arrive, it's with no dramatic gasps or heaves. They've paced themselves, which Georgia should have done, she realizes. Simone has acquired a thick walking stick from somewhere, which she leans on as she appraises the situation. Izzy is wearing a bucket hat and an enthusiastic smile.

"Excellent," says Cecilia, bringing her hands in front of her. She isn't wearing any makeup today, which Georgia usually finds both enviable and slightly sanctimonious from women her age. (It seems, to Georgia, a bit like showing off.) Here, though, on the hill, Cecilia's bare face feels elegant and organic—very Gwyneth Paltrow, whom Georgia also finds a tiny bit annoying despite (or maybe because of?) her excellent skin.

Cecilia says brightly, "How is everyone feeling? Well, I hope?"

No one answers. The 'apapane continues to warble in the distance, the only noise. Izzy taps sweat from her forehead with a pink bandanna folded into a neat little square.

"Wonderful," says Cecilia, seemingly unfazed by their silence. In her dark sunglasses, the group's reflection stares back at them.

"This hike can be a challenge," she says. "In fact, we chose it for this very reason. A journey is only as meaningful as the obstacles we conquer in the process, and now, here, we stand in triumph over those we've conquered today."

She nods to the slope behind them. Izzy turns obediently to look, although none of the other women move. None of them seem especially triumphant.

Cecilia says, "We all face obstacles. In the journey of our lives, this is the only thing we know for certain."

She looks to Izzy, who understands the silent instruction and hustles over. From the tub by Cecilia's feet (which she must have carried, Georgia thinks), Izzy produces a headset, which she hands to Cecilia. Cecilia takes it and examines it for a moment, a strange expression on her face, like a mother receiving her newborn child.

She says, "Yesterday, we spoke of aids. Aids in this beautiful journey we're on. And these"—she taps the headset lightly—"will be our aids today in this space of challenge and triumph."

This is extremely corny, although Georgia is too tired to feel much about it. Her ears are popping now, which is slightly concerning. (Although maybe this is a common thing to experience after exercising. She wouldn't know.)

"These headsets," says Cecilia, holding up the device now so it's eye level, "are capable of extremely realistic projections. As you may have suspected already, however, they are capable of much more."

Have they suspected that already? Georgia looks around with the vaguely distressed sensation of missing a joke, although she doesn't see recognition on any of the other women's faces.

"In your one-on-one sessions," Cecilia continues, "we explored the stimuli *collected* by the devices. We observed the electromagnetic signals produced by your brain and received by the headsets. In a similar way, these headsets are capable of *producing* electromagnetic signals themselves—signals receivable by your brain, communication in its native language. In this complex dance of biology and technology, these devices are capable of both following and taking the lead."

She pauses here with an expectant expression, although no one says anything. In fact, everything seems suddenly very quiet.

"So, like, what does that mean?" Dede says finally, bluntly, although less combative than she has been—perhaps evidence that the afterglow is still lingering.

Cecilia regards her genially. "It means that these devices are capable of acting in harmony with our brains. In our journey to redefine our thought processes, we may allow these headsets to lead the way."

"Lead what way?"

"Direct our thought processes."

"So, what? It's gonna control our brains or something?"

Cecilia smiles. "Exactly."

CHAPTER 35

Later, Georgia will consider that maybe the timing of everything was significant. Maybe there was a reason they did the mushroom capsules right before the mind-controlling headsets, because in what other scenario, besides a postdrug high, would they agree to something like this?

This doesn't occur to her when it's happening, though. When it's happening, Georgia thinks only, *Okay*. Okay, this is not what she was expecting, but what about The Program has been expected so far?

"Uh, seriously?" Dede says.

Cecilia motions for Izzy, who hurries over with another one of the headsets.

"So far, we have been operating the headsets in what we call 'Classic Mode,'" says Cecilia, as beside her Izzy holds up the headset for the women to see. "In Classic Mode, the headset provides visual stimuli only—the projections with which you are all now familiar."

She nods at Izzy, who turns the headset over, revealing a switch Georgia didn't notice before. She flips it, and the little light at the bottom turns from green to pink.

"And now we're in 'Virgin Mode,'" Cecilia says.

Georgia wonders who named it that. It has a faintly gross ring to it, like *sanitary napkin*, which she always assumed could've only been named by a man.

"In Virgin Mode," says Cecilia, "our headsets do more than

simply create visual projections. Here, the headsets *interact* with our brains. Specifically, using highly targeted pulses of electromagnetic energy, the headsets are able to stimulate the parts of your brain that were altered by your transition to motherhood."

Something about the way she says this—the obvious excitement in her voice—is unnerving. It's too real of an emotion, too *human* from someone like Cecilia.

"To put it simply," she says, "Virgin Mode shuts off that part of your brain—your *mom brain,* if you will. By temporarily blocking these neural circuits, the headsets allow us to think the way we did before motherhood."

No one says anything. Georgia has to struggle not to laugh. She does this sometimes. She would be one of those people who laughs hysterically after a natural disaster, making all the rescuers assume she was a lunatic when really she was just in shock.

"So you're saying these headsets have been messing with our brains?" Alice says finally. It sounds so ridiculous, especially coming from Alice. Alice, so pragmatic. Alice, who told Dede that vegetarianism is a "fashion choice." According to Alice, the only thing you get from being a vegetarian is a vitamin D deficiency and a stick up your ass.

"They have not been, no. Until this point, you have been practicing exclusively in Classic Mode."

"But now you want us to use Virgin Mode?"

"Now I am asking you to take the next step on your journey. I am inviting you, once again, outside your comfort zone, for it is here that you will find the life you are seeking. The one you *deserve.*"

Georgia thinks, randomly, of the red bra on her garage door. She wonders if the person who did it—whoever it was—was outside their comfort zone. Were they nervous they'd be caught? Were they nervous about bad karma? She thinks of the journalist, the one who wrote the story in the *Pacific*, and how much she nodded during Georgia's interview. Georgia thought it was nice at the time. She thought the reporter was interested and sincere. Now, though, she wonders if she totally misread everything. Maybe the nodding was a nervous tic. Maybe she knew the risk Georgia was taking, and that made her uncomfortable.

Cecilia says something to Izzy, and Izzy moves to the plastic tub, where she shuffles things around. Cecilia regards the group with a cheerful expression, and Georgia wonders if Cecilia has ever felt uncomfortable before.

Izzy returns to Cecilia's side a moment later, holding something that Georgia doesn't recognize. It reminds her of the sunshade her grandmother used to use in her car, her diligent defense of her beaded seat covers and Saint Christopher pendant on her rearview mirror. Izzy opens it, unfolding it in thirds. It seems to be a screen, which is currently blank, the dark glass acting like a mirror.

"It's connected wirelessly to your headsets," Cecilia says, answering the question no one has asked. "It allows us to see what the user is seeing in real time. We have found this to be an incredibly useful teaching tool."

The screen flickers on. On it appear a pair of red athletic shoes and scalloped-edge socks.

"Whoops," Izzy chuckles, lifting the headset up so it's facing Georgia rather than her feet. On-screen, Georgia's face looks back at them blankly.

"Excellent," Cecilia says with an approving nod. She then turns to Dede. "So, Dede, would you like to start us off?"

CHAPTER 36

"Uh," Dede says, looking around the group. For a second, it seems like she might say no, although when she looks back at Cecilia, she says, "Sure. I mean, whatever, I guess."

"Excellent," says Cecilia as Izzy jumps to return to the tub. She pulls out one of the several seemingly identical headsets. She hurries over and tries to help Dede put it on, although Dede resists. "I've got it," she says huffily, the way Clover insists she has it whenever Georgia tries to buckle her in.

"So we're going to take this exercise inside the pillbox," says Cecilia when Dede has it on finally, looking equally cute and ridiculous. "But we will be with you on the screen, so not to worry. If you need assistance of any kind, just call out."

This strikes Georgia as a strange thing to say. Why would she need assistance? The question seems to pass over Dede's face too, although it's hard to know for sure with half her face covered by the device.

"So just like, go into the—what? The pillbox?"

"Yes, you can go ahead."

"Right." Dede tugs at her ponytail again. Georgia wonders if she's nervous.

She marches around to the front of the structure, where she disappears from sight. Georgia tries to summon the peace she felt after the psilocybin trip yesterday, although it's getting more and more difficult.

Izzy is fiddling with the foldout screen now, which she has set on a rock. It takes a couple of seconds, but finally, Dede's view appears. First, it's the edge of the hill, the grand expanse of blues and teals below.

Then it all goes black.

CHAPTER 37

"Nothing's happening," Dede says dully. Her voice is coming from the screen, as her actual voice is insulated by the cement. The inside of the pillbox is darker than Georgia thought it would be, so she has to squint to understand what she's seeing: a bare, dank wall with weeds forcing their way through its many climbing cracks.

"You're doing wonderfully," says Cecilia. "Just be patient."

It seems as though Dede can hear Cecilia through the headset. She responds to this with a small "Humph." On-screen, one of her arms is visible as she reaches in front of her. Georgia can see enough to make out her manicure—long with a stiletto cut. (It seems like this would make barre difficult, although Georgia is obviously no expert.)

Inside the pillbox, Dede seems to be walking around the perimeter, her hand outstretched. On the outside, all the women huddle around the screen, waiting for something. Waiting for what?

"There's a door here," Dede says finally. "What do I do?"

Cecilia doesn't respond. Georgia looks over at the screen, where there is no corresponding door on the back side of the pillbox. It's not real. Georgia's impulse is to warn Dede, although thankfully she registers this as inappropriate.

Dede reaches toward it, but as soon as she touches the handle, she pulls back with a yelp.

"What the hell?" she says angrily. "It's freaking hot."

The view on the screen swerves. And then Georgia hears it. It's low at first, a grumble. Or is it a growl? A scared cat? Dede can apparently hear it also. She steps toward the door, the view spinning as though she has turned her head to listen.

And then Georgia realizes: It's not a cat. It's a human.

A child?

"Nova?" Dede says, uncertainly at first. And then, more panicked, "Nova Grace?!"

It's not a sound Georgia has heard before. It's somewhere between a moan and a cry. A chill races through her. She doesn't recognize the child, but she doesn't need to, to understand the noise.

Dede reaches out again and thrusts open the nonexistent door, apparently ignoring whatever heat she felt before. Georgia gasps as orange flames illuminate the screen.

Dede stumbles backward. Georgia has never seen flames so big before. They seem to reach for Dede, who has apparently fallen, based on her view.

And then the child again. The first audible word: "Mommy."

Dede scrambles. Her breathing is heavy, desperate.

"Nova!" she shrieks. "Nova, baby girl!"

The child makes another sound, this one not a word. It's a throaty, excruciating bellow, one Georgia feels as much as she hears. Now, Dede is yelling too—also not words, only screeches, as though the pain is hers as well.

"Stop it!" Alice cries, startling Georgia. They all look at her, but she's transfixed by the screen. "Something's happening to her! You need to stop it now!"

Dede's wails are now carrying through the cement, saturating the thin air. The view is becoming more erratic. Dede seems to be circling the flaming door.

Alice is right. They need to stop it. Something is very wrong. Georgia finds Cecilia's face. She's gazing at the screen, looking entranced.

And then, from the pillbox and from the screen, a terrible roar. All at once, the screen bursts into bright yellow, then the connection cuts out, and it's white.

In the distance, the lone ʻapapane trills.

CHAPTER 38

Dede isn't at dinner that night, although no one was really expecting her to be.

"If it was a concussion," says Alice, putting down her fork, "she'd better sue the shit out of this place." She is only halfway through her poke, which she is eating in excruciatingly small bites. Around the table, the other women look at her but don't say anything. Of the group, Alice is probably the only one who has sued the shit out of someone before.

Georgia wouldn't be surprised if it was a concussion. From what she can tell, Dede ran headfirst into the cement wall, so even if it wasn't a concussion, it wasn't anything great. At least she was able to walk out of the pillbox, although it was with much help from Izzy and Logan, who more or less carried her back down the hill. An ambulance met them at the bottom, which Dede regarded with a dazed expression. They took her away looking as though she didn't know how she'd gotten there.

"It's totally ridiculous," Alice says now, snatching her fork back up and stabbing a piece of fish. "It's totally ridiculous that they put her in that situation to begin with!"

Georgia takes a tentative bite of her poke, which is good, although she's not remotely hungry. She is decisively not in the afterglow period any longer. In fact, she doesn't know how she feels. Alice sounds hysterical, but maybe she's right. Maybe it was negligence, what happened on the hill.

"Frankly, I'm of half a mind to just leave," Alice continues, picking up steam. "I mean, this feels like a *serious* neglect of safety precautions if you ask me."

She looks at them with a ferocious expression, and it strikes Georgia then that she's looking for an answer. In fact, she looks desperate, like she wants to be talked into something, or maybe out of something, Georgia isn't sure.

Nostrils flaring, Alice opens her mouth like she's going to say something else, although she's interrupted by the opening of the café door.

"Good evening, ladies," Izzy says brightly, approaching their table. "How are y'all doing? Holding up okay?"

Alice sniffs loudly. The rest of them just stare. Izzy's smile seems to falter, and while she's arguably at least partly responsible for what happened to Dede, Georgia does feel bad for her.

"Well, I wanted to let y'all know that Dede is doing well," Izzy says after a moment, finding her footing. "A little concussion, the doctors tell us, but she should make a full recovery."

"A *little* concussion?" Alice says acidly. She gives the rest of them a look.

"It's very upsetting," Izzy agrees with a sad little bow. "We do have resources here that I encourage y'all to explore."

"Legal resources?" Alice says. "I imagine Cecilia is prepared to defend herself."

At this, Izzy looks at her pointedly. The expression is unlike anything they've seen from her, and Georgia, not even on the receiving end of it, shrinks down.

"I understand how upsetting this has been," she says, "and we will do everything in our power to help y'all through it. I want to make clear, however, that The Program is not at fault for what happened today."

"Not at fault?"

"Yes. Today was a horrible accident, but it could not have been prevented, unfortunately."

Alice gives her a look of disbelief, and Georgia, too, feels skeptical. There was *nothing* they could have done differently? Nothing at all?

"Well, for your sake, I hope you're right," Alice says finally. "And I'm sure the attorneys will sort that out."

Here, she gives Georgia a meaningful look, which is startling. Yes, Georgia is an attorney, but not *that* kind of attorney. Unless Dede needs a pharmaceutical patent, Georgia isn't going to be of much use.

"I'm sure they will," Izzy says simply, her tone once again cheerful. They could be talking about the weather, or the poke, and Georgia has to give her credit: Her optimism, even if it's forced, is unflappable. And yet, this isn't exactly reassuring. It makes Georgia feel the same sense of distrust she feels about politicians, and shampoo ads.

"Like I said," Izzy continues, "we have resources available for anyone who's still a bit rattled from the mishap today. Otherwise, I hope y'all will be ready tomorrow to pick up where we left off today."

And that's it. No one asks for information about the resources. No one says anything at all. Alice glares, and Simone blinks, and Logan looks determinedly down at her nearly empty plate. It's not until Izzy leaves the café that Logan raises her head. Her nose is even pinker from the hike that morning, but whereas the color made her look healthy earlier, now it makes her look agitated.

"She's afraid of fires," she says quietly, looking at no one specifically. "Dede. She said so the first night, remember? When they asked us about our greatest fears? Dede said her favorite aunt's house burned down when she was little, and now she lives in Rhode Island." She twists her hands in her lap. "Do you think they picked fire on purpose?"

No one answers because there's really no need.

CHAPTER 39

When Georgia wakes abruptly later that night, there's no obvious reason why. There's no strange sound, no light that wasn't there before she fell asleep. She's not too hot or too cold, not in a weird position, didn't swallow spit in a way that makes her choke awake. She doesn't even have that heavy sense of dread she sometimes gets for no reason at all.

For a minute, she lies there with her eyes closed, willing herself to go back to sleep. When this doesn't work, she counts backward in her head starting from three hundred. She gets all the way to one hundred and fifty-seven before giving up.

She thinks of Dede's scream from inside the pillbox, followed by that sickening, abrupt silence.

She sits up.

She needs a reset. She remembers the tea she saw in the welcome basket, something herbal with RELAX in big bold letters. (When she first saw this, she imagined the tea bag shouting it at her: "RELAX!!!!")

She's padding across her villa toward the basket when she hears it. At first, she thinks the voices are much closer than they are—inside the room maybe, causing a brief wave of panic. She realizes almost immediately, however, that they are not in the room. The voices are outside but not very far away.

She tiptoes to the window in her kitchenette and, using one finger, separates the blinds. This window, unlike the door, faces away from the water, toward the duplex behind hers.

Here, the voices are more audible, although it's still impossible to make out what they're saying. They're not whispers but murmurs and seem to be male. Georgia realizes then that the only men she's seen at the resort so far are the driver who delivered her from the airport and the captain from their pontoon trip. That hasn't struck her as weird until now.

There's a group of them, shadowy figures on the porch of one of the villas. The way they're angled makes it impossible to see what they're doing. The door to the villa is open, but nothing inside is visible. Does the person inside know they're there? She feels tingly suddenly. Is she witnessing a robbery?

Someone appears in the doorway, followed by another. Between them is something long and bulky that she cannot identify.

She leans closer so her nose is almost touching the window. At nearly the same time, one of the shadows turns. It's indeed a man, and he's facing her. In fact, he seems to be looking her directly in the eyes.

She drops the blind, stumbles backward.

She never does drink the tea, although she doubts that would've helped.

CHAPTER 40

The villa was Dede's. But what does that mean?

CHAPTER 41

Georgia finally falls back asleep a little after four in the morning. She awakes not an hour later already midway into a thought.

The villa was Dede's. Those men were at Dede's door.

But what does that mean? Does it mean anything?

What did she see?

She's so distracted while she's dressing for breakfast, she puts her shirt on inside out. Then, once she's righted that, she puts it on backward. She stares at the mirror for a moment, the tag of her shirt between her collar bones, and tries to decide what she's going to do about it. Is she going to do anything about it? What is *it*?

She decides she's going to ask Izzy and go from there. This seems like a reasonable first step.

She's the last one from her pod to arrive at breakfast. She pulls out her chair, although only Logan looks up. She gives Georgia a small questioning smile, and the thought crosses Georgia's mind that she should tell them now, first.

Alice says dully, "You've got toothpaste on your cheek." She points to her own face, near the corner of her lip. Georgia lifts a spoon and squints at the back of it. Sure enough, there's a bluish-white blob.

She rubs it off and considers whether the other women will have any better insight into this situation than she does. Worst case, she sets off a panic for no reason.

Well, no, that's not worst case. Worst case, Georgia is right about what she saw. A body from Dede's room—that would be worst case. But there's no way that's what it was.

There's just no way.

She looks around the café, where the other pods are chatting among themselves with no signs of distress. Did they also try Virgin Mode yesterday? If they did, it seems none of them had incidents like Georgia's pod. They attend to their chickpea waffles and guava smoothies unworriedly.

When Izzy appears in the café, she doesn't come to Pod Three's table first. She first checks on the pod closest to the door, then lingers at the second table to laugh at something one of them said. And, okay. *Okay.* If those men were taking Dede's body out of the room (she can barely believe this is a possibility), surely Izzy wouldn't be carrying on like this. She's a bit odd, but she's not a *sociopath*.

Georgia feels herself relaxing slightly.

When Izzy arrives at their table finally, she gives them a grand smile.

"G'morning, ladies!"

"Good morning," says Logan, although she's the only one. Her eyes flicker to the empty seat beside Georgia, where Dede should be sitting. Izzy follows her gaze.

"Yes," Izzy says, like Logan has asked a question out loud. "I'm sad to report that unfortunately, Dede has decided to unenroll from The Program."

Georgia's whole body tightens.

"Unenroll?" says Alice.

"Yes. While her injuries were relatively minor, she decided to prioritize her recovery. And of course we support her decision totally."

"Her decision?"

It's Simone who speaks this time, and they all turn to her. Her arms are resting lightly on each side of her plate, but her eyes are blazing.

Izzy cocks her head with a virtuous expression.

"What was that?" she says.

"You're talking about a decision. Something Dede chose herself."

Izzy smiles faintly. The other women are whipping their heads back and forth like they're watching a high-speed tennis match.

"Sorry," Izzy says with an unconvincing lightness. "I'm afraid I'm not understanding. Is there a question?"

"Was it Dede's decision to leave, is what I'm asking. You're suggesting she made that choice on her own, and I'm asking: Did she?"

Georgia holds her breath. Izzy looks both strained and like she's trying very hard not to appear that way.

The moment stretches out just long enough that if Georgia were in Simone's shoes, she would relent. She would sit back, maybe even apologize. *That isn't my business,* she might say. But Simone doesn't. She holds Izzy's eyes until Izzy's flick to the right. Is that the side that means she's lying, or is that the left?

"It was indeed her decision," she says finally. "But I can see that y'all are concerned, and that's understandable." Her eyes move just around Simone's, never quite making contact. "Simone, it might be beneficial if you spoke with Cecilia directly about this matter. She may be able to calm some of your nerves."

Alice leans forward at this, her interest piqued. Simone licks her top teeth without opening her mouth.

"All right then," she says, pushing herself back from the table. Alice's nostrils flare, and it seems like she might ask to come also. Georgia imagines this must be excruciating for her, to not be speaking to the manager herself.

CHAPTER 42

Simone isn't in the van when Izzy picks them up later that morning.

"Cecilia can fill you in," Izzy says when Alice asks her about it. "It's not my place to speak about other attendees' personal details."

Alice frowns, which Izzy doesn't see, as she is staring intently out the windshield. She must understand how contradictory this is, given what she told them about Dede that morning. Georgia imagines herself as a character in a novel, and what she—as the reader—would think about them all in this situation. How would their compliance look to an outside observer? Unreasonable? Unbelievable? She hates when this happens in novels. Sometimes she'll shout out loud at them: "People don't act like that! That's not what people do at all!"

But this isn't a novel, and what are they supposed to do, really? Demand answers? Izzy is probably telling the truth. She probably can't say much, realistically.

Alice, who's standing in the van doorway, seems to come to a similar conclusion. She sucks her teeth, then climbs in. The automatic van door closes behind her, and for a second—just an instant—Georgia is struck with a sense that maybe, actually, she is right to be wary. If she were reading her own character, maybe she would tell her: "Yes! Of course, you nincompoop!" (This is the word she uses now, ever since Clover called a friend at school an idiot and Georgia implemented a family ban of the word.) But she thinks this as the van is pulling away, as Izzy is turning on the radio, so she ignores it. After all, she has never been one to make a scene.

~

"It's a disappointment, of course, but alas, it is to be expected."

Cecilia says this standing on a pier, the sun to her back, giving her silhouette a soft white glow. The way she says it, it sounds instantly reasonable, although it's also possible that Georgia simply wants it to be.

"Frankly, The Program isn't a fit for everyone. The most important criterion for success is the *desire* to succeed, which can be . . . a challenge for some."

At this, Alice nods hard in agreement. And yes, Georgia can see how this is true. Once, when she was in college, she went with a group of friends to a comedy club where a hypnotist was performing. He asked for volunteers to come onstage, from which a few would be hypnotized. "It won't work for everyone," he cautioned, as around the room—at Georgia's table, even, although certainly not from Georgia herself—tipsy hands waved for attention. "To be hypnotized, you have to *want* to be hypnotized. It won't work unless you've bought in."

"It's regrettable," Cecilia says, shaking her head with remorse, "but we do see this with most classes. Here and there, a woman or two will feel their needs are not being met, and they choose to disengage."

Georgia thinks of Dede, her pursed lips and crossed arms. How she bounced her foot impatiently whenever Cecilia spoke. *Disengaged* is certainly one word for it.

"So Simone thought it wasn't working too?" Logan says, her voice so small, it's almost lost in the breeze. Her eyes dart around the group immediately, as though she, too, is surprised by the question.

Cecilia gives her a kind smile.

"I'm afraid Simone took issue with a few aspects of The Program, yes. I was quite saddened by her decision to unenroll, as I thought she was making great progress. But of course, we cannot keep anyone here against their will."

Beside her, Izzy bows her head sorrowfully. Georgia wonders how that conversation went between Simone and Cecilia. She suspects it was quiet but brutal, the sort of confrontation Georgia is not capable of having. When Georgia fights with people—the rare times she does—she has an infuriating habit of crying. Once, with Will, she actually stomped her foot like a toddler. "I'm not crying because I'm upset!" she told him. "I'm crying because I'm mad!"

Cecilia brings her hands together in front of her.

"But as they say, the show must go on."

At this, Izzy raises her head and gives an energetic nod. Because they're on a pier, they're almost totally surrounded by water, a fact of which Georgia becomes suddenly aware. No one has explained what they're doing on the pier, and she was so consumed by the question of Simone and Dede, she forgot to wonder. As Izzy moves to the plastic tub of headsets, however, and as Cecilia gives them a genial smile, she remembers to be afraid.

CHAPTER 43

"Georgia," says Cecilia. "What do you think? Would you like to start us off this morning?"

Izzy is holding one of the headsets—Georgia's, presumably—and for just a moment, Georgia considers what would happen if she said no. She doesn't want to start them off, actually, but what would happen if she said that? Would Cecilia allow it? Would she make Georgia do it anyway? How would it feel to stand up to someone like Cecilia? Would it feel good or just terrifying?

"Georgia?" Cecilia says. She tilts her head.

"Um, yes. Yes, okay."

Logan is standing beside her, and Georgia can feel her shifting her weight. Alice's lips are pressed into a totally straight line.

"Excellent. You're in Virgin Mode today."

Virgin Mode—surely *there's a better name for it,* Georgia thinks.

Izzy hands her the headset, where on the bottom, the little light is pink. Georgia pulls it over her head and her mind floats to Dede: the grasping orange fire in the pillbox, the primordial way she screamed. When they pulled her out, her previously buoyant ponytail had traveled sideways, becoming only a defeated tangle at the side of her head.

"All set?" Cecilia says. "Feels good?"

Georgia finds Cecilia's eyes. Cecilia, so well-spoken and competent, exacting but not unkind. If she is a bad guy, then Georgia has completely lost her ability to spot them.

"Feels good," she says.

"Marvelous."

Beside her, Izzy is unfolding the screen.

"We'll have you in that car today," says Cecilia, nodding over Georgia's shoulder. Georgia turns to look as she adds, "You can go ahead and get in."

It's the only car on the pier, a sunburnt blue hatchback. It's parked along the edge, near the bay door of an abandoned-looking building. The building has a few broken windows and a dark oval above the door, like there was once a sign there that has since been removed. The pier is cement, and it must be sturdy to accommodate a whole building, Georgia thinks.

As she approaches the car, she feels the sun on the back of her neck more intensely. She starts to sweat as she pulls open the driver's side door, where inside she finds a cracked leather seat with bits of foam popping out from the fabric. It's overwhelmingly unremarkable.

She doesn't want to get in. She really, truly doesn't.

She slips inside.

Nothing happens. She looks out the window, where the water dances cheerfully in the sun. She thinks of her grandmother again, randomly. They went to the beach one summer, she and Georgia and her parents, when her mom was still alive. Babcia spent the whole time under the umbrella, reapplying sunscreen. "We're not beach people," she kept saying to Georgia, to which Georgia had no response. What she *wanted* to ask was what Babcia meant by "we." Did she mean her and Georgia? Their whole family? Or was she talking about the Poles generally? Babcia had a habit of that, speaking for the whole of the Polish people. Georgia was seven at the time, and she wanted very badly to understand where in this puzzle she fit.

She looks out the other window, where Cecilia, Izzy, Logan, and Alice stand. They're looking at the screen unfolded in front of them.

Then she hears it.

She swivels around. In the back seat, there's a startlingly realistic car seat, right down to the pulverized animal crackers smashed into the padding. In it sits Clover, her forehead creased.

CHAPTER 44

"Whose car is it, Mommy?" Clover says a second time, when Georgia doesn't answer the first. Georgia doesn't know how to respond. This, though, isn't exactly unusual. The older Clover gets, the more difficult her questions have become. (Where does wind come from? Why can't mommies lay eggs?)

Cecilia Clements's car, honey. She put us in here so I'll be a better mom for you.

"I don't know, baby," she says honestly.

"Is it our car?" Clover narrows her eyes in suspicion, prompting a tinny sound in Georgia's ears. How *realistic* the holographic children are.

"No, honey. It's not ours."

"How did you get it?"

Even the pitch of Clover's voice is accurate, the earnest way she tries to make sense of the world.

"I borrowed it." She doesn't know if this counts as a lie.

"Where are we going?"

Will jokes that Clover would make an excellent investigator. "A lot like her mom," he says.

Georgia's eyes travel to the rear windshield. The only thing visible is the sky, blue and cloudless. Where *are* they going? Clover did not mean this as an introspective question—even for a five-year-old, she is especially literal—but still. How is it that Georgia can't answer it in any capacity?

She turns to her window.

"Should I be doing something?" she says out loud, feeling self-conscious. She knows the women can hear her, but it nonetheless feels weird to be talking to the empty car.

No answer. She again wishes there were more instructions when it comes to these exercises. The truth is, they are more than halfway through The Program, and Georgia still isn't sure, concretely, what changes she's supposed to make when she gets home.

Beneath her, the car jolts abruptly. Georgia cries out in surprise.

"Mommy?" Clover says cautiously.

"Sorry, baby. That just surprised me."

She forgets for a moment that it isn't the real Clover.

She runs her hands up and down her thighs. The car started on its own—or it feels as though it started. Is it possible for the headset to do that? To mimic the rumble of the engine under her seat?

"Can we go to Target?" Clover says. "I've got to get something real quick."

Despite herself, Georgia smiles. It's always such a sweet, terrifying moment when Clover repeats something Georgia taught her without meaning to teach it.

"I . . ." Georgia looks down to the ignition, where a set of keys has appeared. She puts her hands on the steering wheel at ten and two. It feels like she's supposed to be going somewhere, although she has no idea where. Carefully, she presses her foot against the brake pedal and sets her hand on the gear stick. She gives one last glance up to the mirror, where Clover gives her a bright smile.

She puts the car in Reverse.

CHAPTER 45

The first time Georgia tried pot was not, actually, with her intuitive pothead boyfriend. She tried it once before that, at a Halloween party her freshman year in college.

She and her roommate went to the party as slutty bumblebees. Her roommate wore a thrifted yellow camisole, and Georgia uncharacteristically wore a pair of fishnet tights. To this day, she cannot for the life of her remember who offered her the joint. Most of her memories from that night revolve around a secondhand couch in the house's basement, where she found herself with a guy dressed as Waldo, a very skinny stranger with a larger-than-normal Adam's apple and gaping nose pores. He said he was a physics major, except it wasn't regular physics. Astrophysics? Geophysics? Georgia only remembers laughing very hard when he told her because it sounded like a fake degree, and she was high enough that it didn't occur to her that laughing at this was rude. She laughed at that, then laughed at Waldo's little puffball hat, then laughed at herself for wearing fishnet tights.

After she finished laughing, Waldo went into a detailed explanation of quantum entanglement, which he illustrated helpfully with a napkin that someone had used to blot a piece of pizza earlier in the night. Waldo folded the napkin, then jabbed his finger through it, showing her how time could fold, and how it was possible to leap through the folds, jumping through time out of turn. "Like your finger," she noted, no longer laughing. She was totally, impenetrably invested at this point. "Like my finger," Waldo confirmed, pleased with her for catching on. The idea of quantum entanglement felt so very important in that moment, so relevant and profound, and perhaps it was important and relevant and profound, although more than likely, she was just very high.

For a second, just an instant in the car, she thinks of Waldo. It isn't even his face that flashes through her mind but his vaguely effeminate finger jabbing through the greasy napkin. Time can fold that way. One moment, you're sitting on a pier, looking at your daughter, and in an instant, a ripple in the fabric of the universe, you are—here.

You're in the driver's seat, brilliant blue sky spinning out the windshield.

You're in the water, waves lapping playfully against the windows' glass.

You hear a constant, ethereal ringing.

You feel each droplet of sweat forming on your hairline, individual pinpricks of perspiration.

Time can speed up, and time can slow down. Things that normally happen very quickly can stretch out as far as the universe wants. She can see so clearly how it happened. She can see Waldo folding the napkin in his overly moisturized hands. She can even see herself sitting on that couch—the shadow of smudged mascara on the top of her cheeks, how the whites of her eyes are pink. She made bumblebee wings out of two wire hangers and a pillowcase. She curled her hair, which went flat by the end of the night.

She turns her head and feels a little tickle of curiosity at how she seems to be moving at a normal speed even when the world around her is going so slowly. She feels a flash of bizarre giddiness looking out her window at the water, which has crept a quarter way up the glass.

The car reversed off the pier. That's just what happened. And what a thing to have happened! Up close, the water is clear, not blue. Why does water only look blue from a distance? Waldo would know. Georgia feels sure of this.

And then she hears it—a sound fighting to break through the high-pitched ringing in her ears. It sounds faraway and thin, as though she can wave her hand through it. It's familiar, something she knows, and hates. Something she can feel in her stomach.

Clover screaming.

All at once, the world resumes its normal speed. The water outside the car is no longer joyful. It roars furiously at her. Clover is shrieking from the back seat, not her usual cries, but in true terror.

Hardly thinking, Georgia whips around. Her seat belt—sensing problematic movement—locks, thumping her in the chest. Clover's eyes are wild. Her skinny limbs are flailing, making fleshy thwacks against the car seat's fabric. Georgia knows that for the rest of her life, she will close her eyes and hear this sound.

"Clover, I need you to stay calm," she says, barely recognizing her own voice. Clover's eyes flash to her briefly, but there is no recognition behind them. It's as though Clover isn't actually seeing her at all.

There's a part of Georgia that feels drawn to Clover here, a primal force acting on her body. She understands, somehow, that this is the mighty force of motherhood, the collective fury that flips cars, rips open steel. Travels over and over and over again across an electric mat.

And yet, there is a different, larger force acting upon her. It's quieter, calmer. If she were a religious person, if she were Babcia, she would have called it the gentle, leading hand of God.

She frees herself from her seat belt, and in the same movement, she dives for the floorboard by the passenger seat. Later, she will try to remember if she noticed the emergency hammer there before or if it only appeared once the car started sinking. She grabs it. It's heavier than she expected. She uses every fiber of her body to whirl around and slam it into her window. The glass cracks, a web of faint lines concentrated at the point of contact.

She winds up and slams a second time.

She gasps as the water pours onto her lap. The water isn't cold, but the sensation is surprising all the same. She can feel the water in her shoes, saturating her socks. Clover is still screaming. Somehow, Georgia momentarily tuned it out.

"It's okay," she pants as the water around her rises. She turns so she can finally release Clover from her car seat. "It's okay, baby. We're going to be just fine."

CHAPTER 46

They give her a blanket afterward, the foil kind they hand out after marathons. Still, Georgia continues to shake.

CHAPTER 47

After Georgia's exercise, Izzy tells them that Cecilia will meet them back at the resort. "To go over your performance!" she says brightly, although there's a slightly manic insistence to it, the way Georgia gets during the holidays.

They make the rest of the drive back in silence. Georgia can't stop shivering, although as far as she can tell, she's not actually wet. This sensation is almost as bad as the exercise itself. She saw the water. She *felt* it. And yet, when she digs her finger in the heel of her shoe, expecting her sock to be sopping, there's not a drop.

"Ya'll will be in the Shell Room this afternoon," Izzy says when they're back on campus, turning around in her seat. She gives them a hopeful smile, although when no one responds, she seems to falter. "This is the hardest part," she then tells them, this time more sober. "But I promise, y'all are doing great."

It's not entirely clear why the Shell Room is called the Shell Room, as there are no shells in it as far as Georgia can see. It's a freestanding building on stilts and traced by a wide veranda, containing a single room furnished with white chairs and a white lectern, where Cecilia stands waiting.

"Please," she says warmly, "find a seat."

Beside Georgia, Logan gives her a worried look, as though unsure if Georgia will make it to a seat. Georgia is also unsure if she will make it to a seat. She feels very weak, and her ears are ringing, and despite the blanket like a cape around her neck, she continues to shake.

"Excellent," Cecilia says when they're all finally seated. (Georgia has no idea by which metric she has decided that.) Logan is next to Georgia, with Alice one row up.

Cecilia smiles here for a moment, and Georgia allows herself to finally feel annoyed. She wants to stomp her foot and demand that Cecilia stop smiling. She wants to say, *What was the point?* Because what *was* the point? Is she supposed to know something now? Because she certainly does not. As far as she can tell, she has learned nothing up to this point besides that she does in fact hate the water and that these stupid foil blankets are as pointless as they look.

"Georgia," Cecilia says finally, again with that uncanny expression, like she heard all these thoughts. Georgia presses her lips together, the closest to polite as she's going to get. "How are you feeling?"

The question catches Georgia by surprise. It's not the question itself exactly, but the way Cecilia asked it, the sincerity in her voice. Like an actual person.

"Not great, if I'm being honest," Georgia says, unable to stop herself. Something about Cecilia's expression makes her feel as though she can be honest, although in front of her, Alice glances over her shoulder with a disapproving look.

Cecilia raises her eyebrows, but she doesn't look offended.

"Yes," she says simply. "I suspect not."

There's a pause, and in it, Georgia tries to make sense of this answer. A part of her feels indignant, but more than that, she's curious.

"Virgin Mode can be quite a strain," Cecilia says, her eyes gliding over the other women in the room before landing back on Georgia. "Especially one's first few times with it. Most find these early sessions physiologically exhausting."

There's another version of Georgia's life, with another version of

Georgia, where someone like Cecilia Clements says something like this and Georgia laughs. In this universe, she might be beside Julie in a conference room, or at a client lunch. Someone will complain about their physiological exhaustion, and Georgia and Julie will share a look, and for the rest of the day they will say dumb things like *I'm physiologically hungry*, or *I need a physiological shot*.

But this is not that universe. In this universe, Georgia touches her temple and thinks Cecilia is right. She *does* feel worn down—physiologically, but in all ways, really—although it's hard to say if this is due to Virgin Mode or not.

"As I explained earlier," Cecilia continues, "Virgin Mode is a temporary but very real rewiring of your brain. In Classic Mode, your world looks different, but you are moving through it in the way you usually would. In Virgin Mode, however, we temporarily block the brain's maternal circuit from functioning. Again, it's temporary—occurring only so long as the pulses of electromagnetic energy are being produced—but while Virgin Mode is activated, the brain is, quite literally, operating in a way it normally would not."

It strikes Georgia somewhere in the back of her mind that she's no longer shivering. It feels as though every one of her cells has suddenly tensed with attention, oriented toward Cecilia at the front of the room.

"And that's not to mention the practicalities of the exercise," Cecilia continues. "The deliberate ways in which we have utilized your fears."

Here, she dips her chin, as though she's expecting Georgia to protest. Perhaps she's expecting Georgia to cross her arms and pout. It's what Dede would've done, and maybe she would've been right to. For Dede to face fire, for Georgia to face water—it does feel cruel.

"You're afraid of water," Cecilia says, and it's not a question. Still, Georgia nods.

"Why is that, do you think?"

Georgia shrugs. "I don't know. It's just something I've always been afraid of."

She can hear the way she's talking, the brazen curtness in her voice, and maybe she shouldn't be talking this way to Cecilia. And yet, it feels as though she's earned it, at least a little bit.

"Understandable," Cecilia says. If she's troubled by the way Georgia is speaking to her, she doesn't let it show. "And sometimes there are no rational explanations for these things. Sometimes it is simply the way we are wired."

She pauses here, but Georgia can tell she's not finished. Logan, next to her, is totally still. It feels like they are about to learn some great secret—the secret, possibly, that they came to learn.

"But it may also be that our fears speak of something deeper within us," Cecilia continues. "Something of which we are not consciously aware."

She looks at Georgia here as though she is looking down into the deeper, murkier parts of her. Georgia wonders what she sees down there.

"In some cultures," says Cecilia, "water is seen as a symbol of chaos and destruction. And in this context, it is easy to see why water might be feared."

Georgia frowns. She feels oddly disappointed by this explanation, even though she really should not. After all, Cecilia's right: She *doesn't* like chaos or destruction. Still, it feels like a cop-out, or at least so generic of an answer that it really isn't one. She had her tarot cards read once, and the tarot reader predicted a difficult relationship, which was technically true, but true in a way that told her nothing. She and Will had just bought their first house and had a difficult relationship with the raccoon who kept pooping on their deck.

"But, Georgia," Cecilia says, her voice turning softer, "I have a different theory. I may be wrong, but I wonder, Georgia, if your fear of water is actually your fear of the unknown."

She looks at Georgia here like she's expecting her to answer, and Georgia is surprised by how very profoundly she cannot. She has always considered herself a fairly self-aware person—she knows her laugh can be annoying, for example, and that she's mean when she's hungry—but it has never been clearer that she doesn't know herself nearly as well as she once thought.

"I—don't know," Georgia says lamely.

Cecilia keeps looking at her, clearly expecting more, but Georgia simply doesn't have more. Is she afraid of the unknown? Isn't everybody?

Finally, Cecilia breaks eye contact, her eyes sweeping over the other two women in the room. Georgia feels both relieved by the shift and desperate to regain her attention. It's that feeling of being on the cusp of something—an orgasm, a sneeze—but never getting relief. She's missing something, some crucial piece to the puzzle that is her, and if only she could find it, it would all make sense.

"The choice to utilize your greatest fears is on purpose," Cecilia says, now speaking to all of them. She steps out from behind the lectern and strides to the middle of the room. "But it is not a choice to be cruel. No, our goal is to push you further and harder than you've ever been pushed. We want to put you in the most demanding situation possible and see where you come out."

Georgia realizes now, watching Cecilia move around it, that the room itself is shaped like a seashell, the front scalloped and wider than the back. It's beautiful, actually—the architecture, the detail. Nothing Cecilia does is without thought.

"And where did you come out, Georgia?" Cecilia says, looking at her again. This time, though, she's back to her usual self, formal and distant. Georgia can't tell if this is a rhetorical question, and if not, what answer Cecilia is hoping to receive.

"Um," she says.

Cecilia says, to all of them, "In Classic Mode, on the beach, you lost your daughter. Ruby. She was swept out to sea."

No one says anything. Georgia thinks of Ruby, her singular dimple, the whisper-fine hair that sticks to the back of her neck. "I didn't know they came with mullets," Will said when she was born with one, and Georgia smacked him but laughed.

"Because in Classic Mode," Cecilia continues, "your maternal circuit was on and active. In Classic Mode, your brain was processing your surroundings like a mother, with a hypersensitive focus on your child. And in this hyperfocus, you lost the big picture. You were so focused on each and every detail of your children, you hesitated for just long enough for Ruby to be swept away."

Georgia thinks of Ruby the first time she held her, pulling her from the nurses in the hospital, all goopy and screaming and red. "You've got a feisty one," the doctor told her, and in all the time since, that's what she's been: Georgia's beautiful, feisty girl.

"Now," says Cecilia, "imagine what that hesitation would've looked like in the water, in that car. Imagine if you had, for example, tended to your daughter in the back seat before freeing yourself. If you had been similarly focused on her."

But Georgia doesn't have to imagine. The memory is still so real: the water lapping up against the window, the sound of Clover's thighs against the car seat, *thwap thwap thwap*. And when she finds Cecilia's eyes, she sees the answer there too: A moment's hesitation, and they both would've drowned.

"But you didn't hesitate," Cecilia says, her voice still soft, although her face has changed. In her eyes now is an intensity that's unsettling but also beautiful. A mother beholding her child, God looking down on his creation. Georgia's grandmother said she talked to God, and Georgia never really believed her, but looking at Cecilia now, she wonders if it might be possible to feel the divine.

"In Virgin Mode," Cecilia says to all of them, although it feels like she's speaking only to Georgia, "you were not burdened by the maternal circuit. You moved quickly and decisively, which you could not have done otherwise. And *this*, this triumph Georgia experienced in that water today, is what I want for all of you. This, what you did today, is freedom."

CHAPTER 48

Later that night in her bedroom, Georgia lies face-up on the bed, staring at the ceiling. It's late enough that she should probably be asleep, but she isn't. She can't. Even the concept of sleep feels faraway, like someone she once knew but now doesn't recognize.

She thinks of Julie, that time after she went on a trip to the Grand Canyon, where she was caught in a lightning storm. "It was terrifying," Julie told her afterward, back in the safe, ugly walls of their office, "but amazing. Like I forgot for a second I was even human, you know?"

Georgia didn't know, and even now, that's not how she feels. She feels very much human, although she understands now what Julie meant. It's as though she has gotten a peek behind the curtain, to a world she didn't know was there. A world she never even imagined, because how could she?

This is what she's thinking about when she hears the knock on her door.

It takes her a moment to register the sound, and then another for her to understand what it means. Panic then grips her. She thinks of the men on Dede's porch, whatever it was she did or did not see.

She sits up and looks around, taking a quick inventory of her surroundings. There's nothing here that could really be used for a weapon, except maybe her suitcase, which she could roll toward an intruder like a bowling ball.

Relax, she tells herself. She's being ridiculous. Besides, she can't even bowl.

She pads to the door quietly. Unfortunately, there isn't a peephole, which feels like a significant oversight in the room's design.

She presses her ear against the wood.

Nothing.

She clears her throat. "Hello?"

"Georgia? Hello? It's me."

Georgia frowns. She thinks it's Logan, but she's not sure, as they certainly are not close enough to announce themselves as *me.*

And yet, when Georgia opens the door, there Logan is.

"Hi," she says with a nervous smile. "I didn't wake you up, did I?"

She's holding something—two plates of pie. Georgia frowns, confused, which Logan mirrors. She looks down at the pies sternly, like she wasn't expecting to see them there either.

"I brought pie," she explains. "I thought you might need it. You know, after today."

She gives Georgia an expectant expression, and Georgia doesn't know what to do. She is not prepared for visitors. She is not prepared for pies.

"Oh. That's so—nice."

Logan beams.

Georgia, feeling bad, says, "Do you want to come in?"

Logan doesn't hesitate. She steps inside, looking around in amazement, as though she isn't staying in a room exactly like this.

"It smells good in here," she says.

Georgia, closing the door behind her, says, "Oh. Really?"

"Yeah. Like your shampoo."

Georgia touches her hair. She didn't know people noticed her shampoo, although she's not upset to hear it. She is constantly guilted into the expensive stuff at the salon, not because she especially wants the expensive stuff, but because it feels rude not to get it. Like by denying it, she's saying something about the hairdresser's work.

"How are you feeling?" Logan continues, turning more serious. She gives a critical look up and down Georgia's body, which is currently most unimpressive in a pair of Will's old boxer shorts.

"Oh, I'm good. Fine. Just—I don't know." She sighs. "A little shaken up I guess."

Logan nods emphatically. The pies jiggle like they're nodding too.

"Virgin Mode sounds intense," she says.

"Yeah. I don't know. It's mostly weird. It just felt so . . . real, you know?"

When Izzy pulled her from the car earlier, Georgia found herself not in the water but on the pier. Apparently, the car never moved, something she still can't wrap her mind around. It's nauseating in a way, like those awful rides that make you feel like you're zipping and flipping, although in reality you're just being jostled a bit.

"Well, hopefully pie will make you feel better," Logan says, once again raising the plates. "I got one key lime and one, I *think*, is Boston cream pie. That's what it looks like anyway. I got both because I wasn't sure what you like."

"Oh. That's . . ." Georgia searches for the word, but she can't find it. Giving up, she says, "I did like the key lime actually."

"Perfect! Because I prefer the Boston cream."

Despite herself, Georgia smiles. *What an odd bird,* she thinks.

She crosses the room to get them some forks. "Where did you get these?" Georgia says as Logan sets the plates on the little table in the kitchenette.

"Oh, the kitchen," Logan says cheerfully.

"Ah." She hands Logan a fork. "I didn't know you could get desserts from the kitchen."

"Oh, you can't. I mean, I don't think you're supposed to, technically speaking, but I have a key fob." She turns suddenly businesslike. "And one of the girls from Pod Two told me that they throw away the extra pie at the end of the day anyway, so I don't think it's *technically* stealing."

It does seem like technically stealing, although Georgia doesn't say this.

"Where did you get the key fob?" she says.

"Oh, I brought my RFID cloner." She reaches into the pocket of her sweatshirt. From it, she produces a little blue device. "From Amazon. Super handy." She says this the way Georgia sometimes recommends the cord organizer she got on sale last Black Friday, although these two things do not feel remotely the same.

"I don't— A cloner?"

"A key fob cloner. One of the kitchen staff left their fobs out, and I figured, just to be safe, you know?"

She pulls from her pocket a little plastic baggy, in which appear to be more key fobs.

"Blanks," she explains. "For cloning." She frowns for a moment as though considering something. She then holds the device and the bag out. "Here. You take it."

Georgia feels momentarily discombobulated. "What? Take— No. I mean, thank you, but I don't need it."

"You never know when you'll need it," Logan insists. "And I have a bunch of them. Seriously." She shakes the bag. "Just in case."

"Okay. Well, thanks," Georgia mumbles, relenting. She takes the device and the bag and sets them next to her plate. Logan watches her expectantly, although Georgia isn't sure what else she's expecting her to do. She cannot imagine a situation in which she might need a key fob cloner, although saying so feels rude.

Instead, she takes a big bite of pie, although she just brushed her teeth, so the toothpaste remnants make it taste weird. Logan, apparently finding this sufficient, takes a bite of her own pie hungrily.

"So," Georgia says after a moment. "You said you have a daughter?"

Logan brightens.

"I do! She's six. Jo." She smiles to herself, and Georgia softens.

"Jo. Is that short for anything?"

"Yeah—Josephine. Like *Little Women*. The book, you know?"

She gives Georgia a sheepish expression, and Georgia tries not to look surprised. The fact that she finds this surprising is probably in itself highly prejudicial. So Logan has blue hair. So she clones key fobs. So what? She's just as likely to read *Little Women* as anyone else.

"Jo was my favorite too," Georgia says, which isn't exactly true. She liked Jo, but she always had a soft spot for Beth, whom she felt was severely mistreated.

"My Jo is a lot like *Little Women* Jo," says Logan. "So smart. Definitely smarter than me."

She seems far away now, with a faint smile lingering on her face.

"I bet you both are," Georgia says, which seems to bring Logan back. She looks sadder suddenly. She is still holding her fork, but it's resting on her plate.

"No, I'm an idiot actually. First-class, grade A."

"No, you're not," Georgia says, even though she has no idea if this is true.

"No, I am. That's the whole reason I'm here."

Georgia doesn't say anything. She shouldn't be so curious, but she is.

Thankfully, Logan offers on her own, "My ex—Jo's dad—he just started dating this new woman. She's— I mean, don't get me wrong. She's beautiful. Nice hair, perfect body. She looks a lot like you actually."

Georgia is too surprised by this to hide her reaction. She would consider herself a lot of things, but beautiful is generally not one of them, and she would certainly not call her hair *nice*.

"But I don't know," Logan continues, her shoulders now hunched. "I just had this *feeling* about her. You know what I mean? She and her brother sell secondhand jewelry, which is *fine*. I mean, I'm all for environmentalism and everything. Of course."

Georgia frowns. She's not sure what environmentalism has to do with this.

"Some of her clients are just—I don't know. And Jo says they sometimes come to the house, which is maybe normal for secondhand jewelry sales? I don't know. I don't wear jewelry. But the point is, people were coming over when Jo was there, and I just had this *feeling*, like something wasn't right. And I panicked."

Georgia is holding her breath now, waiting. There's a beat, then another, until it becomes clear that this is the end of Logan's story.

"What does that mean, you panicked?" Georgia says finally, unable to help herself. Logan has put the fork down and is now wringing her hands beneath the edge of the table.

"Ah. Well, they were trying to tell me it was kidnapping. But how can you kidnap your own child, you know?"

But Georgia doesn't know. She can't even imagine. Kidnapping. That sounds, on its face, very serious. But Logan is right: How fairly can a mother be accused of kidnapping her own daughter?

Logan says, "So this was part of my probation. A week here. It's better than jail, I guess."

She smiles weakly, revealing a tiny bit of chocolate pie stuck on her tooth. Georgia doesn't know if it's this, or Logan's overall niceness, but she feels the anger rising inside her on Logan's behalf.

"That's not fair," she says, although Logan just shrugs. And maybe that's all they can do. Because it's not fair, but it never is.

How many times has Georgia told Clover that? Life isn't fair. And yet, deep down, does she even actually believe this? Or does she believe the opposite—that all good things will be rewarded and all bad things will see their justice in the end? How does one get through life believing it can be any other way?

"It's not been fair for you either," Logan says after a moment, although it takes Georgia a second to register this, as she's feeling very far away. Even then, when she looks at Logan, she doesn't know what to say.

"I mean, you shouldn't lie," Logan continues, "but I'm sure you had a reason. And people don't need to be so mean about it, if you ask me."

She sounds sad as she says this, and Georgia realizes that she means it, genuinely. That somehow, despite what she knows, and despite what she doesn't, she still believes Georgia is worthy of sympathy.

"I had a reason," Georgia says, "but I don't know if it was a good one."

Logan nods, looking attentive, and Georgia wonders if this is the first time anyone has ever actually listened to her about this. She told the partners at her firm, and they heard what she was saying, but it's not clear if they actually heard her. And even Will, who never judged her, who never even suggested that he was mad, has never looked at her the way Logan is looking at her now.

Georgia says, "When I did it—the interview, I mean—I didn't think I'd be like, the lead narrative. I thought my story would just be one of many they were telling. Kind of like this chorus of voices, you know?"

Logan nods again, but her expression is empty. She doesn't know, clearly.

"The story I told," Georgia tries a second time, "it didn't happen to me, but it could have, and people don't want to talk about that. It's like, MeToo happened, so we must be all good now, but we're not. We're really, really not. And I have two daughters, you know? So when I did it, I felt like I was . . ."

She trails off. She thought she had it, the explanation. It felt so solid, especially after the psilocybin, like it was something in her hands. Now, though, trying to put words to it, she realizes she can't find them. She has opened her fists only to find them empty.

"Like you were helping," Logan says for her. "You felt like you were lying for your daughters, to make the world better for them."

Hearing Logan say it, it sounds so stupid, so naive. And yet.

"Yes," she whispers. "It sounds crazy, but I did."

For a moment, they just sit there, and Georgia tries to imagine what this situation would be like if the roles were reversed. With Logan trying to explain how she thought this lie could be good or helpful. How she thought it could result in anything other than what it did. She wants to believe she would be as generous as Logan is being, although that may be giving herself too much credit.

"Do you think Cecilia can help us?" Logan says after a little while, with a look like she expects Georgia to have an answer.

"I don't know," Georgia says, because she doesn't have one, as much as she wishes she did.

CHAPTER 49

Logan's turn in Virgin Mode is the next morning. They meet in front of the Shell Room, where Cecilia is waiting for them outside. They know the drill by now, so Logan doesn't need instructions. Izzy hands her the headset, and she slips it on.

"Excellent," says Cecilia, summoning actual enthusiasm, like Logan's performance is indeed a thing of excellence. Logan nods uncertainly, clearly nervous. From beneath her headset straps, her blue hair flares out frizzily.

When Logan left Georgia's villa the previous evening, she gave a heartfelt but ultimately ineffective attempt at comfort. It seemed, at the start of an extremely painful sequence, like she was going in for a hug, although by the time Georgia realized she wasn't, they were too close to stop. Logan then attempted to recover with a formal handshake, which only made it worse.

"Now, go on inside," Cecilia instructs Logan, nodding to the Shell Room. "We'll be right here watching the whole time."

Logan looks over her shoulder to the building, then back at Cecilia. Her jaw is tense with worry, and Georgia is struck with sympathy toward her, a feeling that's almost maternal. After last night, she really doesn't know what to make of Logan, although one thing has crystallized: If Logan deserves to be here, then every mom does.

Logan climbs the short staircase to the Shell Room veranda. They watch as she pauses at the top, hesitating. Then she pushes open the door.

The Shell Room seems to be furnished differently than it was last time. Georgia squints and thinks she can make out a long piece of furniture. Is it . . . a couch?

"You can go inside and close the door," says Cecilia brightly. If she registers Logan's nervousness, she has decided not to acknowledge it.

Logan steps inside obediently, and the door clicks closed behind her. Under the veranda, on the small foldout table Izzy set up, the screen turns black.

"Light switch is on the wall," Cecilia says.

Logan flips it, revealing a much different room indeed. This one appears to be a classroom lined with, not a couch, but desks. They're small desks, presumably for children, and at the front, there's a larger one for a teacher—all a projection, of course, but it looks so real.

Logan doesn't move from her spot at the door. Georgia remembers what it felt like in the car by the water, the prickly unease about what would happen next. She glances at Cecilia, who is watching the screen with a mild expression. Beside her, Alice is grimacing.

The moment stretches on. Logan remains motionless. She doesn't even seem to be looking around. She stares straight ahead at the whiteboard, where along one side, a schedule has been taped. *Reading. Math. Social/Emotional. Recess.*

Finally, just as Alice shifts her weight with impatience, there's a sound from the screen.

"Mama?"

Logan looks, the view whipping in the sound's direction. And there, in a corner seat, is a little girl. Georgia knows immediately who it is. She looks like a Jo, somehow. Not the *Little Women* Jo; this Jo is small, delicate, with deep caramel skin and long black hair that falls in a braid over her shoulder. She doesn't look like Logan at all, but for some reason Georgia can't explain, it's obvious she's Logan's daughter.

"JoJo?" Logan says, although she still doesn't move.

"Mama? Why are you here?"

The girl is wearing a navy jumper with bright red apples on it, and while Georgia doesn't know her, she feels like she would do anything to protect her.

"I'm—" Logan starts, but she's cut off by a sound so loud, everyone—everyone except Cecilia, that is—jumps. Alice and Georgia look around, although it becomes clear almost immediately that the sound is the projection.

And then, again. This time, the sound is unmistakable. It's the sound of gunfire.

"Mama?" Jo squeaks, part plea, part question. Logan hurries toward her and pulls her from the chair.

Again, the pulse of gunshots, so close together, they make a single whir. It echoes just outside the door, and for a moment, even Georgia forgets that just outside the door is the veranda, the bay. She and the other women watching from below.

There's a brief pause, silence, followed by the slam of doors. Faraway screams. Another round of bullets Georgia can feel as much as hear.

Jo whimpers. Logan pulls her down so they're crouching. The girl is trembling, and Georgia thinks back to that first night, that first dinner. This is what Logan said she was afraid of. She said she was afraid of people, of crazy people who don't want to be good.

"Mama," Jo whispers desperately. From the hall, there's a slam. A shrill cry lost in another scream of bullets.

"JoJo," says Logan. "I've got to . . ."

Her voice trails off. She scans the room, as though looking for something. The bullets have stopped now, although the sound rings in Georgia's ears. The silence is somehow worse than the noise.

"I've got to call for help," Logan whispers. "I can't do this myself."

"Excellent," says Cecilia, as if to herself.

Georgia looks at her, her heart racing, then back to the screen. And all at once, she sees it. She sees what Cecilia is seeing, the excellence on the screen. Because finally, it makes sense: Everything they're doing is a mirror image of reality.

In reality, Logan doesn't rely on other people. In reality, she rescues her daughter, or kidnaps her, depending on whom you ask. But that wasn't her only option, even if it felt like it was. When she thought her daughter was in danger, she could've told somebody. She could've called the police. She didn't because her vision was clouded, the way all mothers' brains are clouded. But here in the Shell Room, Logan is finally free.

CHAPTER 50

They give Logan one of those foil blankets they gave Georgia after her exercise, which Logan takes looking somewhat dazed. "That was excellent work," Cecilia tells her, to which she just stares back blankly.

"We'll meet back here after lunch," Izzy says as Cecilia heads back inside the Shell Room. And then, to Logan directly, she says, "That was a really good job."

Logan gazes back at her, although this time she nods, a faint look of pride passing over her face. She looks ridiculous wrapped in the foil blanket, like a big human burrito, although there's something distinctly beautiful about her at the same time.

They're then released for lunch, although Georgia hangs back. "I'll meet you at the café," she says to Logan, who nods foggily. Alice, whose turn in Virgin Mode is tomorrow, has already left.

When she's alone, Georgia climbs the stairs to the Shell Room. It registers as she's doing this that it might be out of line, but she can't stop herself. She pulls open the door, and at once, Cecilia looks up. She seems to be flipping through a folder, although seeing Georgia, she closes it.

"Georgia," she says. She sounds surprised, although it isn't a reprimand. "Can I help you?"

Georgia lets the door close behind her. Standing at the back of the room, it's very clearly a seashell.

She takes a deep breath.

"Yes," she says. "Well, I don't know. Maybe. I guess that's . . . why I'm here."

Cecilia cocks her head curiously, although she doesn't say anything. Georgia wishes she had practiced this beforehand. This is the problem with doing spontaneous things, the reason she so rarely does them.

"It's just . . . well, about today's exercise with Logan," she says. "I understand why you were happy with it. And with mine. I get it now, what you're talking about when you say being free of your mom brain. I felt . . ." She inhales, trying to find the word. "Well, free, I guess."

Here, Cecilia nods, her face betraying nothing.

"But what I don't get," Georgia says, "or maybe what I'm not understanding, is what we're supposed to do now that we know this. I mean, I know what I did in the car, and that was great. But I did that in Virgin Mode, and what I don't know is if . . ." She swallows, knowing what she wants to ask but not sure how to ask it. "Well," she says finally, "I guess what I'm asking is if that woman in the car was really even me?"

The last part of the question gets, unexpectedly, stuck in her throat. She didn't expect to get this emotional. She doesn't even understand why she is.

Cecilia doesn't answer for a moment, and as Georgia waits, she tries to analyze this feeling. What it is, she realizes, is fear. Because what if Cecilia tells her what she's afraid of hearing: that the woman in the car *wasn't* her? That she is someone Georgia could've been, maybe even once was, but now is not?

"How much do you know about brain architecture, Georgia?" Cecilia says finally, and Georgia finds herself frowning before she can stop herself. She turns an ear toward her, as though hearing her better might make the question clearer.

"About brain architecture?"

"Do you know much about the parietal lobe?"

Georgia shakes her head. "I don't."

"The parietal lobe is the brain's primary somatosensory cortex. It works to interpret sensory input from other locations in the body."

Georgia just nods in confusion. She seems to have missed some vital connective part of this conversation.

"Oh," she says dumbly.

Cecilia looks at her for a moment, scrutinizing. She then picks up one of the headsets sitting beside her on the table.

"During your exercise," she says, holding it up a little, "I'm sure the water felt real."

She turns the headset slightly so the pink metal catches in the light. Georgia thinks again of the water, of her perfectly dry socks afterward.

"It did, yes."

"And I'm sure you're wondering how that's possible."

Georgia nods. Of course.

"We are able to create these sensations by activating the parietal lobe, as I mentioned. With targeted stimulation to this area of the brain, we are able to produce the *sensation* of sensory input without requiring the sensory input itself."

In Georgia's mind, she sees Dede, the way she howled as she ran into the fire. Georgia felt the water in her own lap. She supposes these were just sensations, although that hardly does them justice. What is life, after all, but just a series of sensations? What is pain, if it's not that?

She finds Cecilia's eyes and feels slightly embarrassed that Cecilia is studying her again.

"So it was all in our heads," she says slowly. "The . . . sensations. The water and fire. None of it was there."

"Yes," Cecilia says.

"But it felt so real."

"Yes," Cecilia says a second time, and the room seems extremely quiet afterward. Georgia can feel the idea forming, can see the fuzzy outlines of its shape, but it remains just past where she can grab it.

Her eyes fall to the headset Cecilia is holding. She thinks of the partner at her law firm, Dana, the one whose client is SHE. She works in the pharmaceutical space, just like Georgia. Does Dana know this technology exists?

"It's one of the more profound pitfalls of modern science," Cecilia says finally. "The common, and incorrect, notion that the external world and our mind's understanding of it are somehow a binary."

She gives Georgia a stern look, and Georgia nods, even if she doesn't understand what this means.

Cecilia's expression softens.

"What I'm saying, Georgia, is that the inner workings of our minds are as real as anything outside them. Just because there was no water as we understand it does not mean the water wasn't real. And yes, just because you were reacting to a certain set of stimulations doesn't mean that the reaction wasn't real either."

Georgia doesn't know what to say to this. She can faintly see what Cecilia is getting at, although she doesn't exactly agree. She cannot, after all, drown in the *idea* of water, can she?

"It's really incredible," Georgia says, nodding to the headset. "It's amazing technology."

Cecilia looks down to the device in her hands.

"It is, isn't it?" she says, a look on her face somewhere between adoration and pride.

"How does it work?" Georgia says. "How do you—how do you get it to stimulate the right parts of the brain?"

When Cecilia looks up at her, her smile has vanished, and Georgia falters slightly. Has she gone too far?

For a moment, the room feels charged, although when Cecilia speaks again, her voice is as gentle as it was before.

"It is quite complex technology, as you can imagine," she says. "We rely heavily on the integration of AI—artificial intelligence, I should say."

Georgia nods, happy to be discussing something she understands, at least to some degree. During last year's election, Julie showed her an AI-generated image of a presidential candidate wearing a baby's diaper. "The pinnacle of human innovation," she said, straight-faced.

"Amazing," Georgia says, and she really does mean it. She means it so much, it's almost scary. "I guess it's just . . . I'm just afraid I need it, I guess. Like, I need Virgin Mode or else I'll stay"—she shakes her head—"trapped."

She looks up, surprised by herself and this choice of word. Is this really what she meant? And if so, is that an ugly thing to admit? Is it even fair to say she's trapped when the only thing trapping her is herself?

She finds Cecilia's eyes nervously, afraid of what she'll see—shock or disgust. It might be disgusting to talk this way, like she's a victim, which she is not. But that's not what she finds. Cecilia is frowning, but it's an analytical expression, like she's been presented with a riddle she's attempting to work out.

A beat passes, then two.

Then, finally, Cecilia says, "You have a background in science, I've been told."

It's not a question, but Georgia nods anyway.

"A PharmD, yes."

"PharmD and juris doctor. Very impressive."

Georgia shrugs.

"I like you, Georgia," Cecilia says. "I like smart women. We need more women like you in the world, I think."

CHAPTER 51

On the last day of The Program, all the pods meet again in Two Dove Hall. Georgia isn't late this time, so she takes a little longer to admire the sculptures outside before heading in.

The doves are objectively beautiful. In high school, she had an art teacher who was adamant that nothing about art is objective, perhaps as a kindness to her class who—for the most part—produced objectively awful art. "To be an artist is to elicit a response," she insisted. "Art is only as good as the depth of the reaction it receives."

But the art teacher was wrong. The doves outside the hall are objectively, unquestionably better than any art Georgia has seen before. She's probably not supposed to do it, but she runs her hand down one of them, tracing the intricate rivulets of each individual feather. It's almost a surprise that the stone isn't soft.

She takes a step back.

EQUALITY IS DIVINITY.

The inscription is in bold block letters, an eye-catching contrast to the elegant birds. It's interesting that Cecilia chose this message—of all the possible messages—to take such a position of prominence.

The auditorium is alive with chatter when Georgia enters. From what she can tell, neither Pod One nor Pod Two has lost any members. Georgia wonders if it was just plain old bad luck the way things happened for her group.

She finds Logan, who is alone in a row near the back.

"How are you feeling?" Georgia says, sitting down next to her. Logan's exercise was two days ago, and she looks completely recovered now.

"Good," Logan says, but she sounds unsure of herself. And Georgia thinks she understands. She feels good too—rested, for one thing, and without the usual acid reflux that plagues her back home—although she suspects this is simply due to enough sleep and guava smoothies. She feels good but not changed.

Alice arrives a few minutes later, and when asked, she's "good" too. Alice's turn was yesterday, and afraid of planes, she was caught in one that was crashing. She handled it, though. She performed all the steps—her own oxygen mask, then her daughter's—with an almost robotic calmness, like she was one of the bored flight attendants doing a demonstration rather than navigating an actual crash.

When Cecilia appears onstage, she's wearing another cape. This one is baby pink and flutters as she walks.

"And here we are again," she says, raising her arms, which raise the cape. The cape is bejeweled, and against the harsh stage lighting, it twinkles dramatically. "Although it's been only a week, together we have journeyed far. We have questioned and struggled, triumphed and lost."

She seems to look in Pod Three's direction here, and Georgia can't help but nod in acknowledgment, although she is surely invisible to Cecilia in the dark.

"When you arrived," says Cecilia, her voice through the sound system coming from both nowhere and everywhere at once, "you carried with you baggage, both seen and unseen. Whether you understood what was holding you back or you came in search of that answer, each and every one of you stepped through these doors with something to conquer. And throughout this past week, each of you has. I have seen each and every one of you face your greatest fears, and in all of you, I have witnessed even greater courage."

In Georgia's mind, there's the sound of the hammer crashing against the car window. The second swing, the crackle of glass. The feeling afterward, like lightning, like something she'd never experienced before.

"But courageousness," Cecilia says, bringing her hands together in front of her, "although necessary, is not rare in the world. Courageousness, in its purest form, is no more than a quality—an admirable quality, but this quality alone will never bring us to true change. What separates those who wander through life from those who take hold of it is what they do with that quality. How can we use it to become active participants in our lives?"

Cecilia stops here, like she's waiting for a response, although no one makes a sound. In the pit of Georgia's stomach, she feels a sense of longing so intense, it almost hurts.

"Some of you," Cecilia says finally, her voice raining down from the speakers above them, "worry that the work we've done here is temporary. That the progress you've made on this island will not translate to your lives back home. It's a serious concern and certainly not baseless."

It may be Georgia's imagination, but she swears Cecilia looks straight at her here, despite Georgia's cover in the darkness. So she admits the worry isn't baseless. What, then, was the point of it all?

"And you may be wondering," Cecilia continues, "if our journey was thus in vain. What was the point of that struggle? Why endure these challenges if we cannot reap the rewards?"

Here, she smiles out at her audience, but it's not her usual enigmatic expression. This one is almost hungry.

"I made a promise," she says, bringing her hands together. "At the start of our time together, I made a promise that change will be available to those open to receiving it. Over the course of this week, I have witnessed this openness, so now it is time for me to keep my end of the bargain."

No one in the room makes a noise. It feels like the auditorium itself is holding its breath.

Cecilia pulls something from her cape's pocket.

"This is my covenant to you," she says, raising her arms up above her. She is holding something, although it's hard to tell what. "The final phase of our journey, the decision to redefine our lives and ourselves. Come with me now as we step into true freedom, which starts here, with Phase Two."

PART TWO

CHAPTER 52

Georgia has the very annoying tendency to always fall asleep on airplanes, even when she doesn't think she's tired, even when she would really prefer to stay awake. She tries to get window seats for this reason, to avoid the embarrassing situation of waking up on someone's shoulder, which has happened more times than she (or the people next to her) would like.

But on her flight home from Oahu, she doesn't sleep. She watches the entire flight out the window, wide awake.

Overhead, the pilot's garbled voice crackles through the speakers, asking them to raise their tray tables, to buckle their seat belts. He tells them they're close to their destination, and Georgia wonders how often a person experiences something like this: knowing life is about to change right before it does.

"Mommy!"

Clover jumps off the stool with an inelegant little thud. It's late, too late for her to be up, but Georgia can't find it in herself to be upset.

She kneels down and receives the little girl into her arms. Clover smells like she always does, like baby shampoo, a little bit of sweat, and something distinctly her. Georgia wraps her up, then squeezes a little tighter. The simulations on the island were good, but holding her daughter now, it's clear that nothing could ever truly capture this.

"Daddy let me stay up," Clover says, taking a step back. She gives Will a stern look across the kitchen, her five-year-old admonishment.

"Well, it's a special occasion," says Georgia, "so I think it's okay for tonight."

Clover seems satisfied with this answer. She throws her arms over Georgia's shoulders and gives her another hug.

"We're glad you're back," says Will when Georgia stands up, opening his arms for his own hug. She goes to him and finds comfort in how well she fits. He's the perfect size for her, just tall enough that when she hugs him, he can rest his chin on the crown of her head. When she was younger, she was convinced that when she got married—*if* she got married—it would be to someone shorter than her, because most men were, and to wish for taller felt, somehow, selfish. It felt selfish to imagine more.

CHAPTER 53

It's usually difficult to get Clover to bed, but tonight is exceptionally difficult. She doesn't physically protest the way some kids do, which Georgia knows from her mommy Facebook groups (those poor moms). Clover's protests are subtler. With Georgia or Will at the doorway, she will go on and on and on, knowing that the longer she talks, the more time she'll waste. "The art of the filibuster," as Will likes to say.

Tonight, she's talking about garbage trucks, and how the men on the back wear reflective vests so they don't get run over, and how it's actually okay that they're not buckled up, even if it's against the law, because they need to get on and off so much, and did Georgia know that once, when Daddy was little, he rode in the back of *his* dad's car without a seat belt, because you were allowed to do that in "old times"?

Usually Georgia finds this exasperating, because usually Georgia has a hundred and one things to do after Clover drifts off. She knows that blue light before bedtime is unhealthy, but there always seems to be *just one last email* she needs to get out. That, or she needs to finish the dishes or take a shower or address the Christmas cards. Sometimes she just wants to read a book before bed, and somehow even this is stressful, the pressure of having enough time to properly unwind.

But tonight, she kneels by Clover's bed until her words get slower and slurred, then eventually stop. Georgia stands in the doorway for a little while afterward, marveling at the miracle of this moment, how fleeting it is, and how sad it would've been if she hadn't noticed that until it was too late.

~

She wants to go into Ruby's room next, although she doesn't, because Ruby still isn't feeling well, and Georgia doesn't want to risk waking her up. Instead, she hovers by the door, her ear pressed against it, although all she can hear is the white noise machine's hush.

In their room, Will is standing at their bed, folding laundry. Watching him do this from the doorway, imagining all the other things he must've done during her absence, makes her feel tender with affection.

"Thanks for doing that," she says, crossing the room. "And for everything else."

He looks up. The circles under his eyes look darker in the overhead light.

"You don't have to thank me," he says as she lowers herself onto the edge of the bed. There's no bitterness in his voice, but she thinks she detects something. Uncertainty, perhaps?

"How was it when I was gone?" she says. "Be honest. Be *brutally* honest. I can take it."

At this, he seems to lighten. He chuckles and shakes his head. "That's between me, the girls, and God."

"Was it that bad?"

"No. I'm kidding. It really wasn't. I mean, it was hard with Ruby being sick, but still not terrible." A pause, then he adds, "But we're all really glad you're home."

She rises and slips her arms under his. He wraps her up, and for a long moment, they stand like this, a pile of folded undershirts on the bed by their side.

"So how was it?" he says finally. "I feel like we've barely gotten to talk."

She closes her eyes and thinks of Cecilia at the front of the auditorium, her arms spread wide.

"It was . . ."

She searches for the word, but she knows she won't find it, because there is no word. It's a word that hasn't been invented yet. And so instead, with a deep breath, she reaches into her pocket and pulls out the little pink bottle, which fits perfectly in her hand.

CHAPTER 54

Georgia didn't go to Catholic school, but after her mom died, Babcia took her every weekend to Catholic Mass.

Before that, Georgia had only had a basic grasp of church—and really, of God. (She had imagined him somewhere between Robin Hood and Santa Claus.) And honestly, she didn't really get much out of the Masses, because she didn't really enjoy them. Mostly, she didn't like how the church smelled, a bit like her grandmother. She didn't like the chanting or the robes or the way the priests held up the Eucharist and told her it was literal blood.

"But not like, *blood* blood," Georgia remembers once saying, driving back one Sunday. She was on her grandmother's beaded seat cover, Saint Christopher keeping tabs from the rearview mirror.

"What do you mean, *blood* blood?" Babcia said, in that no-nonsense way about her, but Georgia didn't know how to explain it better than she had.

She feels that way now, looking at her husband, the bottle of pills in her hand.

"Phase Two," he repeats a third time, and in her head, she hears Babcia. *What do you mean,* blood *blood?*

"It's just a trade name," Georgia says, although she knows that's not what he's asking. And indeed, he shakes his head.

"Is it like psilocybin?"

"No. Not at all. Phase Two is a synthetic neuropeptide."

He gives her a look, and she understands what it means. It's just, these details are important, even if they don't seem so to him.

"You're going to have to walk me through this," he says finally. He has abandoned the clothes, half of which lie unfolded on the bed. She doesn't know how she expected him to receive this information, although a private part of her was hoping for something a bit more welcoming than this.

"I'm trying. It's just—I guess I don't know where to start."

"How about what it is?" he says, but when she opens her mouth to answer, he cuts her off. "Not the science-y explanation. Just explain to me what it does in normal words."

She bows her head, reminding herself what this must be like for him. When Cecilia announced Phase Two in the auditorium, it was surprising but not out of nowhere—the grand crescendo of a weeklong symphony. For Will, it must be different, an unexpected cymbal crashing through silence.

"So I told you about the headsets," she says, and he nods, which she finds encouraging. "They target a certain part of your brain using electromagnetism—basically zapping you with electromagnetic pulses to essentially turn off that part of your brain."

Will nods again. Good.

"Well, this is like that, but instead of electromagnetic pulses, Phase Two shuts off that part of your brain using chemicals—a neuropeptide, specifically. The neuropeptide does what the electromagnetic pulses do from the headset. They essentially block a certain circuit in your brain from functioning."

"The mom circuit," Will says, and Georgia nods energetically, glad that they seem to be on the same page.

"Yes. Exactly."

He looks at her for a moment, but he doesn't seem to be actually seeing her. His gaze is distant as he chews on the inside of his cheek. It's not totally dissimilar to the way Logan looked when

Cecilia first announced the drug, the way Logan gnawed on her bottom lip like she had been asked to do difficult math in her head.

"Okay," he says finally, slowly. "So . . . okay. I guess—I mean, is this safe?"

"Yes. It's been through all the trials. Approved by the FDA."

His expression changes here; he seems to find this compelling. And of course. He's the sort of person who trusts government organizations, which is one of the reasons Georgia fell in love with him. She liked the fact that he defaults to trusting something, possibly because she was raised by a woman who trusted no one but Martha Stewart and Jesus Christ.

"And you think this is . . . a good idea?" he says. She can tell it's a genuine question, and it's yet another reason she loves him so much: He has always valued her opinion, perhaps too much at times, although it's nice to be taken so seriously.

She thinks for a moment about her answer, but she doesn't need to. Her opinion has been formed already, miles and miles away. Maybe before that, if she had bothered to look for it.

"I do," she says, her eyes falling to the little pink pill bottle, in which are many pink heart-shaped pills. "More than good, really. I think this is exactly the answer I've been looking for."

CHAPTER 55

The next morning, Ruby wakes up differently from how she usually does. She usually announces her return to consciousness with a prehistoric shriek, which doesn't stop until Georgia rushes to her room. This morning, however, Georgia goes into Ruby's room just before eight to wake her and realizes with a little start that she's already awake.

"You're awake," Georgia says, pulling her daughter from the crib.

Ruby gives her a look like this is the most obvious thing in the world.

Georgia changes her diaper, then scoops her up and heads downstairs. Ruby rests her head on her mother's shoulder, and Georgia nuzzles her, breathing her in. For as good as Cecilia's VR technology is, this is one major shortcoming: the way her daughters smell. In just a week on the island, Georgia has almost forgotten, or maybe Ruby smells different from how she remembers—fruitier, like Will got them new shampoo.

"She was awake," Georgia says to Will in the kitchen. He's standing in front of the sink, hungrily eating a bowl of cereal.

"Who?" he says.

"Ruby."

"She was awake?"

"Yes."

"Doing what?"

"Looked like her taxes."

He raises an eyebrow. He seems surprised that she's joking,

and Georgia wonders if she's usually so tense that a joke is in fact surprising.

"Well," he says, his eyes traveling from Ruby back to his wife. "How does she seem? Do I need to call in again?"

At this, Ruby lifts her head to get a good look at her father. She doesn't look like Will. She doesn't look like Georgia either. In fact, the person she looks most like is Georgia's grandmother, but in baby form—a tiny, critical Polish woman.

"I don't know," Georgia says, studying Ruby, who is studying Will. "She seems fine, I think. And I mean, if something comes up, I'm so close to the day care."

Will seems to find this persuasive, and so does Ruby, who rests her head back against Georgia's chest—all of them, Georgia included, relieved by a decision so easily made.

Will usually drops Ruby off at day care, but this morning Georgia does after she gets Clover on the bus. "I missed her," she says, and Will seems happy to have the morning off.

Ruby has been going to the same day care since she was four months old, which is the same one Clover went to until she was five. It's right down the street from Georgia's office and costs more a month than their mortgage (but they pay it because the day care is so wonderful).

Ruby's teacher, Miss Amira, is one of the things about the day care Georgia likes best. She's in her early twenties, always smiling, and has an amazing collection of holiday-themed earrings.

"Ruby girl!" Miss Amira cries when Georgia arrives in the classroom, sounding actually thrilled. "We missed you!"

"And she missed you!" Georgia says.

Miss Amira takes Ruby from Georgia, which Ruby acknowledges with a weary smile. This behavior isn't exactly normal, and the thought crosses Georgia's mind that perhaps she still isn't feeling well.

"She seemed okay this morning," Georgia says, "but maybe still a little tired from that bug."

"No worries," says Miss Amira, stroking Ruby's cheek. Ruby looks back at her adoringly.

"If it seems like she's going downhill, just give me a call. I'm right down the street."

"I will!" Miss Amira says. She then seems to struggle with something for a moment before adding sheepishly, "You look great, Mrs. Evans."

Normally Georgia would find this mortifying, the thought that anyone knew where she was. And yet, Miss Amira says this with such sincerity that—coupled with the handprint butterflies hanging above her, Georgia's own daughter snuggled beneath her chin—she finds it difficult to feel anything other than touched.

"Thank you, Amira," Georgia says. "I feel great."

She arrives at her office at just past nine, with plenty of time before her meeting at ten. The meeting is with Dana and the other equity partners, presumably to talk about The Program and what comes next. She knows she should feel nervous about the meeting, as she has no idea what to expect from it. In her mind, she's imagining a tribunal—the Spanish Inquisition, but in the main conference room with its big, awful art. (When a meeting is really boring, she and Julie will text one another their stupidest interpretations of the paintings: *a baby pooping out pony beads*, or *a Cubist portrayal of a lawless Easter egg hunt*.)

But when she sits down at her desk this morning, she's surprised to find that she's not nervous about the meeting, not really, not the way she usually would be. She wonders if this is the Phase Two, and if so, what that says about those feelings in the first place.

She logs on to her computer and sighs at the emails that have accumulated while she's been out. This will take all morning, if not longer, she can already tell. She rests her fingers on the keyboard for a moment, then leans her head against her headrest and swivels her chair so she's facing the window, which is a good but not great view of DC's notoriously busy K Street.

DC is such a contrast to the wild, green world of Oahu. Here, there's grass, but only a geometrical patch of it in Farragut Square, crisscrossed with sidewalks. The square is bustling, food trucks already lining the curb to get the best spots for lunch. Later, it will be packed with professionals eating gyoza from tinfoil, tourists playing with cameras, pigeons being pigeons, homeless people asleep.

And this is what she will start with later, when she's telling the story to Will. She will start with a detailed description of the crowded square, all the people, the depressing concrete. She doesn't usually tell stories like this. "You don't need to set the scene for everything," as she sometimes says to him, but this time it *will* be necessary. It will be crucial for him to understand exactly what she was thinking as she looked out the window just before she got the email, or else it won't have the same impact when she says, "It's like I conjured it myself."

CHAPTER 56

The email is from Cecilia Clements, with the subject line: *Meeting in DC.*

At first, Georgia can't make sense of this. She knows what all the words mean individually, and she understands what they should mean together like this. And yet, that meaning feels totally incompatible with a message from Cecilia Clements.

Cecilia wants to meet in DC tomorrow morning, in the SHE office downtown. She has a "proposal," although that's all she says.

Georgia checks her calendar, which is mostly a formality. She would rearrange her schedule if there was a conflict. She would do just about anything.

Yes, she types. *I'm available. I would be happy to come by.*

She watches the message whoosh away with a feeling of disbelief. She tries to imagine Cecilia in DC, which she knows must happen regularly, as this is where SHE is based. And yet, she can't imagine it. She can't picture Cecilia with her amazing white hair, her grand, sparkly capes, just . . . walking down the sidewalk. Waiting in line for a food truck. Swaying in the metro along with all the regular people in a car that smells like pee.

How many reasons could there be for her to want to meet with Georgia? She closes her eyes to consider this, which is when her phone rings. Her first irrational thought is that Cecilia heard the question somehow and has called with an answer.

The call isn't from Cecilia. It's from Ruby's day care, Academy for Tots.

"This is Georgia Evans," she says, eyeing the time. Her meeting with the partners is in fifteen minutes. She should probably be mentally preparing herself.

"Hi, Mrs. Evans. This is Miss Sullivan from Academy for Tots."

"Oh. Hi, Miss Sullivan."

"Hi. Yes, I'm calling about Ruby. Unfortunately, after morning snack a little bit ago, she was sick."

"Sick?"

"She threw up, poor thing."

Fourteen minutes until the meeting. Georgia bites her cheek and nods.

"Oh my. Okay. Let me call my husband. One of us will be there right away."

"Okay, great. I'm so sorry," Miss Sullivan says, sounding sorry indeed.

Georgia hangs up and calls Will. She waits as it rings and rings before going to voicemail. She calls again, but it's the same thing.

Twelve minutes now. She's annoyed, but somehow, this doesn't feel like a calamity. She wonders if this coolness is also Phase Two, and if every crisis in her life was not actually a crisis, just mom brain.

She sends an email to Dana and the others, asking to reschedule. She apologizes twice in the message but doesn't wait for their response before she leaves.

CHAPTER 57

Will returns her call once she and Ruby are already back at the house.

"Sorry," he says, a little breathless. "The kids were testing. I didn't have my phone."

Georgia and Ruby are on the couch together, and Ruby seems to recognize her father's voice through the phone. She gives it a critical look, which is a bit how Georgia also feels.

But she doesn't say this, because she knows it's not fair. She knows how testing works at the high school, how hard it is for the kids to stay focused, how hard it is for Will to stay focused when his only task is to walk around and make sure no one is cheating or asleep.

"Ah. Well, I'm home with Ruby now," she says. "The day care called."

"What? What happened?" He sounds worried.

"Rubes threw up."

"Threw up?"

"Yeah. After morning snack, apparently."

"Oh man." He is so obviously distressed, it actually is hard to be mad at him. "And you had that meeting with the partners this morning. Did you get to do that?"

Georgia closes her eyes. Dana responded to her message when she was gathering Ruby from her classroom, but she didn't read it until she got home.

"No. I had to reschedule."

"Oh no. I'm so sorry, Gi."

"It's okay. Everything's fine now."

And the strange thing is, it does feel fine. Not ideal, but also, somehow, remarkably *okay*. She's not worried, and she's not mad, even if she normally would be. Normally she'd be angry with Will for not answering, angry at the situation for being what it is. Angry with herself for something that was never her fault in the first place.

~

She tells Will about the email from Cecilia later that night, after the girls are in bed.

"It's like I conjured it myself," she says. "Which, okay, I know sounds ridiculous. But it's also a little ridiculous that she would email me *right* when I was thinking about her, you know?"

They're in the kitchen, which Georgia cleaned up after dinner while Will entertained the girls. Ruby didn't eat much, but she also didn't throw up again, and other than being a bit lethargic, she was acting mostly like herself.

"You were thinking about Cecilia?" he says.

"Well, more about Oahu. I was thinking how different it is from here."

He doesn't have anything to say to this, perhaps because he cannot fully grasp just how different the island is from here—from anywhere they've been before, really. And it's not just that it's an island. Every other summer, they go to the Outer Banks in North Carolina for vacation, which is, per Will, a "real island." It's technically a barrier island, with feral cats and non-chain coffee and no lifeguards on duty. And yet, from their rental, they can see the glowing Dollar General sign across the highway, can hear the bang of trash trucks twice a week. Now that Georgia thinks about it, she didn't see a single trash truck the entire time she was in Hawaii.

"So what did she want?" Will says after a moment. He's still wearing his work things, a gray polo shirt that's tight around his biceps. Georgia often teases that it's a good thing he doesn't teach at a co-ed high school or he'd be the target of all the girls' crushes.

"She wants to meet. Tomorrow."

"Tomorrow? In DC?"

"Yeah. Her company is based here. The office is actually right down the street from my office."

"I see. And why does she want to meet?"

"She didn't say. She just said she had a 'proposal.'"

Saying it, it sounds so formal, although Georgia doesn't mind. She was always happy after Will proposed and people said they were *engaged to be married* rather than just engaged. It felt more romantic, like she was a character in a Jane Austen novel.

"Well," he says, but that's all he says, apparently not knowing how to finish the thought. He is rubbing his chin, looking faraway.

"I have a good feeling about it," she says, answering a question he didn't ask. "About the meeting. About all of it, actually. I feel like good things are finally coming our way."

CHAPTER 58

Ruby is the same the next morning—not exactly normal, although not exactly sick either.

"I don't know," Will says, examining her as she examines some oatmeal on her tray. (She usually likes oatmeal, but today she's only pushing it around.) "I guess she looks . . . okay."

Georgia studies her as well and agrees: She looks no better and no worse than exactly *okay*.

"What do you think?" he says, turning to Georgia. "Should we keep her home today?"

He's already dressed for work, and so is she. Her meeting with Cecilia is early, at nine, and this is one she doesn't want to reschedule.

She looks back to Ruby, who meets her gaze with something very adultlike in her eyes. It's not exactly boredom, but something more wizened, like she's jaded by the morning already.

"We can send her in," Georgia says, making a decision. "And we can see how she feels. If she hasn't brightened up by the time I'm done with my meeting with Cecilia, I'll skip the rest of the day."

Will handles the bus and drop-off later that morning so Georgia can leave early for SHE.

She has walked by the office countless times since starting work on K Street, although she has never properly looked at the building before now. It's old, with a limestone facade and lancet windows punctuated by stately hood molds. It looks like a church, actually, and standing outside it, Georgia can imagine the inside filled with the same statues that were all over the Arcadian Bay Resort.

But that's not what she finds when she steps inside the building. The inside is sleek and modern, with stark white curtains that hang pin straight from thin black rods. The only piece of art is a humongous conch shell painting over a painted white fireplace, and the only piece of furniture is a marble desk in the middle of the room with an elegant waterfall edge.

Georgia approaches the desk, where a woman sits. She has a high, tight bun and amazing cheekbones.

"Hi," Georgia says, feeling nervous suddenly. "I'm Georgia Evans. I'm here for, um, a meeting with Cecilia Clements. At nine, I believe."

The woman gives her a pleasant nod and taps at the tablet in front of her, the only thing on the desk. Georgia feels the urge to ask her something, maybe about why she's here or how they get the curtains to hang so straight. Instead, she keeps silent until the woman looks up and says cheerfully, "Perfect. Let me take you back."

CHAPTER 59

Cecilia's office is at the very back of the building, the only room from a long hall of rooms whose walls aren't glass. Georgia peeks into them as they pass, although they all seem to be empty.

Cecilia is waiting for Georgia in her office, standing behind her desk.

"Georgia," she says warmly, opening her arms. "I'm so glad you're here."

The high-cheekboned woman slips out silently behind them and closes the door, leaving Cecilia and Georgia alone in the office. Cecilia is not wearing one of her great capes this morning, but instead a nice if not unremarkable white suit.

"I'm glad to be here too," Georgia says, the truth.

Cecilia motions for her to sit, which she does in the chair across from the desk. The desk, she notices, has legs that are shaped like conch shells, echoing the painting out front.

"Beautiful, isn't it?" Cecilia says, following her gaze. Georgia agrees; it is beautiful.

"It was a custom piece from a friend in Athens," says Cecilia. "A celebration of The Program's opening."

"Athens. That's— Wow."

Looking around, Georgia notices that there are actually seashells all over Cecilia's office: bookends the shape of nautiluses, a chandelier that hangs with many tiny cowries. She thinks of the Shell Room back on the island and again marvels at Cecilia's thoughtful branding.

"Yes," Cecilia says. "She and I have always been drawn to seashells and their powerful symbolism."

Georgia nods. She has gathered by this point that Cecilia takes symbolism very seriously.

"What do seashells symbolize?" she says.

Cecilia is standing behind her desk, so she towers over Georgia seated in the chair.

"A great number of things, as you can imagine. My friend, the one who gifted me this desk, was quite enamored by their connection with divinity—the divine conception, especially."

Georgia doesn't know what to say to this but, "Wow."

"Are you religious, Georgia?" Cecilia says, catching her by surprise. Georgia stumbles for a moment as she tries to come up with the right response.

"Um . . . not really, no. Well, not personally, but my grandmother was extremely Catholic, so I'm religious adjacent, I guess you could say."

This was supposed to be a joke, but it doesn't seem to land. Cecilia responds with only a serious nod.

"Ah yes. And are you and your grandmother close?"

Georgia shakes her head. "She passed a few years ago. But before that . . ."

She stops, not wanting to say something she doesn't mean. She wasn't *not* close with her grandmother, but it doesn't feel quite right to say they were close either. It was more like they were two people trying to communicate while speaking different languages.

"My mom died when I was pretty young," Georgia does her best to explain, "and my dad . . . had a hard time with that. So my grandmother pretty much raised me, but I don't know that I'd call us *close* exactly."

She stops here, although Cecilia does not appear satisfied with this answer. And so Georgia, wanting to satisfy, goes on.

"And I loved her, but she just had a very strict view of the world, like I guess a lot of people do at her age. She just . . . I don't know. She was big on roles and duties, which isn't *bad* necessarily. I guess it's just that we came from very different times, which made it hard to ever get that close."

Cecilia still doesn't say anything. She's wearing an unreadable expression, and Georgia feels a vague urge to keep talking. She has no more to say, though, so she just lets it end at that.

"Yes," Cecilia says finally, sounding thoughtful. "I can certainly relate to that. I was also raised by two extremely . . . shall we say, *role-oriented* individuals."

Georgia tries to arrange her face into something neutral, although this is difficult. To hear anything about Cecilia's personal life feels rare.

"My mother was very devoted to the concept of roles, a woman's role in particular. So devoted, in fact, that she was willing to sacrifice everything to it. And my father, also a solider for roles in the household, decided that his was authoritarian."

As she speaks, her face seems to change, although Georgia is having a hard time understanding exactly what she's seeing. It looks a bit like anger—subtle but raw.

"Usually human nature dictates that one removes oneself from harmful situations, but that was not the case for my mother. No, her role was subservient wife, martyred mother. To her credit, she played the role very well, right up until the end. I would say she was surprised, but I don't think she was, the day he finally killed her."

These final words are so unexpected, so shocking, that Georgia forgets to compose herself.

"I'm so sorry," she says, horrified. "That's— I'm so sorry to hear that."

When Cecilia looks at her, it's with an odd expression, like she just remembered she isn't alone. She regains her composure quickly, whatever emotion she betrayed now wiped clean.

"No need to be sorry," she says briskly. "For me or for them. We all have choices in life, and that includes what to believe."

Georgia nods, feeling shaken. And it's not just the story, the horror of Cecilia's background. It's that she *has* a background at all. Georgia realizes now that she has never imagined Cecilia having a life before The Program, as though she appeared right there on Oahu, fully caped.

"And that's why I've asked you here, Georgia," says Cecilia after a moment, seemingly back to her usual self. Georgia opens her mouth, then closes it, confused. *What* is why she brought her here?

"You said something on the island that I found very compelling," she explains. "Allow me to paraphrase, but you told me you feel trapped by your roles in motherhood."

Georgia thinks back, and yes, she does remember this. In the Shell Room, after Logan's exercise, *trapped* is the exact word she used.

"I understood that, Georgia," she says. "I think all women, if they are honest with themselves, feel this way throughout their lives."

Georgia thinks of Julie, whose son was born only a little bit after Ruby. How once, in the nursing room at their office, Julie looked down at the flanges on her nipples, the tubing connecting them to the machine, and said, so seriously, "Don't they kind of feel like chains?"

"You made great progress with The Program," Cecilia tells her. "And with Phase Two, I think your potential is far greater than we've seen so far. I wonder, though, if you've allowed yourself to strive for more?"

"More?"

Cecilia nods.

"For the women in The Program, we've seen great success with Phase Two, although as you can imagine, we do not want to stop there. Our ultimate goal is to open access to this regimen to everyone, both those who join us on the island and those who cannot. Critical to that goal, however, is messaging. We need a messenger who is able to grasp the scientific foundation of the drug but who can explain that foundation to the general population. This is quite an ask, as you can imagine—someone who has the technical skills and intelligence but who also understands our mission on a fundamental level." She dips her chin here to look at Georgia seriously over her long nose. "Quite an ask," she says, "and quite a responsibility. But for the right person, this role will allow her to do more good than she's likely ever imagined possible."

CHAPTER 60

When Georgia leaves the SHE office after her meeting, she imagines herself in a Jane Austen novel. Or, maybe not a romance novel, but a romance movie, in the final montage. She passes the girl at the front desk, who looks up with a little wave, and Georgia pictures the whole thing with several jump cuts: her stepping into the sunshine, strangers smiling at her on the sidewalk. The whole time, a Sara Bareilles song plays softly, an invisible audience watching on, satisfied.

She didn't accept the position, even though she wanted to. She wanted to tell Cecilia that she would start tomorrow, even though she knows that's not the way things work. In a rom-com, maybe, but in the real world, Georgia will have to at least talk to Will.

As she pulls out her phone, she decides what she'll start with: the salary, which would be more than what he and she currently make combined. And the housing! Included with her offer! A private community for Program employees, totally paid for.

She goes for his number but stops when she realizes he's called her already. Five missed calls, in fact.

She's standing on the sidewalk outside the SHE office now, a strange feeling passing through her. It's not worry exactly. It's more like confusion. Five missed calls—this is not how the montage usually goes.

She dials and brings the phone to her ear. He answers after the first ring.

"Hi," he says, breathy. "Where are you?"

"I just finished my meeting with Cecilia."

"Oh. Right. Well, I'm with Rubes at Capital Kids Urgent Care."

"What? What's going on?"

"I don't know." Overhead, a little bird is whistling, unaware that the montage is now over. "Day care called. I think they tried to call you too. She threw up again, but she's also acting . . . strange."

"Strange? What does that mean?"

"Just . . . I don't know. Kind of listless."

Listless. Such an English teacher's word.

"Okay. Well, should I meet you there?"

"If you want. You don't have to. I'm fine either way."

Georgia looks up at the sky for a moment, as though she might find the answer there. She's surprised, and a little embarrassed, by the disappointment she's feeling. This isn't the way it was supposed to happen. She wishes the bird would stop, at least.

In the end, she decides to meet Will at the urgent care, which is crowded because it's always crowded, because kids are always sick. She finds him on a chair near the window, Ruby curled in a little ball on his lap. As she approaches, she thinks Ruby is sleeping, although as she gets closer, it becomes clear she is not. *Listless*. That's the exact right word for it.

"Hey," she says, her eyes moving to her husband. He doesn't look anxious necessarily, mostly just resigned.

"Hey. They checked us in, but there's a wait."

"How long?"

"They couldn't tell me."

Georgia sits down. Ruby's eyelids are fluttering, like it's taking great effort for her to keep them up.

"What did they say? When you checked her in?"

"Nothing really. Just that there's a wait."

"Did you tell them what's going on?"

"Yeah."

"What did you say?"

"Just what happened. That she's been throwing up, and now she's weirdly tired."

Georgia nods. Hearing it, it does not sound very compelling. She imagines they will not be high on the triage list.

She reaches over to cup Ruby's cheek. With a little sigh, Ruby closes her eyes.

"What'd they say at the day care?" she says. "Was she acting weird there?"

"Not really. They just said after morning snack, she threw up."

"Can I hold her?"

Will nods, shifts, and transfers their daughter like a rag doll. In Georgia's arms, she feels different than usual—lighter, maybe. She *smells* different, like she did the day before.

"Did you get the girls new shampoo?" she says.

"No. Why?"

But they're interrupted by the woman at the front, calling for Mr. Evans. She wants to see his insurance card, she says.

Will stands and reaches for his wallet. Ruby turns her head toward him, but it's a slow, empty movement.

"Are you okay, baby girl?" Georgia says, stroking her daughter's hair. Ruby just closes her eyes.

"Honey," comes a voice from beside them, although it takes Georgia a moment to realize it's directed at her. "Honey," the woman says a second time, "I'd take her to the ER if I were you."

Georgia looks at the woman blankly. A boy is playing a video game on the chair beside her, looking about five or six, and Georgia's first instinct is irritation. What right does this woman think she has, giving this opinion? But then she looks down to Ruby—Ruby, hunched over and possibly a bit pale, now that Georgia really looks. And while this still does not feel like an emergency, Georgia also can't help but wonder if the woman sees something she and Will don't.

CHAPTER 61

In Will's car, heading to the ER, she wonders aloud if they should be more worried. In response, he only glances at her from the driver's seat, looking confused. She's never asked him whether she should be worried before. Usually she just is.

It's because Ruby isn't gasping, she decides as they approach the hospital. She would feel more urgent, more *something,* if Ruby sounded the way Clover did the day Georgia left for The Program. Then, there was something very obviously the matter, whereas now, it's much less clear. She agrees that *something* is up, but it's quite possible it's just a bug or just exhaustion. It's possible that the mother at urgent care has her all worked up for nothing at all.

Will drops them off at the ER doors, then pulls away to find parking. Ruby seems awake, although she offers no assistance with moving her body. The only indication she's aware of her surroundings is the slightest exhale at the sound of Georgia's voice in the ER lobby as she explains to the receptionist why they're there.

The receptionist peers through the plexiglass window, assessing. Looking down, Georgia can see Ruby how the woman might—a beautiful, sleepy child.

"And you said she was vomiting?" the woman asks, kind but businesslike.

"Yes. But also, she's just . . . very tired. *Listless,* really."

The woman nods, and Georgia considers telling her that Ruby also *feels* different. That she smells different, somehow. But even in her head, this sounds ridiculous.

The woman then says something else, but Georgia doesn't hear it, because just as she starts to speak, Ruby's eyes fly open.

For a moment, she looks at her mother, and Georgia feels a sense of relief. *She's okay.*

No sooner does she think this than Ruby closes her eyes and starts to convulse.

CHAPTER 62

Georgia looks down at her daughter's tiny body, dry heaving in her arms, and the only thing she can think is, *This isn't right.*

She looks up to the woman through the plexiglass window. The woman's face is different now. Rounder, more alert.

"We'll get someone down here," she says, picking up her phone. Georgia nods. Yes, they do need someone. This is clear. In her head, she tries to run through a list of all the reasons her daughter might be convulsing but cannot come up with a single one.

Someone appears beside her. A nurse? A doctor? Georgia barely glances at him. Ruby's eyes are open now. She's looking at Georgia with a wide, trapped expression, and Georgia feels like something inside her is fracturing: how things should be happening, and how they are happening right now.

"Ma'am," the man says.

"Sorry," she says, turning to him, helpless. "I don't . . ."

"Let's get you back into a room," he says, and she nods, grateful for a concrete step to be taking. In her arms, Ruby convulses a second time, and all Georgia can do is hold on.

The man guides Georgia from the waiting room, and she's struck by how quiet it is. When it was Clover, she remembers everything being very loud—squeaky wheels and beeping machines and rubber-soled shoes on the floor. Now, it's like a church.

"Let's get an IV," the man says, and Georgia nods dumbly, not realizing that he's talking to the nurse behind Georgia, not her. The woman tells her how to hold Ruby, who's growing agitated now, although her protest is spiritless.

The woman can't get the IV in. Ruby's arms are so tiny, the veins too small.

They'll have to use the scalp, which Georgia doesn't understand. The scalp? What do they mean by that? The nurse lifts Ruby from her arms, and then she gets it. An IV in the scalp.

Ruby finally summons a roar.

Georgia watches the woman place Ruby on a bed, slide the needle beneath the skin of her scalp. It reminds her of a blunt knife gliding through soft butter, and somehow, this is worse than everything else so far.

Ruby's eyes are huge now, terrified. They only close as she dry heaves again, her entire body shuddering. She's so small, so fragile.

How is this happening? What did Georgia miss?

CHAPTER 63

Will keeps running his hands through his hair, over and over and over again. Georgia just watches, not knowing what else to do. What can they do but wait for the doctor? Georgia wishes now she were more religious. She wishes she could honestly pray.

"Mr. and Mrs. Evans?"

The doctor is in the doorway of the room where they're waiting, where Ruby lies between them on the bed.

Will puts both hands on his armrests as though bracing himself.

The doctor is young, younger than they are. As he approaches, they both stand.

"Sit," the doctor says kindly, which neither of them do. The doctor nods once, as though they voiced their protests out loud.

"So Ruby has diabetes," the doctor tells them.

"Diabetes?" Will echoes, like he's never heard the word before.

"Yes. Type 1."

Type 1. Is that the good type or the bad type? Georgia went to school with a girl who had the bad type. She carried around a blood sugar monitor, even to recess.

She almost laughs. A blood sugar monitor. It feels so, so irrelevant.

"You think she has diabetes?" Will says, in a way that makes Georgia no longer feel like laughing.

"We're sure of it. Her blood sugar is extremely high. Over six hundred."

Georgia feels herself nodding as though this means a single thing to her. Six hundred? Out of what? She feels a budding sense of irritation. Why is the doctor talking about numbers? Why is he talking about *diabetes*? What is wrong with Ruby?

"Six hundred?" Will says. "What does that mean?"

The doctor's face is sympathetic. She wonders if that's real emotion or if he learned to fake it in his doctor training.

"To be frank, it's dangerous. In healthy children, levels don't get much higher than a hundred. We're having Life Flight come to transfer her to Children's National. The helicopter will be here shortly."

Helicopter? Georgia thinks.

"Helicopter?" Will says.

The doctor nods.

"It's critical to get her blood sugar under control."

"How? What happens if we don't?" Will is white.

The doctor says something about a coma, and Georgia looks down at her daughter, a buzzing sound filling her ears. She doesn't understand. What did she miss?

"I'm sorry," the doctor is saying now. His voice comes back into focus like she twirled a radio knob, catching the right wavelength. "But the helicopter can only fit one."

The doctor looks at her. Will looks at her. They are waiting for her to say something.

"Do you want to go, Gi?" Will says after a moment.

"It's not very far," says the doctor. "Your husband can meet you there."

They want her to get in the helicopter, she realizes. A helicopter. She looks down at her daughter on the bed between them. Ruby is so little and so gray. Was she this gray the entire time? Surely, *surely*, Georgia would have noticed that, would have noticed the way her baby's rose petal lips look chapped. She looks not entirely human, which is only accentuated by the cords and tubes, and again, all she can think is, *What did I miss?*

CHAPTER 64

The helicopter is louder than she expected. She has never been this close to one before, but she expected it to be like the movies, a happy *thwap thwap thwap*. In reality, the noise is transcendental. The engines and rotors, a breathtaking roar.

Mouths move. Directions are given. Georgia obeys numbly, her eyes locked on Ruby. It's a short flight, just like the doctor promised, and she stares at her daughter the entire time, afraid of what will happen if she looks away.

CHAPTER 65

No one explains which cords are connected to what or why. No one explains the machines, the monitors, the source of the persistent beeping. People work quickly. Ruby is moved. Ruby is handled. Georgia offers to help. No one answers. Maybe she didn't say it out loud. What can she do anyway?

Will arrives at some point. It seems like only a second has passed since she last saw him, and like she's lived an entire lifetime since she left. He asks for an update from nobody, like he is offering the question up to the sky. Is her blood sugar stabilized? Someone says something, but Georgia can't tell if it's an answer. A crash cart is wheeled in, but Georgia doesn't realize it's a crash cart. She will learn that later, like so many other things, once it's all over. Now, Georgia sees the cart's red doors and thinks only, *It's red.*

CHAPTER 66

Her blood sugar is stabilized.

A doctor tells them, and when neither Will nor Georgia reacts, he touches Georgia's hand and says, "You can breathe."

Will starts to cry then. Georgia watches him in a daze and tries to remember the last time she saw him cry. She can't. At their wedding, maybe, but even that wasn't really crying. More like a photogenic glisten.

"Can we see her?" Georgia says numbly.

The doctor says of course.

~

You wouldn't know what happened, looking at Ruby as she sleeps. The color has returned to her face, making her previous paleness that much more obvious, and her expression is serene. She doesn't look like someone who was just in crisis, someone who was so close to being dead.

Finally, it all seems to hit Georgia at once. She makes an involuntary noise, considering what could've happened. Considering how differently things could've turned out. Without saying anything, Will reaches down for Georgia's hand and gives it a squeeze.

A nurse offers them a separate room, a place with beds where they might get some sleep. Will says no thank you, speaking for them both without having to discuss it. There's no world in which either of them will leave Ruby now. Will's mom has Clover, so here in the hospital, they keep their solemn vigil, each on their own side of the pediatric crib.

Eventually, Will leans over and rests his forehead on the crib's slats.

Georgia, though, doesn't feel tired. It's so late, and she should be exhausted, but she's so full of adrenaline, she can't imagine sleeping. She thinks of the woman back at Capital Kids Urgent Care and wonders how long she had to wait to be seen. The boy next to her, presumably her son, didn't look that unwell, but at the same time, neither did Ruby.

"How did we miss this?" she says quietly, knowing that Will is possibly sleeping. But he isn't. He raises his head, his hair shooting out at many funny angles.

"The diabetes," she says, her gaze falling to Ruby. "How did we miss something this big?"

The smell was the diabetes, as she learned later. It can make a person's breath smell fruity, apparently. "I thought it was a new shampoo," she told the doctor afterward, to which he just nodded sympathetically.

"She didn't seem that sick," Will says, but it's like he's trying to convince himself as much as her. She thinks again of the woman at the urgent care, of that little boy beside her. The truth is, Ruby didn't seem that sick to them, but she seemed that sick to someone. She seemed that sick to some random mother who'd never met her before.

"Cecilia offered me a job," Georgia says, her eyes on Ruby through the slatted crib walls. Her chest rises and falls, rises and falls. "This morning, at the meeting. She offered me a job with The Program."

She looks up to find Will nodding slowly, like he's unsure of something, although she doesn't know if it's about what she just told him or the fact that she's telling him right now at all.

"It sounds like a great job. A really, really amazing opportunity. But I just . . ."

She stops for a moment, but the room isn't noiseless. All around them, machines keep time with their beeps. She doesn't want to say it. Even speaking the words feels like something irreversible, a bubble being popped.

"What if it was the Phase Two?" she whispers finally, hardly able to get the words out.

She finds his eyes. He's looking at her hard, like he's considering this question or perhaps considering her.

"I don't know," he says after a moment, sounding thoughtful. "Maybe. But I mean, even if you weren't taking Phase Two, were you really going to suspect *diabetes?*"

It's a serious question, like he really expects an answer, and so she asks herself: Would she? Maybe. But maybe that is giving herself too much credit. She might've suspected *something,* but diabetes still seems so far outside the realm of possibilities, even now, knowing what it is.

"And, I mean, I'm not taking Phase Two," he adds, his voice growing stronger, "and I still didn't see it. It'd be different if I saw something you didn't, but I missed it just like you."

She's aware that his confidence here might be only for her benefit, although it's possible he actually believes the words himself. And to her great relief, she realizes he's not alone. What he's saying makes sense, objectively speaking, and looking at him across their daughter's bed, she believes it too.

CHAPTER 67

This is what diabetes looks like:

Before each meal, a blood sugar check. Then comes the insulin—a pinch of silken skin, a quick jab, sometimes a slight wriggle or disgruntled squeal. Meal, not too long after. Check again, then repeat. And repeat. And repeat.

There are two different types of insulin. When the doctor first said this, it was in a way like Georgia might already know. (She didn't.) "Here's your fast-acting," said the doctor, "and the Lantus is your basal." Georgia wrote this down on the notepad she keeps with her now.

Clover doesn't understand. She thinks the Pop-Tarts have become poison. Georgia reminds her over and over that they're not. That Ruby is not hurt or even sick. She doesn't want Ruby to grow up thinking of herself as defective. "She just needs to eat differently from us," Georgia says, which Clover finds an unsatisfactory explanation.

It's all so much, Georgia and Will have barely discussed Georgia's job offer. They've talked about hardly anything other than schedules and carbohydrates, blood glucose and insurance. Georgia called Cecilia to let her know what happened, to ask for a little more time to make a decision.

"Take all the time you need," Cecilia said without hesitation.

Georgia thanked her, then gave Ruby another insulin shot.

On the third day home from the hospital, Georgia tells Will it's time to make a decision. They're in their room, and at this announcement, he lowers himself to the edge of the bed, preparing himself. He doesn't ask what she means by this, what decision—in a long stream of nearly constant decisions they've been forced to make lately—she is talking about.

"What do you think?" she says. "Give me your initial thoughts."

"I'm pretty far past my initial thoughts at this point."

"Okay, well, what *were* your initial thoughts?"

He goes silent for a moment.

"I don't even remember, to be honest. It was too many thoughts to process. A thought overload. I gave up and threw them all out."

Georgia nods, smiling at the inside joke. It's from the very early days after having Clover, when she was sterilizing some bottle parts. She was boiling water and something happened, causing her to drop a nipple onto the burner—melting the nipple, setting off the fire alarm, waking up Clover, probably creating cancer-causing fumes, or so Georgia cried later. She was so disgusted and so overwhelmed, she didn't bother fixing the situation; she just threw the whole pot out. (They can laugh about it now, but besides being unhelpful, this fit of irrational anger was also very expensive.)

"Well, I remember my initial thoughts," she says, and Will raises his eyebrows, looking intrigued but also tired. He has been meticulous about everything since coming home from the hospital, even more so than Georgia. He, for example, has started counting his own carbohydrates, "just for practice."

"I want to take the job," she says, surprising him. Surprising herself, in a way. "I mean, the salary for one thing. It's a lot of money. And the location—Hawaii is Hawaii. And just the idea of being someplace new, you know? Don't you think we could use a fresh start?"

Will agrees they could use a fresh start.

"And what Cecilia's doing," she says. "What *they're* doing at The Program. I think it's important. I really believe in it."

She says this with gusto, and when she's finished, she marvels at how easy it was to just *say* what she really feels. It was so easy, in fact, she wonders why she hasn't tried it before.

"*Do* you believe in this?" he says, in a way she can't quite interpret.

"I do. Why?"

But he doesn't say why. He doesn't say anything. It reminds her of her dad, in that confusing time just after her mom died but before she went to live with Babcia. How he would just look at her sometimes with an expression not so different from the one Will is giving her now. It was a look that seemed to say, *How did I get here?* Or maybe, *How did* you *get here?* She remembers the look because it was then that she realized her father actually did not have an answer—not for what happened or for what they would do next.

"I mean, I know I had some doubts in the hospital," she says, "but it's like you told me: Would I have ever thought of diabetes? I don't think I would've. A mother's intuition is one thing, but I would've needed like, a medical degree to identify that."

He nods slowly, absorbing this like he's not the one who first said it.

"All right," he says. "You're right. It's just . . ." But the sentence floats off.

When he speaks again, his voice is firmer.

"Clover's going to be pissed about changing schools, you know."

And this is true. Clover loves her kindergarten, her class, the school bus driver who brings the kids tiny chocolate reindeer for Christmas, jelly beans for Easter. Georgia hadn't thought about that.

"But she'll be in Hawaii," she points out.

"She will be in Hawaii," Will agrees.

But then another thought occurs to her.

"But you'll have to leave your school too," she says. Somehow, she hadn't thought about this either, at least not very deeply. It crossed her mind, but it was in the same systematic way she has considered all the other logistics, like what they'll do with their furniture.

"I will," he says, in a voice like this is not his first time considering it. And of course it's not. For Will, his job is not just his job. It's not even his profession. He's the type of teacher kids bring up well into adulthood, saying things like, "He taught me more than literature," or "He saved my life." (One boy said this once literally, in a letter he wrote Will years after graduation. Georgia found the letter later, pressed neatly between the pages of a book on his desk.)

She meets his eyes, not knowing what she'll find there. Resentment? Resistance? She doesn't know what she'll do with either of these responses, although in the end, what she might've done doesn't matter. Because in the end, he just smiles faintly.

"But I'll be in Hawaii," he says.

CHAPTER 68

Georgia gives her official notice to work the next morning. She frames it apologetically, like she knows the news will be surprising and upsetting, although none of the partners seem particularly surprised or upset. The last one she tells is Dana, who—like the rest of them—doesn't ask many questions. She says only, "This is unexpected," but it's without emotion, the way someone might comment on the unexpectedness of a light rain.

She then talks to HR, where a stern woman tells her they'll need to schedule an exit interview as her younger, nervous-looking colleague writes down notes. The last office she goes to is Julie's, although Julie doesn't answer when she knocks, and when Georgia peeks her head inside, the office is empty and dark.

On the way back to her own office, she has to pass the firm's room for nursing mothers. Without planning to, she stops in front of the door, which is shut. It was a big fight for the mothers of the firm to get this room; since there are so few women attorneys, the firm didn't see it as a worthwhile investment. (It apparently didn't occur to them that the other female staff might also need it, as though their babies didn't nurse, or maybe just didn't exist.) The thing that finally swayed them was the realization that if they didn't set aside the room, they'd have to put locks on all the doors so women could pump in privacy, so in the end they decided it was easier just to give them the room.

Georgia looks at the room now and wonders, if she could tally it up, how many hours she has spent in it over the years. The room is a small, somewhat sad space with bad lighting and no windows. (Before it was the nursing room, it was the room where they kept the extra printer paper.) Inside, there are two chairs separated by a small table, which they have to move to make room for their knees when more than one person is pumping at a time.

But you wouldn't know any of this from the outside. From the outside, it's just a door like all the other doors with a placard that says MOTHERS ROOM. There wasn't enough space on the placard to include NURSING, or even the apostrophe at the end of MOTHERS (although Julie speculates that the missing apostrophe was on purpose). ("It's not our room," she likes to say. "It's the room where they store the mothers.")

Georgia should probably feel something about this room, with all the grief it's caused her, but looking at it now, she realizes she doesn't. She walks away without even taking a last look inside.

"Oh, excellent," Cecilia says when Georgia calls her later. "I'm so pleased to hear this, Georgia."

Georgia has just told her that her firm was happy with only two weeks' notice, although *happy* might be a kind way of wording it. *Relieved* probably would be more accurate.

"We're so thrilled to have you on board," Cecilia says, in a way that makes Georgia even more sure of her decision. *This* is the way an employee should be treated, she thinks. She deserves an employer who would not exclude the apostrophe.

When Cecilia asks about Ruby, Georgia is happy to report that Ruby is doing well, all things considered.

"It's a bit of a learning curve, but we're managing."

"Naturally," Cecilia says.

They end the call by going over next steps, which include a weeklong orientation on the island in a couple of weeks.

"We'll go over everything and get you settled in the Village," Cecilia says.

The Village is the private housing just outside the resort, reserved for employees at The Program. Cecilia has emailed her a picture of the houses, which are more like mansions.

"And I'll make a public announcement, if that's okay with you," Cecilia adds. "To celebrate the new addition to our family."

Georgia says, "I would love that."

The announcement goes live on The Program's website the following day, and from there it travels quickly through all the usual places. Georgia tries to stay away from these places, but she can't help but take a small peek at Reddit. She's disappointed by how they identify her there: *Georgia Evans, of the infamous piece in the* Pacific. It feels unfair to use this as her singular most defining characteristic, although she supposes to them that's all she is.

It's that afternoon that Georgia gets a call from Julie. Georgia is in her office, and she did stop by Julie's again earlier, although it was still dark.

"Heath is sick," Julie explains when Georgia asks her about this. "I've been working remotely"

"Ah. Poor guy."

"Is it true? You're leaving?"

Through the open door of Georgia's office, she can see the busy heads of the staff workers, typing diligently away at their cubicles. She swivels her chair around so she's facing the window.

"I am."

Julie makes a sound, but Georgia isn't sure what it means.

"I'm sorry I didn't tell you," she adds. "It's been . . . busy."

"Yeah, I bet."

Julie seems to struggle for a moment, like she wants to say something else.

"What is it?" Georgia says, looking down at the street below her. Same food trucks, same busy sidewalks.

"It's . . ." She sighs. "I don't know. I just . . . ugh. This whole article ruined everything, didn't it?"

She sounds so defeated, and Georgia pictures her at home alone with the sick baby. Julie's plan was to marry Heath's father, whom she'd been dating for years when she got pregnant. The boyfriend, though, decided it was all too much. Now he lives in Miami.

The funny thing is, it was only a few weeks ago that Julie might've said this and Georgia would've agreed. It certainly felt that way, like everything was ruined. Now, though, she barely recognizes that woman or what that felt like.

"It didn't ruin anything," she says to Julie now, and hearing the words, she knows she believes them. "I know it sounds crazy, but I think it needed to happen. I think I ended up exactly where I'm supposed to be."

PART THREE

CHAPTER 69

The night before Georgia is supposed to leave for her orientation, she gets an email from Logan, although she doesn't realize it's from Logan at first. The email comes from Logan Kensington-McCoy, and for some reason, Georgia can't see the Logan from The Program as a Logan Kensington-McCoy (although she supposes she doesn't know what a Logan Kensington-McCoy should look like).

Georgia gave Logan her email address their last day on the island, not having the heart to tell her that she didn't really plan on keeping in touch. Georgia is historically awful at keeping in touch with people, even those she's known for more than a week.

Logan's message is long. She starts with a meandering story about Jo, then goes on to ask about Will and the girls, then whether Georgia is still taking "Cecilia's medicine." (Logan stopped because it was giving her gas.) Georgia starts to skim the rest of the message until she gets near the bottom, when something piques her interest.

> I saw you're going to work for The Program! That makes me feel better. After talking to Simone, I started getting a bad feeling about the place.

Georgia doesn't know what to make of this. Her first thought is to wonder how Logan got in touch with Simone, although this question is quickly crowded out by the next: What does she mean by *a bad feeling about the place?*

Downstairs, she can hear Will and the girls. Will is making dinner, spaghetti tonight, which Clover almost always likes, except when she doesn't. Georgia's suitcase is still only half packed on the floor beside her, some of what she wants to bring still downstairs in the dryer. She really doesn't have time for this.

And yet.

Hi, Logan! It's so nice to hear from you. It sounds like you're doing well! Yes, I'm excited about the position. You said you talked to Simone? How is she?

She adds a few more sentences about Will and the girls, how yes, she is still taking Phase Two, but her stomach is fine. She considers asking whether Logan has talked to anyone else from their pod—Dede, for example—but she decides to keep it brief.

She sends the email and is surprised, but also not surprised, when Logan's response is instantaneous.

Hi! Would it be okay if I give you a call?

Georgia can't help but smile to herself. Logan is so forward, which Georgia usually finds off-putting. Usually she would find it odd and overbearing, someone wanting to call her, someone showing up unannounced at her room with pie and a key fob cloner. And yet, none of this really bothers her about Logan. She suspects she can go the rest of her life and never find someone quite like her again.

She responds with her phone number, and as expected, a few moments later, her phone starts to ring.

"Hi, Georgia," she says when Georgia answers. "It's me."

It's me. Georgia shakes her head.

"Hey, Logan. How are you?"

"I'm good. Really good. How are you? How are Clover and Ruby?"

Georgia lowers herself onto the corner of her bed.

"They're good. Ah, well—good enough. We had a bit of a scare with Ruby recently, but we're all good now."

"A scare? Is she okay?"

"Yes, yes. She's fine. I mean—well, yes, she's fine, but it turns out she has diabetes."

"Oh, wow. Diabetes? That's unexpected."

Georgia thinks of Dana, when she gave her notice. That's what she said too: *unexpected*. This is interesting, mostly because this is not a word that's generally used in relation to Georgia. Georgia is famously very expected, which was the way she liked it, before now. She thinks, randomly, of Cecilia in the Shell Room: *I wonder if your fear of water is actually your fear of the unknown.*

"Yes," she says. "It was unexpected. It is still, I guess. But we're getting used to it. What else can you do, you know?"

"That's right. What else can you do?" There's a pause before she adds, "But I know you can do it. Handle it, I mean. You're so strong like that."

It's such a kind thing to say, and Georgia can't help but feel flattered, although the honest part of her also understands that the compliment is mostly meaningless. The truth is, Logan doesn't know Georgia well enough to know *what* kind of person she is.

"Thanks, Logan. That's— Well, thanks. I'm sure we'll adapt."

"You will. And you'll adapt to Hawaii too!"

"Ah yes. Well, Hawaii will hopefully be a little more pleasant than diabetes."

This is a joke, but Logan doesn't laugh. Georgia considers explaining the sarcasm, but she decides to let it go.

She says instead, "Speaking of Hawaii, you said you talked to Simone? Since we left?"

"Oh yes. I found her online after I got home. You know, on her university's website. We talked on her work phone for a little bit; then she gave me her real number."

There's a beat, then another.

"And how is she?" Georgia says at last.

"Good. Her wife is a cop, and she just got off the night shift. Honestly, I don't know how she did it—the night shift, I mean. I wonder if you eat dinner food in the morning then, since that's technically your dinner. I wouldn't. I feel like that would be gross, but I don't know. Maybe it isn't?"

Georgia tries to remember what exactly Logan said in the email. Something about Simone worrying her about The Program. Did she say more than that?

"Anyway, they're on a normal schedule now," Logan continues, "and they seem like they're doing good."

"That's good. I'm glad to hear that." Another pause before Georgia says, "So you said something in your email about something Simone told you? She was concerned about The Program, I think?"

For a moment, Georgia holds her breath. When Logan answers, though, she sounds breezy.

"Oh yes. So apparently that story about Simone choosing to leave was totally bogus. Simone says she didn't choose. She says Cecilia kicked her out!"

"Kicked her out? Why?"

"You'll have to have her tell the story. Basically Cecilia said she was snooping in her office and got super ticked off."

"Simone was snooping in Cecilia's office?"

"That's what Cecilia said, but I don't know. Izzy let Simone into the office, so I think it's a little unfair to say she was *snooping*, you know what I mean?"

Georgia doesn't really know what she means.

"Right. But I mean, Simone was looking around her office though?"

"I don't know. Simone said . . ."

Logan trails off. Georgia bounces her foot.

"What did she say?"

"I don't know. You should talk to her. I don't want to talk bad about your employer."

"What do you mean?"

"Talk to her. I can give you her number."

Georgia rolls her neck. She actually does not want to call Simone right now.

"Okay. Well, yeah, if you could forward me her info, maybe I'll give her a call."

She has barely finished the sentence before her inbox dings.

"Done! She's really great, actually. I don't know if you guys talked much on the island, but she's totally cool."

"Ah. Yes, I believe that."

"I told her we should all get together sometime. Like, a big reunion. Wouldn't that be fun? Except I think Dede is on the West Coast, so I don't know if she would come."

"No," Georgia agrees, "probably not."

CHAPTER 70

Georgia tries to tell Will about her call with Logan over dinner, although tonight is a night that Clover doesn't like spaghetti—*hates* spaghetti, in fact—so this is difficult.

"Clove, we just had spaghetti last week," Will tries to reason. "Remember how much you loved it then?"

But Clover does not remember how much she loved it then.

"It tastes funny," she says.

"I had some. It doesn't."

"It's red."

"It's always red."

"I'm not hungry," she says with finality, pushing the plate away.

Ruby, in solidarity, throws a fistful of mashed noodles off her tray. They've switched to whole wheat pasta since the diagnosis, and while Georgia will not say this, privately she agrees that the whole wheat pasta is not as good as the regular kind.

"That's fine," Will says, summoning an admirable level of patience. "You don't have to eat it, but I don't want to hear that you're hungry later."

"Fine," Clover mutters, crossing her arms.

Ruby slams her fist into her tray and shouts, "Bah!"

Will and Georgia's eyes meet over their plates, and she can see what he's thinking because she's thinking it too: *How lucky are we?*

Georgia calls Simone as Will is giving the girls a bath, although she doesn't expect Simone to answer. Georgia wouldn't, if it were her. A part of her isn't even sure she *wants* Simone to answer. The truth is, she still finds Simone intimidating.

But she does answer, on the third ring.

"Georgia?" she says when Georgia identifies herself, which is somewhat embarrassing. It hasn't been *that* long since they were on the island, after all.

"From The Program?" Georgia prompts.

"Oh, right."

"Yes. Good." She feels off-balance now. She tries to remember her script. "I'm calling because . . . well, Logan gave me your number. Logan, from The Program. She gave me your number because we were talking about something, and she said I should ask you about it. Something about The Program."

Simone still doesn't say anything. Georgia wonders if she's regretting answering the call.

"And, I don't know if you saw it," Georgia says hesitantly, "but Cecilia offered me a job with The Program."

"I didn't see that," Simone says.

Georgia presses her lips together, doing her best not to be annoyed.

"Right. Well, yeah, I'm actually heading back to the island tomorrow, but when I talked to Logan today . . . I don't know. I guess I was just . . . curious, I suppose, to hear from you about what happened."

She makes herself stop here. Simone is also quiet. Georgia can hear Will and the girls in the bathroom. It's such a beautiful, ordinary sound.

"What do you want to know?" Simone says at last. Her voice

isn't kind, although it's not so unkind that Georgia is afraid to continue.

"Well, I guess I'd like to know why you decided to leave."

"*Decide* is not the word I'd use."

"What word would you use?"

"Cecilia told me to go. It wasn't a suggestion."

This, of course, is not a surprise to Georgia, and yet, she feels a little tickle of something hearing it out loud from Simone herself.

"Why, though?"

"Why did she tell me to go?"

"Yeah."

"I mean, do you want the reason she gave me or the real reason?"

"They're not the same?"

This wasn't a rhetorical question, although Simone treats it like one. Georgia wonders how this conversation went between her and Logan, whether Simone was any more forthcoming. Probably. Logan seems to say the unexpected, which makes Georgia uncomfortable but has proven to be a good way to get people to talk.

With a deep breath, Georgia says, "I heard the reason she asked you to go is because you were snooping around her office."

Her voice cracks a little at the end, betraying her. She has very little practice saying the unexpected. She usually goes out of her way not to, in fact.

And then, suddenly, the thought occurs to her that this approach might backfire. Logan saying the unexpected is one thing—Logan, so clearly innocent and good. It might sound much different coming from Georgia.

When Simone answers, though, she doesn't sound offended.

"That's what Cecilia said, yes."

"But you weren't? Snooping, I mean?"

"No, I was."

Georgia opens her mouth, then closes it. She wishes she could see Simone in this moment. What does she mean by this? Is she joking?

"You were what?"

"Snooping. Looking around. Whatever you want to call it. Izzy let me into Cecilia's office, and I took that opportunity."

Georgia thinks of Cecilia's office, how pristine the all-white everything looks in the sunlight. When Georgia was there, she felt self-conscious about just breathing in it, as though that was taking too much.

"Ah," she says, unsure what else to say. She feels both taken aback and, in a strange way, relieved. This situation feels very uncomplicated: Cecilia caught her doing something she shouldn't, and her reaction, while harsh, wasn't unreasonable.

"But what I think really pissed her off," says Simone, "is that I asked her about it."

"Asked about what?" Georgia realizes her mind is floating off already, which is wrong of her. She should not be treating this conversation like an item on a checklist.

"The list."

"What list?" She panics. Did she say that out loud? She forces herself to focus.

"The one on her desk. I'm assuming Logan told you about it."

Georgia thinks back to everything Logan told her on the phone and in her email. In her message, she talked about Jo and about her new apartment. About the golden pothos in her window in a new, interesting kind of pot that apparently allows the plant to water itself. She didn't say anything about a list. Georgia would've remembered.

"I'm not sure if she said anything about a list. A list of what exactly?"

"Who knows? Believe it or not, Cecilia didn't tell me."

"But what was on the list? I'm confused."

"It was on her desk. Cecilia made a big show of how I was apparently digging around for it, which is bullshit, but I guess that's how she rolls. I think she was embarrassed she left it out."

"But what was it? What was on the list?"

"It was a list of names."

"Whose names?"

"I have no idea. Like I said, she wasn't very chatty."

"What else was on the list?"

"Nothing. It was literally just a list of names, and that's it."

"Was there anyone on it you knew?"

"A few."

"Who?"

A beat.

"Dede, for one."

CHAPTER 71

It does sound weird," Will says once they're lying in bed later that night. She just briefed him about everything, as it's the first chance they've had to really talk about anything all night. "But I mean, a list of names could really be anything."

"Literally anything," Georgia agrees.

It's late, later than they normally go to bed, because in the end, Clover did get hungry after not eating dinner, although she was hungry in a way that could only be satiated by Goldfish. It was a battle Will and Georgia were destined to lose, although they put up a good fight.

Will says now, "It could be a list of people who still owe money."

"Or a list of people who overpaid."

"It could be a list of people who have medical conditions."

"A list of people with allergies."

"Nut allergies are rampant," Will says, and Georgia giggles.

"A real epidemic," she says, causing them both to laugh.

Then they both go quiet, because no, Dede is not allergic to nuts. Georgia knows this because she knows Dede had a tuna roll with chopped pecans at Opening Dinner. She remembers because Alice pointed out that fish were animals, and wasn't Dede a vegetarian? ("Not *that* kind of vegetarian," Dede told her, to which Alice did not have a response.)

"Should I be worried about it?" Georgia says after a moment, serious now. "Is this a red flag?"

She can hear Will breathing as he considers this, although it's dark enough that she can't see his face.

"I don't think so," he says at last. "I mean, a list really *could* be anything, so that doesn't tell us much. And yeah, it sucks that Cecilia kicked her out of The Program, but it sounds like she probably deserved it. So, I don't know—interesting, I guess, but not necessarily a red flag to me."

Georgia closes her eyes as Will speaks, like he's singing to her. And it is so soothing, hearing him list out facts as objective as these.

~

But later that night, she can't sleep.

She agrees with what Will told her. She believes it. And yet, it feels like there's something lurking just beyond what she thinks and believes. It's an infuriating feeling, like having a word caught at the tip of your tongue.

In the darkness, she pulls her phone from the bedside table and turns the brightness all the way down. She doesn't know what she is expecting to find when she searches for Dede. Maybe nothing. Maybe this feeling is just a lingering paranoia from missing Ruby's diabetes.

What she finds is unremarkable. The first link is to *The Bar*, a barre studio "owned and operated by Dede Chomondeley." The home page is chic with lots of black-and-white photos of attractive, fit women smiling in tight clothes. Dede is personally pictured in three separate places, all of the photos similar but with slightly different poses. On the contact page, she's looking off to her side with a satisfied expression. She seems to be gazing lovingly at the contact form next to the photo, below which is an email address.

CHAPTER 72

From: GeorgiaEvans90@gmail.com
To: Hello@LAthebar.com
Subject: Hello

Hello! I was actually hoping I could get in touch with Dede Chomondeley. My name is Georgia Evans. I was with Dede in Hawaii for The Program. If she could send me an email, I would really appreciate it.

Thank you,
Georgia

PS: Your website is very chic!

CHAPTER 73

Georgia wakes up at three o'clock in the morning to check her phone, but of course Dede hasn't responded yet.

CHAPTER 74

When Georgia leaves for the airport the next morning, Dede still hasn't answered her email, although this is not exactly shocking. It's nine in DC, which is only six in LA, and Dede does not strike her as the sort of person who is checking her email at six in the morning.

"Are you sure this is okay?" Georgia says, standing in the doorway, where Will is holding Ruby. Clover is there too, intrigued by the idea that Georgia will soon be seeing an airplane.

"Of course it's okay," Will says. "Don't worry about us."

"But what if something goes wrong?"

"Nonsense. When has anything ever gone wrong before?"

Georgia rolls her eyes, then leans over to kiss Ruby on the head. "I'll be back in a week," she says to her daughter, who frowns, having no concept of time. Clover then asks if Georgia can bring back some dried pineapple like she did the first trip, and she promises she will.

"What would you think about having our own pineapple tree?" Georgia says cheerfully, but Clover doesn't get it. She was born and raised in DC, where fruit comes wrapped in plastic, and it strikes Georgia as she's leaving that even she doesn't know if pineapples grow on trees.

~

She arrives at the airport early enough to stand in the long line at Starbucks, where she waits behind a woman with a small child who looks to be between Clover and Ruby in age. The girl is whining for a cake pop, which the woman, looking at her phone, either doesn't or has chosen not to hear.

Inspired, Georgia gets a cake pop when it's her turn to order, along with her usual latte. She eats it happily on the way to the gate.

Finally, settled in her seat, she checks her phone and is excited to see a response to her email. The response, though, is not from Dede but from whoever is checking The Bar's inbox.

> Hello, Georgia! Thank you for reaching out to The Bar. Unfortunately our business account is not managed by Dede personally, but I will pass along your message. Peace and light!

Georgia does her very best not to find this response annoying. After all, this woman cannot be blamed for not being Dede. (She possibly can be blamed for signing her email "peace and light," but that's irrelevant.)

She considers responding to the email to let them know that actually, so sorry, but this is a bit critical, and could they please forward Dede's personal email address as soon as possible? But that then raises the question of whether this is indeed critical, and no, it is not. Georgia is curious, but to suggest it's any type of emergency situation would be a lie.

This is what she's thinking about when the woman first appears. It's not obvious at first that she's intentionally in front of Georgia, as the airport is busy, and Georgia assumes she is one of those impatient people who want to board the plane first. But then she says something, and it seems to be directed at Georgia.

"Sorry," says Georgia. "What was that?"

"You're Georgia Evans," the woman repeats, and it's not a question. Georgia frowns, feeling uneasy. This is someone she knows, obviously, but who? There was a mortifying incident a few months back where she ran into someone from her high school—which wasn't all that big of a high school—and Georgia could not for the life of her remember the woman's name.

"I'm sorry," she says, "have we met?"

"I read your article in the *Pacific*. I've been following the whole thing."

"Oh." Georgia's voice goes flat. She has the passing thought to correct her—it wasn't *her* article—although she suspects this correction would be counterproductive, given the look on the woman's face.

The woman takes a small step forward. She's wearing a pair of ankle-high Ugg boots, which Georgia notices for God knows what reason. The woman is young and cute with shiny auburn hair.

"I felt bad for you," says the woman, her voice low so only Georgia can hear it. "When it first happened. I have a six-month-old. I could understand going a little insane."

The woman doesn't look like she has a six-month-old, although she does look a little insane.

"I assumed you were sorry too," the woman continues. "I thought, *She probably feels so bad*. But then I read you got a promotion. A *promotion*, after what you did."

There's a teenaged boy sitting next to Georgia, although he doesn't seem to be aware of what's happening. He's wearing a pair of large headphones and bopping his head to an inaudible beat. Georgia opens her mouth, then closes it again. A promotion? She didn't get a promotion. She got a new job. If this woman is going to confront her like this, the least she could do is get her facts right.

"Do you feel bad?" the woman says, taking another step closer.

She's too close now. Georgia can smell something on her—perfume or lotion. "Are you sorry?"

The smell is overwhelming. It's floral, but not a good kind. It reminds her of her grandmother, or a church. This woman is much too young to smell like a grandmother or a church.

"Would you mind giving me some space?" Georgia says, leaning back a little. "Your perfume is a lot."

The next thing happens so quickly, Georgia doesn't even see it. It's like the woman is standing there one second, glaring at her, and then, seemingly without moving, her drink is all over Georgia's lap.

Georgia gasps. The boy beside her notices finally. He leans away from her and says, "Dude."

The drink is hot. Scalding. It burns through the thin fabric of her pants.

No, it's not.

It's very cold. Ice cubes puddle in the space between her legs. She looks up at the woman blankly. The woman stares back. She's holding—Georgia can see now—a cup from McDonald's.

The woman just dumped a *drink* on her *lap*.

"What the hell?" Georgia breathes, standing abruptly, causing the ice cubes to scatter.

The woman hisses, "You're worse for women than any man will ever be."

CHAPTER 75

Georgia has never been in a fight before, at least not physically. She's never actually *seen* a fight besides the fake ones on TV, which she had assumed were dramatized, until Will once told her about a fight he got into in middle school. "Did the other kids circle around you and chant?" Georgia said, kidding, but Will just shrugged, looking pleased with himself.

Georgia has never been in a fight, but in this moment, she could be. She feels like she could punch someone or kick someone or pull this woman's nice, shiny hair. Later, a part of her will wonder what would've happened if she *had* started a fight. In terms of size, Georgia would have the clear advantage, but the woman would benefit from the fact that she's crazy enough to dump a drink on a stranger's lap.

In the end, they'll never know who would win the fight, because airport security shows up.

In an act of heroism, or perhaps an act of boredom, the boy next to them explains what happened. Georgia and the woman can do nothing but stand there, chastised. The security guard nods, as though this is exactly as he suspected. Georgia wonders how many airport fights he has actually witnessed before.

His partner joins them at some point. He's the one who asks Georgia if she wants to press charges, but Georgia doesn't. What she wants is to be finished with this situation. She's boarding soon, and her clothes are soaking, and she doesn't have a spare pair in her carry-on, because why would she? She's long past that era of her life, traveling with newborns, when the risk of diaper blowouts was ever-present.

When she says all this, the guard nods, looking slightly overwhelmed. Behind him, the woman glares at Georgia unapologetically. Other than the glare, though, the woman looks very ordinary. She does not look like the sort of person to throw a drink at you, although maybe she is. Maybe she's a serial drink thrower. How can you know?

"I really can't miss this flight," Georgia says, ignoring the woman, speaking directly to the security guards. "So if you'll excuse me, I need to get new pants."

With her chin held high, she wheels her carry-on past the guards, past the woman, to the gift shop, where she pays $56.99 for a pair of sweatpants that say WASHINGTON DULLES INTERNATIONAL AIRPORT on the butt.

Her plan is to change out of the sweatpants at the resort before meeting with Cecilia, but this turns out to be a grave miscalculation, as Leila is waiting for her when she arrives.

"We'll get your bag to your house," she says both to Georgia and the driver, who presumably will be in charge of that.

"Oh," Georgia says helplessly as the driver hops back into his car, her suitcase full of clothes in the back. "Well . . ." She doesn't even get a full sentence out before he's off.

It is through this series of unfortunate events that Georgia finds herself in Cecilia's office a few minutes later with WASHINGTON DULLES INTERNATIONAL AIRPORT in bright blue across her butt.

Cecilia gracefully ignores this.

"Georgia," she says, holding her arms up. She's wearing another cape today, this one a deep red that gives the illusion of flames when she moves.

"Your flight was satisfactory, I hope?"

Georgia thinks of the woman at the airport. *You're worse for women than any man will ever be.* With some time to cool off, she no longer knows how she feels about the situation. Her anger has melted into something more subdued, although she's not sure exactly what.

"Yes. Well, mostly. At the airport, I had a bit of an . . . incident."

Cecilia raises her eyebrows, and Georgia wonders if the unidentifiable feeling inside her is shame.

She tells her about the woman, about how angry she was for no reason, and then about the sweatpants. Cecilia absorbs it all with wide-eyed attention. She doesn't say a word until Georgia is finished.

"I'm so sorry that happened," she says, giving her head a small, sympathetic shake. "What a shame it is when people don't understand your heart."

Georgia nods, not knowing how else to respond. Without meaning to, she glances past Cecilia to the desk, where a small stack of folders sits. She thinks of Simone, the list. Did Simone misunderstand Cecilia's heart?

When Georgia looks back to Cecilia, Cecilia is looking at her strangely, and she has the unpleasant sensation that she's been caught. Her cheeks redden, and Cecilia cocks her head, curious.

"I'm sure you're anxious to get cleaned off," she says, "but are there any questions I can answer before we get you settled?"

"I . . ." She debates whether to say it. "Well, actually, there is something I was curious about."

Cecilia gives her a small nod, approval to continue. Georgia does before she can overthink it.

"And I hope this isn't out of line, but I talked to Simone recently—Simone St. Clair. She was in Pod Three with me?"

The smile is gone from Cecilia's face now, although she doesn't look agitated. She looks at Georgia with polite attention, the same way Georgia looks at her doctor when he's talking about the multivitamins they both know she's not going to take.

"Well, she told me . . ."

She hesitates for another moment, unsure how to say this without accidentally implying something else.

"She was telling me about why she left The Program," she lands on finally. "And I mean, I know she was probably embellishing the story the way people do. But she did seem concerned, I think, about Dede. From our pod? She also left early?"

She doesn't know why she says the last parts as questions. She prays for Cecilia to show her mercy, to answer the question she really wants addressed without Georgia having to ask it. Cecilia, though, gives her only a pious blink.

Georgia says, "Anyway, she—Simone—seems to think there's some list somewhere. Something to do with Dede? I'm not sure exactly. It's just, she just seemed concerned, which made me—curious, I guess, about what she was talking about."

There's a beat that seems to stretch out forever before Cecilia says, "Yes, of course."

She moves briskly back to her desk, her cape waving behind her. There, she shuffles through the stack of folders, in search of something. Georgia watches on with confusion. It's like Cecilia expected this.

Finally, she makes a sound of satisfaction as she pulls a paper from one of the folders.

"This, I believe, is what Simone may have been referring to."

She strides over to Georgia. It takes Georgia a moment to

understand what she's doing: holding out the paper for her to take, which, hesitantly, she does. At the top is printed The Program's logo, and sure enough, beneath it is a list.

"Disenrollments from The Program," Cecilia says heavily as Georgia scans the page. There are six names on the list, with Dede Chomondeley near the top. "It's not a record I wish to keep, as you can imagine, but alas. In any program such as this one, one must expect there to be a certain number of incongruities."

Incongruities. That's one way to put it.

Georgia scans the list. Under Dede's name, Simone's is near the bottom. Beside each name is a phone number and another name—partners, apparently. Beside Dede's is Brooks Chomondeley, a name that somehow seems to exactly match the picture of him Georgia has in her head.

"Please, feel free to keep it," says Cecilia, who is watching Georgia with interest.

"Keep . . . the list?"

"Yes. Transparency, in my opinion, is the sister of trustworthiness, and this relationship can only function with total trust."

Her voice is light, and there's nothing aggressive about her demeanor. And yet, Georgia feels uncomfortable, as though Cecilia is accusing her of something.

"Oh, that's— I don't need this. I trust you."

She tries to give the paper back to Cecilia, but Cecilia shakes her head.

"I insist."

"Okay. Well—okay. I appreciate that."

Cecilia smiles, revealing a pair of very pointy incisors. They are, like her, not so much beautiful as they are striking.

Georgia folds the paper and slips it into the pocket of her sweatpants.

CHAPTER 76

The Village is about a mile from the main resort campus, which Leila and Georgia travel after her meeting in a pink Program golf cart. As they're zipping past the resort entrance, they pass a black SUV with tinted windows. Georgia tries to see inside, but it's too dark.

The Village is at the end of a leafy dirt road that is protected by a tall wrought-iron gate.

"Who are they trying to keep out?" Georgia says as Leila taps at the keypad. Leila gives her a little frown, not registering the joke.

Through the gate, they chug beneath a canopy of koa trees. Yellow and white hibiscus flowers dot the roadside like pockets of confetti, interrupted every few feet with curvy lampposts. The air is thick with salt, but it's pleasant. It feels clean and nourishing, so different from the brittle, smoggy air back home.

Eventually, the trees part to reveal a giant cul-de-sac around which are six houses. Leila takes them to the far end, past the statue in the middle, a sister to the Aphrodite sculpture at the resort. They come to a stop in front of a three-story mansion with barely pink shutters and a glossy swiss cheese plant out front.

"Wow," Georgia says, mostly to herself. Leila isn't looking at the house. She keeps her eyes trained straight ahead with an odd expression, as though allowing Georgia privacy.

The house appears to be unlocked, as Leila pushes the door open without a key. They find themselves in a grand, sunny foyer with black-and-white marble floors and a regal staircase.

"This is incredible," Georgia says, and this time Leila makes a sound in response. It seems like acknowledgment, although she appears mostly unmoved. And of course. Leila has surely seen houses like this many times before.

"Do you live in one of these?" Georgia says as Leila directs her through the foyer and into the high-ceilinged kitchen.

"Lower staff don't live in the Village," Leila says simply.

On the counter—a grand slab of veiny white marble—sits a vase of flowers. Attached to it is a note from Cecilia: *Welcome home!* Georgia feels a knot forming in her stomach. She shouldn't have asked about the list, she thinks. Or, at the very least, she should've waited. It should not have been the very first thing she said, not when she is receiving all this.

"Can I get you anything right now?" Leila says. She stands by the doorway as though hesitant to come all the way inside.

Georgia looks around the room, at all the beauty that is somehow hers.

"Do you know where there's a trash can?" she says.

"They're usually in one of the cabinets by the sink."

Georgia finds it, lined with a trash bag already. No detail spared, she thinks.

She pulls the list out of her pocket, and even though Cecilia isn't there to see her, she makes a big show of crumpling it up and throwing it inside.

CHAPTER 77

Whoever brought Georgia's suitcase to the house also took the liberty of opening it. It waits splayed out in her room on a luggage rack by a huge window that overlooks the cul-de-sac. She doesn't like the idea of someone doing this, although maybe this is common for the fabulously rich. She wouldn't know. She's never been fabulously rich before.

The house has five bedrooms, each of them grander than the last. The primary is the size of her entire first apartment out of college, its buzzy boob light swapped here for an elaborate chandelier. The furniture is all complementary pieces of dark carved wood, and in the corner, by the window, is a statue of a woman wearing an expression not totally dissimilar from the Aphrodite statue back at the resort—anger, possibly, although here it's dulled slightly by the woman's mismatched eyes, the left one darker than the right.

For three silent minutes, Georgia sits on the edge of her new bed, just looking around. She then unpacks her suitcase, something she never does on vacation.

The bathroom is so big that the shower is totally open on one side. She stands in it for a moment—water off, clothes on—trying to imagine how it will feel to use it. The vanity is far enough away that there seems to be no real risk of water getting on it, but it's angled so that Georgia can see her reflection in the mirror. She pictures herself naked and feels immediately vulnerable. She wonders if this is something the fabulously rich are also used to.

After all this, she calls Will, although he doesn't answer. It's dinnertime at home, which has become a stressful multistep process. She sees she has fifteen unread messages on Instagram, which she decides not to open, and no emails from Dede, which she chooses not to read into.

When she goes downstairs and looks in the fridge, she finds it stocked with food: bowls of fruit and whole milk yogurt and a pitcher of freshly squeezed orange juice, all labeled. Next to the fridge is a café menu and a delivery number. Ordering delivery feels too indulgent, although she's too tired to make anything or attempt the trek back to the resort.

In the end, she calls the number and requests, apologetically, a poke bowl and guava smoothie. It is, as Will would call it, a "Georgia dinner," which is just his way of saying not enough meat.

But it's only for tonight, she tells herself. When he gets here, they'll eat something more substantial. They'll probably cook more and cook better. How could they not, in this kitchen? Everything will be different in a place like this.

At three o'clock in the morning, she sits upright. She was dead asleep, but it feels like she was awoken midway through a fully formed thought.

It was literally just a list of names, and that's it.

That's what Simone told her. That's what she saw on Cecilia's desk, the reason she was kicked out. It was literally just a list of names, and that's it.

There was nothing next to the names.

There were no partners.

There was no Brooks.

Georgia feels a strange, disoriented feeling, like déjà vu. Like watching a movie she is pretty sure she's seen before but can't quite remember. That heady sense of knowing what is about to happen a split second before it does.

The list Cecilia gave her earlier, and the one Simone found: They are not the same list.

Without thinking, she swivels. Her feet hit the cold tile, and a shiver races through her body.

In the kitchen, she goes to the cupboard with the trash can by the sink. Her poke from earlier came in a plastic bowl, which she threw away when she was finished. In it still swim little bits of green onion in a puddle of low-sodium soy sauce.

She pulls the bowl out, sets it on the counter. She moves aside the cardboard smoothie cup, dried guava remnants looking gross on the lip. Below that are some used napkins, and below that, what she's looking for.

It's crumpled, but she can still make out the names.

She remembers just before she calls that, unlike DC, LA is only three hours ahead of Oahu. There, it's not even six. She doesn't know what type of person Brooks Chomondeley is—an early riser or a night owl—but she suspects he will not be happy by a crack-of-the-morning phone call from a stranger regardless.

And so she waits. First she gets back into bed and pulls the covers up to her chin. She closes her eyes and feels not the least bit tired. Then she gets up, straightens the bed, and—tiptoeing for no reason she can explain—examines all the other rooms in the house. The next biggest one, the one that will probably be Clover's, also has a chandelier that is not much smaller than the one in Georgia's. It drips with crystals and intricate steel flowers, which she examines with wonder as she lies on her back on the floor.

No chandeliers in the other rooms, but they're all still very nice. Wainscoting in what will be Ruby's room. A whole wall of sturdy built-ins. She pulls open all the drawers and pushes them shut, but they're the expensive, soft-close kind, so they close without a sound.

Finally, at six o'clock, she decides it's an appropriate time to call someone in California. She dials Brooks Chomondeley's number from the corner of the bed she straightened hours earlier, pulling the sheets as tight as she could.

She wonders, as the call is ringing, whether Brooks will answer, and if so, whether he will talk. She wonders if she would talk if the roles were reversed. She thinks of the woman at the airport and wonders how much she knows about people at all.

Brooks does answer. He clears his throat and says, "It's Brooks."

His voice sounds scratchy and full, like maybe he just woke up. She should be tired too, but she's not. It's six in the morning her time, and Georgia feels like she could kick down a wall.

"Hi, Brooks. This is— My name is Georgia Evans. I, um, was in Hawaii with Dede a few weeks ago."

Silence. Georgia is afraid for a moment that he hung up, but when she pulls the phone away from her ear, she sees he's still there.

She says hesitantly, "Hello?"

"What do you want?"

His voice is gruff. She suspects this isn't because of sleep.

"Oh. Yes—I'm sorry. I, uh . . ."

What does she want, actually? This would have been an excellent thing to nail down before calling.

"I just wanted to get in touch with her, I guess. Dede, I mean. To see how she's doing. I know she left The Program after a . . . difficult situation."

Well, there you have it. She's talking like Cecilia already.

Brooks makes a sound she can't interpret, somewhere between a grunt and a snort.

She says, "I guess I just want to make sure she's okay."

"That's a *great* question. If I were you, I'd ask her."

"Yes. Well, I would. I just . . . I haven't been able to get in touch with her."

"That's annoying, isn't it?"

Georgia has no idea what this means. She switches the phone from one ear to the other.

"I'm sorry. I know this is an intrusion."

"How about this? How about you call me back if you hear from her?"

"Hear from her?"

"Dede."

"Yes. Are you—? Is she not with you?"

He makes that sound again. She thinks maybe it's a laugh.

"Not with me. Confirmed."

"Where is she?"

"Hell if I know. She said she's taking a *sabbatical*. Like she's the queen of mother-fucking England."

Georgia's mind is racing, crowded by images of Dede in the headset, the men on Dede's doorstep. The actual queen of England, who seems to have been unfairly brought into this conversation.

"Oh. That's— So, wait. Did she come home after The Program?"

"No. She called me from the airport to say she's taking more time off."

"Called you?"

"FaceTimed."

"Okay. So you saw her then? On the phone?"

"Yes." He sounds impatient now.

"Okay. That's just— I don't understand."

"Yeah." The word is acidic, although it's hard to blame him for that.

"But you talked to her?"

"*Yes*, I talked to her. And a lot of good that did."

CHAPTER 78

Georgia makes herself breakfast that morning with the things already in the fridge—fresh mango slices, tangy vanilla yogurt. She finds lotus-shaped dishes in the cabinet and carefully lays the mango in a starburst shape. She doesn't know where the spoons are, and so lost in thought, she pulls open the same drawer three different times before it registers what she's doing.

She finds the spoon, and with it, she takes one bite of yogurt before realizing she's not at all hungry. She feels bad wasting such good food, so she puts the lotus bowl in the fridge.

Sabbatical. That's the exact same word Simone used when she told Georgia about her colleague. And that's odd, right? There's no way she can talk herself out of that. It's strange that two different women, in two different situations, would make this very unique decision. That they both would use the word *sabbatical,* like they're the queen of mother-fucking England.

But Brooks talked to Dede. He *saw* her, and he didn't seem worried. He just seemed mad. And if something was really wrong, he would be more worried than mad.

As Georgia brushes her teeth afterward, she wonders where she would take a sabbatical, if she decided to take one. Somewhere beachy and warm, probably.

It strikes her then that she *is* somewhere beachy and warm.

Maybe Dede is fine.

"You wanted to take a sabbatical too," Will says when she calls him later that morning. "Remember that?"

Leila is supposed to come get her soon to give her the "new employee" tour, which should take most of the day. Georgia is dressed and in her room, ready and waiting.

"I mean, I wasn't serious," she says. "I wanted to take a sabbatical the same way I want to buy a Ferrari."

"You want to buy a Ferrari?"

"No. You're not— That's not the point."

Will sighs.

"Sorry," she says. "I'm just . . . I don't know."

"I know. I get it. I guess I'm just trying to figure out what the point is."

She picks a piece of lint off her knee. After her tour today, Georgia will be attending Opening Dinner with the newest class on the island. It will be her first official event as an employee of The Program.

"I am too," she admits. "I don't know. Maybe there isn't a point, really."

Will says, this time gently, "I'd trust your gut here, Gi. Do you think there's a problem?"

In her mind, she sees the woman at the airport, her ankle-high Ugg boots. She doesn't know why she remembers this detail or why it feels so important. It's just, the woman seemed so *ordinary*. In those boots, she could've been anyone.

"I don't know," she says honestly. "I guess not, no. Not really."

"Well, okay then. That's good. I wouldn't second-guess yourself."

~

Leila is, as she always is, very talkative on the tour. A lot of what she tells Georgia seems to be from a script, but some of it doesn't, like when they're behind the Arcadian Bay Café and she points out the spot where they once found a feral wallaby that seemed "not quite right in the head." She tells Georgia this chattily, then about how they had to call animal control and some other agency she can't remember the name of. It was, according to her, "a whole ordeal."

When Georgia is back at her room later, she is exhausted. She has two hours before she has to leave again for Opening Dinner, and she is tempted to use this time for a two-hour nap. She can't, though, as she's very sweaty from getting in and out of Leila's golf cart all day, and she refuses to be smelly for her first official event for The Program.

The shower is exactly as uncomfortable as she expected, as it's difficult not to make eye contact with her reflection over the vanity, and the lack of a door or shower curtain makes her feel very exposed. She doesn't bother drying her hair when she's finished, admitting preemptive defeat to the humidity. Instead, she rubs her new and special mousse through it, hoping to achieve the chic island look. She then stands in front of the beautiful armoire, staring at all the clothes she brought for the week.

She bought a new dress specifically for tonight's Opening Dinner, a blue and white shift dress that looked amazing on the hanger. It's different from what she would usually buy, a bit more fashionable with less structure than she normally likes. It's the sort of thing she used to think only worked on a certain type of body—someone like Dede, for example.

She thinks of Dede, wonders where she is now. Maybe she's in Bali. Maybe she's in Italy, eating olives and getting a marvelous tan.

Her eyes fall to her suitcase, which sits under the gaze of the stern stone statue in the corner. She has unpacked nearly everything from it—everything except one thing, in the little pocket in the front, which is stained where a travel bottle of hand sanitizer exploded in it.

She goes to it. Opens it. And there it is, right where she left it. She hasn't touched the key fob cloner since she put it there. "Just in case," as Logan said that night.

Just in case . . . what? When Logan said it, it felt so ridiculous. In what scenario would Georgia ever need this?

If someone was lying to her? If someone was in trouble and needed her help?

Even in her head, it feels ridiculous, because it *is* ridiculous.

She pulls out the cloner and drops it into her purse anyway, just in case.

CHAPTER 79

Izzy greets her at Opening Dinner that night wearing a silk lei.

"I have one for you too!" she says merrily, holding up a second one. "Staff perks," she adds with a wink. And indeed, across the cabana, Georgia can see that the other staff members are also wearing them, although they look much less happy about this than Izzy.

"Oh," Georgia says. "That's— Okay."

Izzy puts it over her head without asking. "Looks great," she says, appraising her work

"Thank you so much," Georgia manages, to which Izzy gives a grand smile.

"So let's get you back to the staff table. How *exciting*, right?"

She does seem genuinely excited, and Georgia tries to match this energy, although she suddenly feels uncomfortable in the shift dress, which looked better in the store than it does tonight. She holds on tight to her purse, which is bejeweled and in the shape of a seashell. This is also a new purchase. (When she brought it home, Will looked at it and said only, "Wow.")

Izzy gestures for Georgia to follow, which she does, passing the other tables at which sit an array of nervous-looking women. Georgia thinks back to her first night on the island and how unsure of herself she felt, and how amazed she was by someone like Dede, who didn't seem to suffer from the same affliction. Dede, who marched through her time in The Program like it existed only for her to march through.

"It's different being here not as an attendee," Georgia says to Izzy, who is half a step ahead.

Izzy smiles over her shoulder. "I bet!"

She stops in front of the staff table and turns, looking expectant. Georgia's fingers play with the zipper on her purse.

"Do we keep track of all attendees once they leave the island?" she says. "Or only the ones taking Phase Two?"

Izzy frowns slightly. They seem to be momentarily insulated by the humid night air and the low hum of forced chatter from the other women.

"We try to stay in touch with everyone," Izzy says, her voice betraying nothing.

Georgia nods. "What about Dede Chomondeley?"

At this, something seems to pass over Izzy's face, but it's so slight and so quick, Georgia isn't able to interpret it. She could be convinced it wasn't even there.

"Dede from your pod?" Izzy says.

"Yes."

"Hmm." Izzy brings a finger to her lips. "I'll have to see about that one! She left early, so we might not have done our usual follow-up."

Her voice is cheery. Georgia can't tell if it's forced.

Izzy taps the chair in front of her.

"Here's your seat. Right next to mine!" She announces this with the gusto Georgia uses to sell her children vegetables. "Why don't you get settled?"

Georgia hesitates for a moment, debating whether she should press her harder. If anyone would know about Dede, other than Cecilia, it must be Izzy. And yet, something about her expression, the furious enthusiasm with which she is patting the seat back, makes Georgia suspect that even if she does know, she will not be revealing that information.

And so she sits.

There are five women at the table, not counting Georgia. They introduce themselves one by one with kind smiles and easy confidence. One is the outreach director. One takes care of housing. One—the one who, somehow, looks the least like a doctor—is an MD. When they finish their introductions, they all look at Georgia with the same waiting expression. Georgia tries to mimic their confidence as she explains her role at The Program, and while it's not her best performance, it's also not her worst.

"That's wonderful," the housing lady says emphatically. She has a perfectly round face and buoyant hair, and she gives Georgia an approving nod before turning to the woman beside her, the doctor. The doctor is young and beautiful and has hair that is, unlike the housing woman's, seemingly impervious to the humidity. The housing lady asks her a question about a trip she has apparently just taken.

Before the doctor can answer, Izzy appears back at their table. She leans over her chair, her hands on either side her plate.

"We're going to be starting in a minute. Everyone okay?"

The women all make sounds of confirmation. Izzy stands back up, looking satisfied. Georgia doesn't know if it's her imagination or if Izzy is intentionally avoiding her eyes.

As Izzy leaves again, the attention turns back to the doctor, who starts to answer the housing lady's question. Georgia, though, doesn't hear it, as she sees what the other women either haven't or have found unimportant: Izzy's keys.

She left them there, right next to her plate, a big loop with a collection of fobs.

The idea comes to Georgia slowly but also all at once. It feels like her body is buzzing. Her shell purse is hanging from the back of her chair, and it suddenly feels like a ticking bomb.

The doctor (Georgia thinks her name is Sarah, but it could be Sasha) is saying something about ayahuasca now. Georgia nods, but her eyes are on the fobs. One of them is labeled DIAMOND. She can't read the rest.

"We're looking at it as a potential alternative," Probably Sarah is saying, although Georgia can now barely hear over her own heartbeat. She puts her elbows on the table, leaning in as though she's rapt with attention. No one looks her way.

Is she really going to do this?

She inches her elbow over just the slightest bit, and it makes contact with one of the fobs. She looks around, which no one seems to notice. The woman on her other side is also leaning forward slightly, entranced by Probably Sarah and the ayahuasca.

Georgia moves her elbow farther. The keys scratch against the table, but again no one reacts.

Probably Sarah says that ayahuasca is usually drunk as a beverage. The other women are surprised by this.

Georgia inhales, coughs. In the same motion, she flinches her elbow, sending the keys off the edge of the table and onto her lap.

Probably Sarah stops, and Georgia can see the whole thing unfurling in front of her at once. Probably Sarah saw it. She knows. And of course she does! She's an MD! She can spot a real cough when she hears one. Of course she knows Georgia's was fake! She's going to tell Izzy, who will tell Cecilia. She imagines Cecilia in her office, shaking her head in disappointment. Leila, silent, as she drives her away from the Village for the very last time.

The beat seems to last for years. Millennia. The entire existence of humanity, in this pause.

Then Probably Sarah says, "Bless you," apparently having confused Georgia's fake cough with a sneeze. She smiles slightly, then to all of them says, "Anyway, yes, it's been used for centuries in indigenous spiritual medicine."

Georgia nods enthusiastically, covering the keys with the napkin on her lap.

~

It is, as Logan told her it would be, very easy to copy the key fobs with the cloner once she gets them to the bathroom. And this—getting them to the bathroom—was much easier than getting them to her lap. All she did was slip them into her purse under the table as Probably Sarah was telling them about a spiritual ritual she recently witnessed in Bolivia, and no one around her even blinked.

The fobs are all labeled, and she decides to copy a few of them: one to the Shell Room, one to Cecilia's office. Each takes only the press of one button, then another. *Write success!* the device cheers when it's finished, and despite herself, she almost laughs. To be congratulated by a tiny robot. To be cloning key fobs in this luxury bathroom. The bathroom smells like pineapple, but just a faint, tasteful hint. It's all so ridiculous.

When she returns to the table, the women have moved on from ayahuasca. They're discussing the housing woman's goldendoodle puppy, who is "supposedly hypoallergenic," but she "has doubts." Georgia slides into her seat and joins the chorus of dismayed tongue clucks.

No one sees her put the keys back on the table, and when Izzy returns a little while later, she does not seem to suspect anything amiss. "Ah!" she says, snatching them up. "There you are!" As though reprimanding a misbehaved child.

As the dinner starts and the attendees line up for their drinks and sushi and rice, Georgia can focus on little but the contents of her purse. The feeling is a lot like nerves, but it's not quite that. It's something else. She can see now why people become criminals. She wonders if some people don't even do it for the money but for the high of it, the *rush*.

She thinks of Will and what he would say if he could see her. *I'd trust your gut here, Gi.*

She doesn't think this is what he meant.

When Georgia gets back to her house later that night, the first thing she does is open the shell purse. She is half expecting the fobs not to be there, to discover that the whole thing was just a hallucination. But no, there they are, right next to her spare tampon and ChapStick.

She doesn't touch them. She brings the purse upstairs, holding it slightly away from her body, then hangs it on the crystal knob of her armoire. She wonders if just having them is a crime. Probably. She imagines trying to explain herself if she were caught. "What were you planning to do with them?" they would say, pens poised above notepads, expecting some diabolical reveal. But Georgia would just look at them and say, honestly, "I didn't have a plan. I did it just in case."

And she *doesn't* have a plan, other than going into her great big bathroom and brushing her teeth and washing her face. She's wearing more makeup tonight than she usually does, and the mascara is hard to get off. When she's finished, there's a miniature crime scene in her sink.

Then she tucks herself onto the very end of her huge bed, where she has a full view of the armoire and the purse still hanging on it. She closes her eyes but still has the sensation that she's being watched.

CHAPTER 80

The next morning, Leila picks Georgia up outside her house. It's the first full day of The Program, starting with the infamous edification mods in Two Dove Hall.

"Sleep good?" Leila says, sounding perky.

"Great," Georgia says, even though she didn't. In the end, she moved the shell purse from the armoire, first to the handle on her door, then under a pile of towels where she couldn't see it. Still, throughout all this, she never touched the key fobs inside.

"Excellent," Leila says before smashing her foot on the gas. Georgia, thankfully, is holding on already. (She learned early yesterday that Leila likes to go fast.)

They zip through the clear morning, the wind just loud enough that they can't really talk. They slow as they near Two Dove Hall, where at the entrance waits a group of women, probably nine or ten in all. As Leila and Georgia pass them, a few look up, squinting slightly against the morning sun. Georgia averts her eyes, which only registers as the wrong thing to do after she has done it. She is, technically, a staff member now. She should be treating these women as her clients.

Leila takes her around to the back of the auditorium, to an entrance that is nearly hidden by a pretty tulip tree. "Cecilia said she'd meet you inside," she says, and smiles.

She drops Georgia off, letting Georgia go in on her own. Georgia easily finds Cecilia backstage in a makeup chair. A girl—woman, she supposes—is sweeping a fluffy brush over her face. Cecilia spots Georgia and waves her over.

"Georgia," she says, eyes closed now as the woman dabs something onto her eyelids. "I'm happy to see you this morning."

The woman steps back and appraises Cecilia. Cecilia doesn't seem to notice.

"I'm happy to be here," Georgia says, and she's caught off guard by how much it sounds like a lie. She *is* happy to be here actually. It's not a lie.

Cecilia seems to register this too. A single crease appears between her eyebrows.

"That will be all," she says to the makeup artist, not unkindly, but with a note of finality. "It's wonderful. Thank you."

The woman gives Cecilia a small bow. She doesn't look at Georgia as she scuttles away.

"Georgia," says Cecilia. She leans forward slightly so her elbows are resting on her knees. Her makeup is tasteful, accentuating rather than fighting her features. "Something is bothering you," she says.

In her head, Georgia hears Brooks Chomondeley: *A lot of good that did.*

When she doesn't say anything, Cecilia raises her eyebrows, and Georgia considers lying. She's never been a good liar, though, even to people who are easier to lie to than Cecilia.

"I talked to Brooks Chomondeley," she admits, which feels a little bit scary, although at the same time, also a relief. "Yesterday. He was on the list you gave me."

"Ah," Cecilia says, and Georgia notes that she doesn't look angry, although she also doesn't look especially surprised.

"I just wanted to know how Dede is doing. You know—since she left."

"Yes, yes. Of course. And did Mr. Chomondeley ease those concerns?"

Like she's the queen of mother-fucking England. No, he didn't ease those concerns, although perhaps that was expecting too much from someone like Brooks Chomondeley.

"I guess so. I mean . . . I don't know. He said Dede took a sabbatical after The Program?"

Cecilia nods. She does not look particularly moved by this information either. She looks, in fact, like this is not new information at all.

Georgia says, "Have you heard anything about that?"

"I have, yes."

"Oh," Georgia says, feeling stupid.

"Yes. Belize, if I recall. She has some family in the area."

"In Belize?"

"Yes. I do apologize if it seems as though I was keeping this information from you. As you can imagine, attendee privacy—even after they depart—is an utmost priority."

"Oh. Right."

From beyond the curtain comes the twang of a string instrument. Cecilia and Georgia both look toward it.

"Ah," Cecilia says, closing her eyes and lifting her chin. "This is always my favorite part." She stays like this for a moment, looking serene, and Georgia has no idea what to do, where to even look.

"Soon enough, it'll be you out there," Cecilia says at last, opening her eyes.

Georgia nods blankly. "Yes" is all she can think to say.

Cecilia smiles. Most of her makeup is subtle, but on her lips is a dark red stain. It makes her incisors, sharp and bone white, all the more noticeable.

"I'm excited to be working together, Georgia. I think we will make an excellent team."

She stands, touches Georgia lightly on the shoulder, then brushes past her and onto the stage.

Georgia hoped the rat videos might be different the second time—less shocking, more clinical. They're not. She stands at the corner of the stage, in the shadow of the curtain, and feels just as unsettled as she did the first time. She's closer to the screen now than she was in the audience and can see each individual fiber of the rat mother's fur. The ends of her whiskers quivering. Her tiny, translucent nails that click against the floor.

A shiny spot of saliva caught on her teeth as she widens her mouth to scream.

CHAPTER 81

Babcia had many thoughts about life, but one of her favorites was this: *There is no devil greater than a little god.* Georgia first assumed this phrase was from the Bible, although she later learned it wasn't. It was, apparently, from a pig farmer back in Poland, whom Babcia knew before she left. The adage journeyed with Babcia from Poland to America, from raising her own children to raising her daughter's. Georgia heard it mostly when she was worrying, which she did a lot, even as a child. "There is no devil greater than a little god," Babcia would tell her, by which she meant, "Nothing is worse than trying to control your life." And for the most part, this is what Georgia heard in her head whenever things went wrong. Whenever her plans went awry, she would think of Babcia and the Polish pig farmer, how they had warned her not to play little god.

This is what Georgia is thinking about later that night, after all the edification mods are over, after having another dinner delivered to her house. She sits on her bed, her purse on her lap, and thinks of Babcia and the Polish pig farmer. She imagines both of them in the room with her now as she lays the evidence out before them.

Cecilia gave her a list and said it was the same one Simone found. It wasn't.

Cecilia said Dede went to Belize because that's where she has family, but that is not true. Georgia knows it's not true because all of Dede's family lives in California—all of them except for one, her favorite aunt, who lives in Rhode Island.

Georgia imagines presenting this to her dead grandmother and a faceless Polish farmer, her little two-person jury. Even in this imaginary scenario, she knows what they'd tell her.

So there are some questions—some *incongruities*, to use Cecilia's word. It's something to be aware of, but it is no reason to do something drastic. It is no reason to play little god.

And yet, the thought occurs to her now, alone in her room, that maybe Babcia misunderstood the farmer. What if the farmer wasn't offering a warning but an observation: No devil is greater than a little god.

What if the greatest thing one can do is take control of one's situation? To want more? To *demand* more from those who withhold it? What if playing little god is the only way to make it in a world like this one?

What is the lesson of The Program, after all, if it isn't this?

Under the cover of darkness, Georgia hurries down the main path, along the road that connects the Village to the resort. There are some streetlights, but they are dim and staggered, so they are hardly helpful. She is wearing a pair of sweatpants, and her face is bare. She feels wild, and scared.

She feels very alive.

She reaches the iron gate, and for one disappointing moment, it seems that her only option is to climb it. (And this, really, is not an option, as Georgia is not the sort of person who can climb anything.) Thankfully, she finds a control box nearby with a button helpfully labeled OPEN.

She presses it, and the gate obeys.

She slows as she reaches the resort, creeping carefully toward it, although it does not appear that anyone is out. Some of the villa windows glow a muted orange from behind drawn curtains, while others are dark. It strikes Georgia suddenly that she doesn't know where Cecilia stays. Is she also in the Village? The thought makes her uncomfortable.

The climb up to Cecilia's office is somehow easier in the dark. Maybe it's because she can't see how steep the stairway is, or maybe she has just grown used to it. Maybe she has gotten stronger over the last few weeks.

Cecilia's office is dark, as Georgia hoped it would be. (For a second, she was worried Cecilia stays in her office at night.)

But Cecilia isn't here. Georgia is alone.

She opens her purse. Inside are five cloned fobs, none of which she labeled. She tries them one by one until the fourth one works.

The little light turns green.

A click.

She hesitates for a moment, hovering in this rare slice of time between before and after, between the world she's in and the one she's about to create. She considers the fact that she can still back out. Nothing undoable has been done yet.

She takes in a breath, then takes a step.

CHAPTER 82

She considers turning on the light but realizes, thankfully before she does it, that this is a bad idea. It strikes her then that not only does she not have any experience with breaking and entering, but she also does not have the right instincts. She is not the type of person who has an uncanny awareness of the world around her. She is the type of person who stubs her toe regularly on the same pieces of furniture in her house.

She creeps forward. Cecilia's desk is clear of everything except a single notebook in the middle, with a pen lined up perfectly parallel with one edge. Not even a computer, which is a good thing. There is no chance she would be able to successfully pull off a computer hack.

She rounds the desk and pulls out the chair. In a moment of inspiration, or perhaps a moment of weakness, she lowers herself into it. It's firm but comfortable, with a seat back that lends itself to good posture. She looks across the dark office, imagines a knock. *Just a moment!* she imagines herself calling out busily.

She scans the drawers in front of her. Each one has a unique shell-shaped pull. She pulls at one of them, but nothing happens. It's locked. She tries another, but this one is locked too. It occurs to her that she shouldn't be surprised by this, and that she is in fact a horrible criminal.

She sits back, thinks. Considers her options. She had a boyfriend in high school who could open any lock with only a bobby pin and a tension wrench. Or was it a bobby pin and a screwdriver?

She supposes it doesn't matter. She could have all these tools, and she would have absolutely no idea what to do with them.

Logan would have a solution. Georgia feels very sure of this. She wonders if she would be able to work up the gumption to do this a second time after consulting Logan.

Then she hears it.

She freezes.

Did she imagine it?

Her heart is beating in her throat.

Outside the door, on the landing, there's a movement. A sound. It's a person. She can see their shadow through the window.

And then, a click.

CHAPTER 83

She doesn't think. She just moves.

She dives beneath the desk into the space meant for someone's legs. At the same time, the office is flooded with light. Her hands feel both numb and prickly, every nerve saturated with adrenaline.

She holds her breath.

Whoever it is doesn't move.

She tries to peer out but can see only the legs of whoever it is. They're wearing pink pinstriped pajamas.

How did they know? But of course, there must be a security system. *Of course.* How did she not think of that?

She starts to feel lightheaded from not breathing. She lets out a careful exhale. The pant legs remain standing. She prays—desperately, pleadingly—that whoever it is (Cecilia?) will find the empty room sufficient without further investigation.

Another moment. And then another.

Is it possible? Could she be that lucky?

She makes a deal with God: *Let me out of here, and I'll never even jaywalk again.*

Longer still.

Maybe?

But then, Cecilia's voice.

"Georgia, please come out from under there."

CHAPTER 84

Georgia doesn't move at first, although it's not because she chooses to stay still. It's more that the signals reaching her brain—the sight of Cecilia's pajamas, the smooth, almost playful sound of her voice—cannot be processed in any meaningful way.

"Georgia," Cecilia says again.

She shimmies out backward. Stands. Dusts off her thighs. Makes herself look Cecilia straight in the eye. Cecilia's button-down pajamas have pink tubing at the edges and a monogram on the breast pocket. This compared to Georgia's drawstring sweatpants and the oversized sweatshirt she stole from Will.

"Georgia," Cecilia says a third time. She doesn't sound angry or even that surprised. She sounds disappointed, but it's mild, the way the dentist sounds when Georgia lies to him about how often she flosses.

Georgia wants to say something, but she doesn't know what. What does a person say in this situation? Is there anything she could say now that would change the result?

Finally, Cecilia says, her voice heavy, "I was so hopeful it would not get this far."

Georgia opens her mouth, then closes it again. Cecilia nods as though Georgia actually said something. It's a slow, regretful movement, like Georgia has let her down.

Will she call the police? How serious of a crime is this? She would be a pitiful prisoner, even worse than she is as a criminal.

"I'm . . ."

She starts to say *I'm sorry*, but she can't bring herself to do it. Curiously, Cecilia cocks her head. Georgia's mind goes to Ugg woman, the look of resignation on her face as she stood over Georgia, like she had no other choice but to dump her drink.

"I feel like there's something you're not telling me," Georgia says, which is a wild thing to say, given her position. Cecilia raises her eyebrows slightly, perhaps thinking the same thing.

They stand like this for a moment, neither of them speaking. Georgia remembers Simone's similar standoff with Cecilia, not that long ago. How impossible it seemed at the time, and now look at her.

Now look at her.

"Yes," Cecilia says finally. "Yes, I suppose we couldn't have expected any less from you."

What does that mean?

Wordlessly, Cecilia turns to the door.

Over her shoulder, she says, "Come with me."

CHAPTER 85

Cecilia doesn't look back to see if Georgia has heard or is following. She doesn't even hold the door. She sweeps out of the office with complete confidence that Georgia will come with her, and Georgia—because she can think of no alternative—does.

The night is soupy and dark enough that the small pinprick stars are visible overhead. It's a beautiful night. Picturesque. The strange, unnerving thought occurs to her that a night as beautiful as this one would be an ironic time to die.

Cecilia doesn't take the stairs Georgia climbed to get there. Instead, she disappears around the corner of the building, following the wraparound porch into the shadows. Georgia follows.

The porch, it turns out, doesn't wrap all the way around the building. It stops near the back at a gate that Cecilia breezily pushes open. Again, she doesn't turn to explain to Georgia where they're going, or even to see if Georgia is in tow. Georgia considers turning back around, although that then begs the question of where she would go and what she would do after that.

The gate leads through a thicket of scraggly kiawe trees. There aren't lights along the path, although this does not seem to slow Cecilia. Georgia stays close behind.

The path opens eventually to a small paved cove where a golf cart sits. It's not so dissimilar from the one Leila drives, although perhaps a bit bigger. Cecilia strides over to it, and only then does she glance back at Georgia.

"Shall we?" she says.

And finally, Georgia allows herself to feel annoyed. She understands she shouldn't. How annoyed can she be, after all, with someone who just caught her breaking and entering? On the other hand, Cecilia's lack of transparency—this total confidence that others will accept her unquestioningly—is not without blame.

"Where are we going?" she says.

Cecilia gives her a sympathetic little smile, which Georgia finds even more irritating.

"You feel I have been keeping something from you, no?"

Georgia bites the inside of her cheek, then begrudgingly, she steps forward. Cecilia gives her an appreciative nod and mounts the cart with a swiftness that belies her age. Georgia has barely buckled her seat belt before they're off.

CHAPTER 86

Georgia recognizes the white building immediately. It is, after all, nearly impossible to forget the place where you first did magic mushrooms.

When they reach the door, Cecilia pulls the keys from her breast pocket as the kiawe trees around them bristle in the breeze. She looks back at Georgia, her face marred by shadows from the light above the door. Her expression is one of intrigue, as though curious to see whether Georgia might finally protest.

When Georgia doesn't, Cecilia pushes the heavy door open, revealing the dark entryway that Georgia has been in only once before. She motions for Georgia to lead the way, and Georgia obeys, stepping into the darkness. The door shuts hard behind them, and for a moment, Georgia can see nothing. It's barely enough time for her to feel afraid, however, before Cecilia turns on the lights.

"You will recall White Hall?" Cecilia says. She sounds conversational.

Georgia nods.

"Excellent. Follow me."

She brushes past Georgia, down the hall toward the room where Georgia and the other women took their trips. Again, Georgia keeps close—so close that when Cecilia makes an abrupt stop, Georgia almost runs into her back.

Cecilia lifts the keys. Georgia doesn't understand what she's doing, doesn't even notice the door camouflaged by the wall, until Cecilia swipes the fob and it pops open.

"After you," she says.

Georgia hesitates. Through the door, nothing is visible. It's just a yawning mouth in the wall.

She steps inside.

CHAPTER 87

When Cecilia closes the door behind them, a dim light flickers on. It's a single sconce on the wall, barely illuminating the hallway.

Georgia turns to Cecilia, who is unrecognizable in the shadows.

"Please," says Cecilia, motioning as though she would like Georgia to continue walking. Cold fear races through Georgia's body. There is no visible handle on the door they just came through, no way to open it, and who knows how thick the walls are? If she screamed, would anyone be able to hear?

"Where are we?" she says.

"Ah. Yes. We call this the Diamond."

DIAMOND. Georgia remembers Izzy's keys.

"What is it?"

"Please." Cecilia motions again. "Much will become clear in a moment."

And what else can she do at this point but obey? So she does. She moves slowly, cautiously. Cecilia follows a step behind her, their footsteps echoing in the hall that is who knows how deep in the building. When they come to a spiral staircase, Georgia looks back at Cecilia, who gives her a cheerful nod to continue. Georgia descends carefully, arriving at the bottom with only the whisper of her shoe against the cement floor.

The room is, appropriately, diamond shaped. It's also dim, but not as dim as the hallway behind them. Around the perimeter are evenly spaced red up-lights, which create an eerie glow on some type of machinery, a complicated system of screens and wires. On one wall, there's a corded telephone. Her eyes move to the middle of the room, where there is something she can't identify.

She looks at Cecilia, who nods slightly, as though granting permission. Georgia creeps toward whatever it is.

She's close enough to understand what she's looking at before she can say it.

"Is that . . . ?"

A sweeping, visceral feeling overtakes her, and she wonders if it's possible she has been this wrong about something for a second time.

CHAPTER 88

"What is this?" she says, the only thing she can think to say, even though she can see what this is. What this is, is three women arranged on gurneys in the middle of the room, their heads toward one another, creating a kind of starburst shape. Their eyes are closed, their palms splayed lightly at their sides. Asleep, possibly.

She doesn't recognize two of them. The third is Dede.

She turns to Cecilia, who does not appear fazed by what they're seeing. But how? Is Georgia missing something? She feels disoriented suddenly.

"Did you know, Georgia, that the hypothalamus is roughly diamond shaped?"

Cecilia is speaking coolly, her eyes on Georgia, not the women in the center of the room. Georgia opens her mouth, then closes it again. She did not know that, does not know why it matters. She feels lost.

"And the hypothalamus, of course, is the 'heart' of the brain."

She can hear now the quiet *whoosh whoosh* of machinery, which she didn't register before. She places the sound—the steady, predictable beat of a machine doing a human function. Breathing.

"And as the hypothalamus is the heart of the brain," says Cecilia, "here we have the heart of The Program."

"The heart of The Program?" Georgia says blankly. "What . . ." She trails off. She doesn't even know what to ask, where to begin.

"Research, Georgia. Real, unflinching research. At the heart of

The Program is research into those areas that, throughout so much of human history, have been maliciously ignored."

"Research," Georgia repeats dumbly. "They're here for research?"

Cecilia nods. In her mind, Georgia sees Rat Mother Number Two, the trapped look in her eyes. Like she knew where she was, knew how it would eventually end.

"I don't . . ." Georgia begins, but she stops. The questions seem to stick together in her head, a tangled mess of thoughts. "Here? Why are—? I don't understand."

Cecilia gives her a small nod, as though this were cogent.

"There are certain hurdles," she says, "as I'm sure you are aware, when it comes to research that involves human subjects. Some of them necessary, of course, although some challenges are merely the symptom of bureaucracy—the same bureaucracy, unfortunately, that has for so long neglected this critical area of the human experience."

Georgia tries to understand.

"So this isn't—approved by anyone? This research?"

Cecilia cocks her head. Smiles.

"But what are you doing? What are you researching? I don't understand."

Georgia can't look at them, the women. At Dede. Their presence here is unnerving, although it's not just that. It's what they're wearing: each a boxy peach medical gown. She can imagine Dede's horror at being caught in something like this, and this indignity feels as wrong as anything else.

"These women are those whose brains exhibited the most resistance to our regimen," says Cecilia. "They did not respond to Virgin Mode, as you may recall from Ms. Chomondeley's performance, and we would like to understand why that is. To explore what it is about their maternal circuits that renders them so durable."

Georgia thinks of Dede, the sound she made right before she ran into the concrete structure. *Durable.* Is that what she was?

"So you're studying them?"

"An unsophisticated way to word it, but in essence, yes."

"But why— I still don't get it." A thought then occurs to her, followed by a sickening realization. The men in Dede's doorway. The lies. She feels lightheaded as she manages, "Are you *keeping* them here? Did they agree to this?"

"Of course they agreed to this," Cecilia says, a slight slip in her demeanor.

"But Brooks—Dede told him she was taking a sabbatical. A *trip*."

When Cecilia speaks again, she has regained her composure.

"We do require a certain commitment to discreetness, as I'm sure you will understand."

Does she understand?

"I don't, actually. I'm sorry, but you have to see how crazy this looks. They're here for—what? Secret research? It seems so . . . so . . ." She struggles for the word before landing on, "*Unnecessary*."

But that isn't right. Unnecessary is Clover wearing a cape to the grocery store. Clover accepting a sandwich only if it's cut the right way. Those things are unnecessary. Unnecessary is not three women in some secret basement for . . . *what*?

She finds Cecilia's eyes, again feeling off-kilter. Has Cecilia lied to her? Is she lying to her now?

Cecilia studies her for a moment as though she's trying to decide something as well.

"There are certain . . . challenges," she says, "when it comes to this area of research. Risks that have been deemed outside the lines of acceptability. Of course, those lines are drawn by those with no interest in the work we're doing here. Who don't understand it or how crucial it is."

"So you're keeping it a secret because of the risks?"

"Because the world is not ready for this research, Georgia. You know this. You know this as well as anybody. On any journey toward change, there will always be those who refuse to understand your mission."

She thinks of the woman in the Ugg boots, the stale smell of the airport. *You're worse for women than any man will ever be.*

"And in life, Georgia, there are always risks," Cecilia continues. "It is the only guarantee on a mission such as this. This area of research in particular requires an intimate relationship with certain parts of the brain—a crucial relationship, although when you are dealing with the mind, there is always the risk of unintended consequences."

It takes a moment, but these words eventually register. When they do, Georgia's stomach twists.

"And what are those consequences?" she croaks.

Here, Cecilia gives her an unexpectedly warm smile.

"I understand your concern, Georgia. Naturally. But the question you should be asking is, When it comes to freedom, is there any risk that's too high?"

Yes! Georgia thinks. *Yes, of course there is!* Of course there is, and how can Cecilia even ask this? Cecilia, standing there so confident. So *sure*. Georgia must be missing something. She must.

She turns to the women, to Dede, who looks paler, almost waxen, although no less beautiful. Like a sculpture of a woman, almost but not quite mirroring the real thing.

"And these women—agreed to this?" Georgia whispers.

"These mothers," says Cecilia, "have come to us because they are in pain. Because society has withheld from them what they need and what they *deserve*. Perhaps they did not understand this when they arrived, could not see clearly the ways in which they have been imprisoned, but we believe strongly in the power of education. And once educated, these women came to understand the urgency of this work. That it is bigger than them, bigger than any one of us individually."

"But why?" Georgia says. "I don't . . ." She shakes her head. "I thought Phase Two was approved already. I don't get it. Why do you even need them here?"

She turns away from the women toward Cecilia, feeling desperate for an explanation. Desperate for a way this makes sense.

Cecilia doesn't say anything for a moment. The faint sound of mechanical breathing counts out the beats.

"Your daughter," she says finally, "Ruby. She was recently diagnosed with diabetes, correct?"

Georgia feels the instinctive urge to recoil. It feels wrong—*vicious,* even—for Cecilia to say Ruby's name here.

"Yes."

"And I understand that it was quite traumatic. That the diagnosis came dangerously late."

Georgia licks her lips. She's not sure what she's feeling now: Is it indignation, or is it shame?

"Yes," she says again.

"And perhaps you doubted Phase Two because of this. Perhaps you wondered whether you might have caught it sooner had you been operating as you were before the treatment? With, as we call it here, a mom brain?"

Georgia doesn't say anything. She wonders if there's anything Cecilia could do or say to surprise her at this point.

"A very natural thing to wonder," Cecilia continues. "And the answer, of course, is yes."

Georgia leans in closer, sure she misheard.

"You indeed *would have* caught the diabetes sooner," says Cecilia, "had you not been taking Phase Two. Almost certainly. A mother's intuition is a very powerful thing."

"I don't . . ." Georgia struggles. She can't quite articulate what she's feeling, although it feels very big. "That's the whole point, though. To stop the maternal circuit. That's—that's why we're here."

Is it anger she's trying to wrestle? Betrayal? She thinks of Ruby in the helicopter and wonders if the feeling is rage.

"No, Georgia, that's not why we're here," Cecilia says, this time with a note of frustration. "Our goal is not to rid humanity of the maternal circuit. To do so, I believe, would be a great tragedy. Maybe even our downfall, as you have discovered yourself."

Georgia wants to stomp her foot. It's such a juvenile, silly reaction, but still.

"Then why am I taking Phase Two? What's the point of"—she waves her arms—"*this*? Any of this?"

"Georgia." Cecilia's voice is gentler now, but it's clearly a reprimand. "The goal here is not to get rid of motherhood. No. Our mission, the *point*, as you say, is freedom. It's the freedom of choice. Phase Two is critical, of course, as it allows mothers to opt out of what does not serve them, but this is only one side of the coin. The other, just as crucial, is the freedom to opt *in*."

Here, Cecilia finally looks at the women. She smiles softly, but in the red light, at this angle, it looks like a leer.

"The *point*," she says quietly, "lies in joining Phase Two with its natural sister, Phase Three. We have successfully freed mothers from their biological prisons with Phase Two, but we must not stop there. True freedom is choice, and where is the choice for those who *desire* a life guided by maternal chemistry? Who are constrained by biology, but in a different way—who want the maternal circuit but cannot have it? Are these mothers any less worthy of freedom?"

She looks at Georgia here, expectant. Georgia stares back wordlessly.

"Phase Two is the starting point," says Cecilia, "but Phase Three is the way. Of course, to create a mom brain is much more of a challenge than to stop one's function, but here, with this research . . ." Her gaze falls again to the women in the middle of the room, a faint smile still on her face. "We are close to understanding it. So close. And once we do, *all* mothers will have the freedom to live authentically as they choose—whether that is with a mom brain or not, whether they have birthed children or are child-free. There is a price, yes, but there always is for freedom. And soon, Georgia, we will all be free."

CHAPTER 89

They don't say anything on the drive back to the Village. It's not a cool night, but by the time they arrive back at her house, Georgia is covered in goose bumps.

They left the Diamond the way they found it: red lights on, the machines humming diligently away. Georgia stopped at the top of the staircase to look over her shoulder as they were leaving, and from there she could see the women. She wondered why she didn't notice them on the way in.

The golf cart comes to a stop in front of Georgia's house, where the upstairs lights are still on. Through the big window, it's like a showroom, her open armoire on display to the street below.

When Cecilia speaks, she almost sounds sad.

"This work requires sacrifice, Georgia. It's true. But those women understand that. They understand that it is only through this sacrifice that we will ever be free."

Georgia shifts in her seat to see Cecilia gazing up at the lit bedroom window, and from this angle, in this light, she looks as fragile as anyone else.

"You know I can't be a part of this," Georgia says finally.

Cecilia turns, meeting her eyes. Cecilia's, Georgia notes, are clear.

"Oh, Georgia," she says, shaking her head. "Of course you can. You already are."

When she gets upstairs, the first thing she does is close the curtains. She may be trapped, but she can at least deny Cecilia the satisfaction of seeing her afraid.

~

She could try to call Will, but what can he do? What can anyone do?

She knows—the same way Cecilia knows—that she is not involved with the women in the Diamond. That she would never be involved with this if she had known what was going on. But just as she knows this, she knows what Cecilia meant on the golf cart: Who would believe her at this point? Who is going to believe a liar?

She stands in the middle of the bedroom that doesn't feel like hers and brings her hands to her head. She presses them into her temples and directs herself to think.

Think.

She must leave. Of course she must. Whether or not anyone believes her, she cannot be involved with this. Women here being used for research—willingly, according to Cecilia, but who knows if that's true? The last time Georgia saw Dede, she was in no position to be making important decisions, and before that, she certainly wasn't risking anything for Cecilia's work. And really, how willingly can someone ever make a choice like this? A choice to . . . what?

Devote yourself to a cause? Risk your life for something bigger? Take action for what you believe in? *Is* that actually so hard to believe?

She thinks again of the woman in the airport, how she looked at Georgia just before she dumped out her drink—like Georgia wasn't a stranger, like she knew something about Georgia that Georgia didn't even know about herself.

And she thinks: What if those women *did* choose this? What if Cecilia is right, and they *were* willing to risk everything for this mission? For freedom? It might feel wrong to Georgia, but maybe that's because Georgia is wrong. Maybe that woman in the airport saw her for what she really is, even if Georgia couldn't see it herself.

No sooner does she think this, though, than she sees Dede's body in her head: motionless, limp. Splayed out without defense. And she knows it isn't true. She knows it in the only way certain things can be known, a truth that lies below thought. Because this thing—whatever it is—isn't about freeing women. It's about taking from them. It's about using them to reach an end goal, one that's built on a lie. Because if these women are the sacrifice, even a willing one, this can't be *for* them.

And maybe it was never supposed to be.

CHAPTER 90

The first thing she does is try to look for flights out of Hawaii, although her phone doesn't have service and the Wi-Fi won't work. She then opens up her laptop, but this doesn't work either. The Wi-Fi, it seems, is out.

She wonders if this is a sign.

The thought crosses her mind: She *could* wait until tomorrow. After all, the women aren't going anywhere. Tonight, she could prepare herself—mentally, physically. She could take a warm shower, apply her new eye cream. She could slide into the luxurious sheets in this luxurious mansion, knowing that down the road, Dede and the others lie bare.

She imagines telling this story later to some faceless investigator. *Yes, I was so very distressed by the discovery, although I chose to apply my eye cream first.* Who would believe that? *She* doesn't believe that.

She'll go to the main road, she decides, try to find some service. Get a taxi, get to the airport, figure it out from there.

She starts to pack her suitcase, but halfway through, she realizes it's pointless. It's a mile to the main road, not to mention how far she'll have to walk after that. Plus, a lot of it is gravel. The suitcase will have to stay.

She stands, feeling weirdly, somewhat worryingly, detached. Should she feel more panicked right now? More urgent? Should she feel *something* about this?

She grabs her purse, her wallet, and heads to the front of the house. Overhead, the brilliant chandelier twinkles goodbye. She reaches for the heavy door, tugs it open to where the muggy night air envelops her.

And there, on the front porch, stands Izzy.

~

Georgia lowers her hand silently back to her side. Izzy also doesn't say a word. Her eyes move over Georgia's purse, then back to her face.

Finally, Georgia says, "I'm leaving."

"Shh!" Izzy hisses at once. She gives Georgia a meaningful look that Georgia doesn't understand. Izzy puts a finger to her lips, then reaches over to what Georgia assumes to be the button for the doorbell. Using one fingernail, she plucks it off.

Beneath it, like a beady black eyeball, is a camera lens.

~

Izzy pulls her inside, and Georgia lets her, not knowing what else to do. Izzy is looking around, in search of something. More cameras? She finds what she's looking for in a plant by the base of the staircase. She pulls the lens out, drops it to the floor, and stomps on it.

"You've been watching me?" Georgia says indignantly.

At this, Izzy gives her a disbelieving look, as though the question doesn't dignify a response.

"Cecilia put me on observation duty tonight," she says. "You're lucky. But my shift is ending in an hour, and then . . ."

She doesn't finish the sentence, as though she's made her point. As though anything about what she just said makes sense. Georgia's *lucky*? In what world?

"I take it Cecilia's on her way then?" Georgia says, her voice stronger than she feels.

Izzy, though, shakes her head slowly, her eyes wide.

And it strikes Georgia then: Izzy is afraid.

CHAPTER 91

We have to be fast," Izzy says, stepping past Georgia and toward the staircase. "If my shift ends and I'm not back . . ."

She doesn't finish the thought as she starts to ascend, and Georgia feels herself growing irritated. Izzy has come here with very little explanation—and no desire to offer more explanation, it seems—and expects Georgia to simply trust her. It's the first time Georgia has identified any similarities between her and Cecilia.

Izzy is halfway up the stairs now and doesn't look back to make sure Georgia is following. And Georgia doesn't have to. She could leave now, like she was planning to, and do . . . what, exactly? She sees now the gaping holes in her previous plan, primarily that the plan had very few concrete steps.

And so, because it seems like the best option, or perhaps the only option, she follows Izzy up the stairs.

Izzy seems to know where she's going, which Georgia finds surprising only until she really thinks about it. Izzy, of course, knows this house. She has presumably watched Georgia in it: Georgia lying on the floor of the spare bedroom, digging through the trash. She doesn't know if she feels mortified or outraged, knowing someone was watching all of this.

They turn into Georgia's bedroom, which is in disarray, the suitcase still half packed on the floor. "I was in a hurry," Georgia says apologetically, embarrassed by the mess. To this, Izzy responds with only a bewildered glance.

Izzy heads to the corner with the statue, where she drops the bag she's carrying. Georgia stands awkwardly a few steps behind her, not knowing how to help.

From her bag, Izzy pulls out one of the headsets. She holds it up to her eyes, scanning the bedroom. Over her shoulder, the stone woman watches on with her solemn expression and her mismatched eyes.

One eye is a camera, Georgia realizes, and as soon as Izzy raises the headset over it, it's clear what she's about to do.

Izzy presses the side of the headset. Above the statue's perfect porous nose, a pinprick lightbulb glows green.

"Show me Georgia Evans," she says, "in the bed, going to sleep."

~

"I don't understand," Georgia says as she follows Izzy back down the stairs, toward the front door. "They're going to know it's not me tomorrow when I don't show up."

"That's enough time," is Izzy's only cryptic reply.

Georgia doesn't know what this means and is having a hard time keeping up with Izzy to ask. Izzy's out the door now, flying down the driveway, where at the end she has parked her golf cart.

"Enough time to leave?" Georgia says, running to catch up.

Izzy nods without turning around.

"I tried to book a flight out," Georgia pants. "But the Wi-Fi wasn't working."

"Yeah, Cecilia shut that off."

Georgia stops. For some reason, this of all things feels like a line crossed.

"She *shut it off?*"

Izzy hasn't stopped. She jogs toward the front of the cart without looking back.

"Yeah. Until tomorrow. She wanted to make sure you didn't leave, I guess."

At the front of the cart, she stops finally to look at Georgia. Georgia looks right back.

"Well, I do want to leave," she says, feeling childish.

"Clearly."

"So, what? You think she's going to try to stop me?"

"That's exactly what I think."

The directness of this answer is so startling, it takes Georgia a moment to react.

"Well, okay. But how? What's she going to do?"

"I don't know. Use your imagination."

"I've never been very imaginative."

Izzy raises an eyebrow, and Georgia feels herself falter. Her anger is not going to save her, and they can both see it.

"So what are we going to do then? Will you take me to the airport?"

"No. She'd find us before you'd get a flight."

Georgia nods, suspecting Izzy is right. She can't imagine there are more flights out this late, which means she would be waiting there until tomorrow.

But would Cecilia really try to stop her there, at the airport? In public?

She thinks of the women in the Diamond and realizes she actually has no idea what Cecilia would do.

"Okay. Right. So what's the plan?"

Izzy frowns, and the thought crosses Georgia's mind that there is no plan. That it's just them and a golf cart and their cell phones without service or Wi-Fi.

But then Izzy says, "The pontoon captain from our snorkeling trip—I know him. He's a good friend. He lives in North Shore. He'll be able to get you to another island tonight."

"The pontoon captain?"

"Pika."

"Excuse me?"

"His name's Pika."

"Oh. Pika. Right."

"Get in," Izzy says, nodding to the golf cart, but Georgia doesn't move. Pika, with the pontoon boat. She looks up at the sky, the swirl of clouds and faraway galaxies, like an ocean. A dark, deep ocean, somehow darker and deeper at night.

"I don't . . ."

"We don't have time, Georgia. Get in."

Georgia doesn't know if it's Izzy voice or the look in her eyes or just the sound of her own name. Whatever the reason, Georgia obeys.

"Not the front," Izzy barks, turning on the ignition. "There are cameras everywhere in the Village. Get in the back."

Georgia nods. This side of Izzy is different, almost comforting. It gives the illusion that *someone* is in charge, at least.

CHAPTER 92

The back of the golf cart is not meant for passengers. It's a flatbed with a black hose curled loosely in the corner.

"Hold on," Izzy says at the same time that she presses on the accelerator. The cart makes a cartoonish squeal as they speed out of the circle. Georgia notices that none of the windows in the other houses are illuminated, and for some reason, this makes her feel very alone.

She bumps and jostles in the back of the cart as they speed down the dimly lit drive. She keeps her eyes trained on the black hose in front of her, which in the shadows looks more like a snake. She tries to conjure Pika in her mind but isn't able. When she thinks of their pontoon trip, all she sees is water.

She lifts her head. In the front seat, Izzy is leaning forward slightly, like a horse jockey. It's so ridiculous, so Bonnie and Clyde, that Georgia feels a laugh swelling up in her chest. It dies there, though, never coming out.

The gates to the Village are open, and the cart doesn't slow on the way by. The main road is smoother than the gravelly driveway, so Georgia stops clanking her head into the side of the bed, at least.

They drive for what seems like forever, although Georgia doesn't check her phone to figure out how long. Finally, the cart starts to slow, and she lifts her head to look around. She thinks she recognizes where they are, but it's hard to tell.

When they come to a stop, Izzy jumps from her seat and grabs her bag.

"Wait," Georgia says, getting her bearings. "This is—"

Izzy turns around. "You stay there."

They're at White Hall, where they did the magic mushrooms. Where three women currently lie in the basement. Or, she's pretty sure that's where they are, although White Hall is tucked into the trees so deeply, she can't be sure. There are no lights here, so Georgia can only see Izzy from the moonlight.

"Are you kidding?" Georgia says. "I'm not staying here."

Izzy sighs loudly.

Georgia says, "I thought we were going to North Shore?"

"No. That's too far for my cart."

"I'm not staying out here by myself."

Izzy seems to consider her for a moment, her lips pinched.

"Fine," she says finally. "Let's go then."

She starts jogging toward the trail, into the dark.

CHAPTER 93

Georgia catches up with her just as they reach the front door of White Hall, which is thankfully illuminated by an overhead light.

"What are we doing here?" she says, panting. She's wearing a sweatshirt, and in the humid night air, she has started to sweat.

"We're calling Pika," Izzy says without turning around.

"Calling Pika? Do you have service?"

"No. No one does here."

"But the Wi-Fi . . ."

Izzy is flipping through her key fobs, leaning in close to read them.

"There's a phone in the Diamond," she says. "A landline. We'll call him from there."

She seems to find the one she's looking for. She swipes it, and the door clicks. She pushes it open to reveal the long, dark hall.

She holds up her phone, using it as a flashlight. Georgia almost suggests turning on the light, but she thinks better of it. There are probably cameras here too.

"Once we get in touch with Pika," Izzy says, motioning for Georgia to follow, which Georgia does, "we'll go meet him somewhere close. My shift will probably be over, but you should have a little more time before they figure out what's happening."

She says this in the same matter-of-fact way she has talked about so much on this island—the headsets, the Phase Two. It was this matter-of-factness that made her so believable.

The thought strikes Georgia suddenly, probably much too late: Can she really be sure Izzy isn't lying to her now? As soon as she thinks it, she can see the rest of it like it all actually happened: Cecilia and Izzy watching Georgia together. Cecilia sending her here, feigning help. Leading her to the Diamond. *The Diamond*, where three women are currently in the basement, unconscious.

She comes to a stop.

"Why are you doing this?" she says, the sharpness in her voice catching even her by surprise.

Izzy stops too. Slowly, she turns around.

"Doing what?" she says.

"Helping me. This. Why would you do this for me?"

As she says this, a second realization hits her: She has no backup plan. She doesn't even know how she'd get back to the main road from here. As Izzy seems to search for an answer, Georgia considers the outrageous, but possibly only, option of getting the golf cart keys from her by force. Will this be the scene of Georgia's very first fight?

"You didn't lie in that story," Izzy says at last, but it's like she's wrestling with something, like she hasn't made up her mind about what to say. "In that article in the *Pacific*. You lied about it happening to you, but the story wasn't a lie. It happened to your friend."

For a moment, Georgia forgets where they are, what they're doing. She can register only what Izzy said. She opens her mouth to protest, but there's a look on Izzy's face that tells her protest would be pointless. And so she doesn't say anything, just presses her lips together.

How does Izzy know this? Did Julie tell her? When? How? Why?

"Cecilia," Izzy says, hearing her unspoken question. "And that partner at your law firm. Daniella, I think her name is. She told Cecilia she thought there was more to your story, and Cecilia got it out of your friend. I mean, she had to. She wasn't going to hire a crazy person, after all."

Georgia's mind is spinning.

She says, stupidly, "It's Dana."

"What?"

"It's Dana, not Daniella."

Izzy frowns.

"But . . . I don't get it. Why do you care? What does that have to do with anything?"

Izzy sucks on her teeth. Around them, the hall is perfectly silent.

"Those women," she says finally, "in the Diamond. It's not fair, what Cecilia did to them. She . . . I don't know. She manipulated them. She pushed them when they were so weak and so confused, and made them think . . ." She trails off, shaking her head. "And she doesn't even want to help them," she adds, her voice turning harder. "She says she does, but if she gets her way, we're not going to help them. We're going to *erase* them. It'll mean nothing, being a mother, and that's what she wants. She wants motherhood to be replaced by this . . . this . . ." She struggles. "This hollow copy of motherhood that means nothing."

She closes her eyes, and for a moment, everything is still. It's so quiet, Georgia can hear her own breath.

"And I can't stop it," she says finally, quietly. "I'm in too deep, and I just . . . can't. I don't know how, and I'm not strong enough. But you . . ."

Georgia stares, waiting for her to finish the sentence. But she doesn't. She lets this hang in the air for a moment before turning back toward the hall.

Georgia wants to stomp her foot. *But me what?* Does Izzy think that *she's* going to stop Cecilia? Why? How? What makes Izzy think she could do that?

"But," she starts, although her voice is drowned out by something, a sound.

The sound of the door.

CHAPTER 94

Ladies," says Cecilia, more of a purr than a word.

From somewhere, a pinched yelp echoes down the hallway. It takes Georgia a second to realize that it came from her.

She whips around. Against the light now pouring in behind her, Cecilia in the doorway is only the shape of a woman, a ghost.

She found them.

How did she find them?

How did they think she would not?

Georgia doesn't think about what to do next. She must escape.

And so she does.

She turns, starts to run. Stumbles. Catches herself. She has the disorienting sensation that she is watching this all from above: herself scrambling. Cecilia in the doorway, featureless with the light to her back.

She passes Izzy and instinctively reaches out. Georgia's impulse is to flee. Izzy's, apparently, is to stand frozen, her expression slack. Georgia pulls at her wrist, but Izzy doesn't move, so Georgia releases it and continues to run.

"Cecilia," Izzy says from behind her, both a question and a plea at once.

At first, there's no response. And then, a thud so loud Georgia nearly trips again, startled by the sound.

She regains her footing and keeps going without turning back around.

At the end of the hallway, she finds herself in the room with the many colored chairs. Near the windows, Logan's egg chair. In front of Georgia, the chaise. She dives behind it. In her ears, there's an ethereal ringing, but around her, silence.

Her heart is beating so fast, she can feel it. She puts a hand to her chest, trying to still herself.

What is she going to do? What is she doing right now? She's not going to outrun Cecilia. Does she need to? Is Cecilia actually a threat?

Well, her answer's in the hallway, isn't it? She heard once, on a true crime podcast, that the sound of a body falling—even a small body—is much louder than you would think, and they're right.

She notices the edges of her vision getting darker suddenly, the world around her tunneling fast. Is she going to pass out? She has never passed out before. At least she wouldn't have to make a decision then, she supposes, and she almost lets out a manic laugh.

And then, through the ringing in her ears, she hears the sound of footsteps. They're soft, unhurried. Not someone running for their life.

"Georgia?" Cecilia says.

Georgia is crouching behind the chaise, and she can't see Cecilia. She doesn't know if Cecilia can see her.

A few more steps, then the sound stops. Another long stretch of silence.

"Georgia?" Cecilia says again. "Georgia, please come out."

There's something almost playful in her voice, and Georgia can envision her face: the beautiful lines of her features, the sharp points of her teeth.

The sound of Cecilia's footsteps again, moving closer. Every muscle in Georgia's body tenses, a spring coiled tight.

Nearer, nearer they come.

And then, past her. Georgia is able to peek past the edge of the furniture, where she sees Cecilia moving to the other side of the room, toward another hallway.

Georgia moves swiftly, silently, back toward the front entrance. She doesn't hear Cecilia behind her, although it's hard to hear much through the sound in her ears. She hurries down the hall, eyes on the door. If she can just get out of this hall, this building. Maybe then she'll have a chance.

She stops.

In front of her is something dark, crumpled.

"Izzy," Georgia breathes.

She bends down. Izzy's eyes aren't open, but she's alive. She's breathing, at least.

"Izzy," she says again, touching her shoulder. She doesn't see an injury—no sign of blood. By her side, out of an open palm, is the ring of key fobs.

And then, behind Georgia, a noise.

Cecilia.

Georgia grabs the fobs. Doesn't think.

Beside her is the door to the Diamond, barely an outline. Visible only if you know where to look.

She swipes, pushes.

Runs.

CHAPTER 95

The walls of the hall are stone, so they echo Georgia's desperate scramble through them. The darkness is disorienting, nightmarish. She is falling as much as she is running.

She's at the spiral staircase when she hears Cecilia behind her.

"Georgia," she calls. It's such a contrast, her voice. A lullaby in the corridors of hell.

Georgia bounds down the stairs, holding tight onto the railing as her feet slide beneath her. She sees the three women in the middle of the room. Around them, the mechanical sound of a breath in, a breath out.

"Georgia," Cecilia calls again. She's at the top of the stairs now, her head cocked, a small smile playing at the corner of her mouth. The red lights shine upward on her face, obscuring her eyes in shadow.

"Georgia, please. Let's stop this."

Cecilia starts down the stairs, one hand lightly on the rail. She isn't running or falling or scared. She lands at the bottom of the staircase with a noiseless step.

Stops.

Georgia looks at her then—really looks at her. Somehow, despite everything, she still doesn't look like a monster.

"Georgia," Cecilia says again, only this time there's an edge. It's not a threat exactly, but a reprimand. The way Georgia might speak to Clover when Clover is being unreasonable.

Georgia takes another step back, and Cecilia's eyes flash. And that's when she realizes where Georgia is headed: the phone.

Georgia reaches out and picks it up.

"*Georgia.*" There's no mistaking it now. This is a threat. Georgia thinks of Izzy, slumped upstairs.

She brings the handset to her ear, the cord from the wall offering only the lightest resistance. On the display, a red button blinks.

"Georgia, I want you to think very carefully about what you're doing," Cecilia says. She has regained her composure, fixed the slight slip of the mask. "Think about what you're doing and what that would mean for you and your family. You are a part of this now. You know that, don't you?"

"I'm not part of this," Georgia snaps, surprising herself. It's pointless to argue this here, with her.

"Aren't you, though?" Cecilia says gently. "Will anyone believe that? Believe *you*, Georgia? It'll be my word against yours, and how many people, Georgia, are still willing to believe your word after everything you've lied about?"

Georgia opens her mouth, but she can't say anything because she knows—the same way Cecilia knows—that she's right.

"It was tough for you these past few months," Cecilia says, taking another step closer. "Now imagine what you will be putting your family through, being associated with something like *this*."

And in her mind, Georgia can see it: the red bra on her garage door. Her phone, pages and pages of cruel messages filling the screen. The woman at the airport. The drink in her lap.

"You can leave," Cecilia says softly, taking a step forward. "I won't stop you. You can leave now and be free of this."

She thinks of Julie in her office, right after her assault in the nursing room. The dazed look on her face. She was trembling, and when she looked at Georgia, she was looking right through her. Georgia thought, then, that she looked so young. She thought, *She could be anyone. Anyone's mother, anyone's daughter.*

She could be mine.

She reaches for the dial pad.

"Georgia." Cecilia's voice is higher now, and Georgia hears the panic. She thinks of Izzy, upstairs in the hallway.

"I'm sorry," Georgia says, and the strange thing is, she actually means it.

That's when Cecilia starts to lunge.

CHAPTER 96

What happens next seems to happen all at once. Cecilia coming toward her. And then not coming toward her. Making a small, almost comical *oomph*.

Cecilia on the ground—two people on the ground. Two individual bodies.

"Izzy," Georgia says dumbly.

Izzy looks up. She's splayed out over Cecilia's body, and there's something slightly repulsive about it, like an animal over its prey. Under her, Cecilia appears unconscious.

"Well?" says Izzy. "Are you going to call them or what?"

"Call . . . who?" Georgia feels disoriented. She thought Izzy was hurt upstairs.

"The cops. You're calling the cops, aren't you?" Izzy is wheezing as much as she's talking.

Georgia looks down to the phone in her hand, remembering. Actually, she wasn't going to call the cops. She was going to call Will, which in hindsight was not the best option. She makes a horrible criminal, and an even more horrible hostage.

She looks back to Izzy, who has seemingly just registered that Cecilia is unconscious beneath her. She scrambles to her feet, looking horrified.

"I just tackled her," she says, but it sounds like she's talking to herself. She holds up her own hands to look at them, befuddled. "I just *tackled* Cecilia."

She meets Georgia's eyes like she's looking for confirmation.

"Yes," Georgia says. "But she was going to hurt me."

"She was going to hurt you," Izzy repeats, but her voice is hollow. She presses her eyes closed hard and touches her temples. "She was going to hurt you."

Georgia can't tell what she's doing. Is she trying to convince herself? Is her brain broken? Should they call for the police or for an ambulance?

Izzy opens her eyes, and when they find Georgia, the fog in them is gone.

"*Was* she going to hurt you?"

"Yes. I mean, I think she was. She hurt you."

Izzy shakes her head. "She didn't hurt me."

"But upstairs . . ."

"I fainted. I faint when I'm shocked."

"Oh," Georgia says. That would've been a crucial piece of information to have earlier.

In unison, their eyes fall to Cecilia. She seems to be breathing, but there's a hairline trace of blood coming from her nose.

"I tackled her," Izzy whispers, and Georgia wishes she would stop. It isn't helping. It's actually making things worse.

"*I* tackled her," Izzy says a second time, only this time she looks at Georgia hard. "Who knows what happened down here? An argument. Something. I was with Cecilia, and I tackled her, or I pushed her, and she hit the ground."

Her eyes are wide and meaningful. Georgia doesn't understand what she's saying.

Until she does.

"No, Izzy," she says, but Izzy shakes her head vehemently.

"You have a family. Two daughters. And you . . ." She takes a deep breath, and in it, her face hardens, as though she has decided something. "You were asleep in your house in the Village when it happened."

"Izzy . . ." Georgia says, but Izzy holds up a hand, and for a horrible instant, it seems like she might cry.

She doesn't, though. Her voice is steady and clear when she says, "Go, now. Go back home, where you were asleep. You didn't know about any of this."

PART FOUR

CHAPTER 97

It's been one week since Georgia returned from the island—one week since The Program shut down temporarily, although most speculate it's for good. First to leave was Cecilia, whom the paramedics carted away with screaming sirens. Everyone else was quick to follow after that.

There were no public announcements about what happened, although that didn't stop the news from leaking. It started immediately, although it came bit by bit. First, that there had been a medical emergency. Then, that Cecilia was in critical condition. Then came the rumors about who was there and what had happened—that Cecilia had fallen, and possibly how. And after that . . .

"Will," Georgia whispers into the darkness now. They're in bed, and it's very late. They both should be asleep, although Georgia feels like she hasn't slept in a week.

She holds her breath, not knowing if he heard her. Will's week hasn't been any easier than hers, but unlike Georgia, he is able to sleep.

She has resigned herself to the fact that he is sleeping when his voice breaks through the darkness.

"Yeah?"

She swallows, her throat already thick.

"I was just thinking," she says, her voice brittle. "What if Cecilia would've let me go? In the Diamond?"

She bites her finger, which he can't see. He clears his throat. The sound is raspy, and she wonders if she did wake him up.

"What?"

"What if Cecilia let me go? She said she was going to. What if she was telling the truth? What if she was never going to hurt me?"

They've had this conversation already. They had it the first night, then every night after in some variation or another. In the beginning, it was Will asking, mostly—collecting information, attempting to understand exactly what had happened that night. And Georgia told him, as honestly as she could. The problem is, as the days march forward, she feels less and less sure herself.

"I don't know, Gi," he says, not unkindly, but he sounds exhausted. "It's possible, I guess. But it's also possible she *would've* hurt you. I mean, look what she did to those other women. She was obviously capable of it."

Georgia knows what he means by *those other women*: Dede and the two with her, Wendy and Christine. Christine was in the hospital for only a day after they woke her. Dede is still there.

"I was scared," Georgia says, the same thing she has repeated over and over in her head since that night. She's disappointed that it sounds exactly the same said out loud. "We both were. We *thought* she was going to hurt us. We didn't mean to . . ."

But she can't say the rest of it. She can't say *kill her*.

"I know," Will says, but his voice is lost now in her crying. She's crying so hard, she can't hear him as he rolls over, doesn't realize he has until he reaches out and pulls her in.

"Shh," he says into her hair, but she doesn't.

She cries for Cecilia, who deserved a lot of things, but not the ending they gave her. Not the undignified way she went, her head hitting the cement at just the right angle with just the right level of impact. *A perfect accident,* they would say online later, which would really only make things worse. An obvious killing, at least, would be straightforward. There would be nothing to speculate about in that case. Now, no one knows for sure what actually happened, the only guaranteed way for everyone to have an opinion on what did.

But of course, she's not just crying for Cecilia. She's also crying for Izzy, who hasn't been officially charged with anything but also hasn't not been charged yet. Izzy, who forced the golf cart keys into her hand just before the ambulance arrived. Georgia sped away from the scene, away from one version of her life and into another. And the truth is, she's crying for that woman too, even if that woman is the last one who deserves it. She cries for how that woman's life might've gone, the alternate way things could've turned out. Because what if she hadn't run when Cecilia first met them in the hallway? What if she hadn't hidden? Maybe Cecilia would've hurt her, but maybe she wouldn't have. Maybe, if she had done something differently, the ending would've changed.

"Gi," Will says, once her crying has dissolved into pitiful hiccups. "Gi, listen to me. Don't do this to yourself, okay? You did the best you could at the time, and it sucks what happened, but part of that is on Cecilia. Okay? You need to believe that."

She nods into his chest. She does believe that, but it doesn't help.

"I just feel so bad for Izzy," she says, and with these words, another sob. "She . . ."

But she can't finish the sentence. How could she? How do you capture with language how it feels when someone has saved your life?

CHAPTER 98

On the ninth day after Georgia's return from the island, Julie invites Georgia over to her house.

At first, Georgia doesn't want to go. She wasn't officially implicated in Cecilia's death, but that is an uninteresting detail to the media in front of their house. They've been camped out there for over a week now, although thankfully they've recently started to dwindle. Now only a couple of vans arrive each morning, and even they leave for lunch.

Georgia doesn't want to go, but Will thinks she should. It's a Saturday, so he's not working, and today not even the last straggling vans have shown up. (A few days ago, to everyone's horror, one came to Will's school. The police were called. The reporter didn't look ashamed.)

In the end, she decides to go because she doesn't have anything else to do. She goes because Ruby is sleeping and Clover is practicing her reading with Will on the couch. Because she can't browse the internet or turn on the TV without seeing Cecilia. Because she's getting tired of walking the halls of her house like a ghost.

She gets ready to leave, but as soon as she steps out the front door, one of the vans reappears. Someone, a reporter, recognizes the opportunity and nearly falls from the front seat before the van even comes to a stop.

"Georgia Evans?" he says, waving a hand as though she could've possibly missed him. Georgia stops dead in her tracks, her entire body cold. The van is big and purple. The reporter has a lot of gel in his hair. She realizes she can't say anything. She's paralyzed.

"Hey," comes someone's voice from over the boxwoods, and both Georgia and the reporter look over as one. There stands Darla Hildebrandt in her driveway, holding her keys, dressed like she's about to go to the gym. Georgia hasn't talked to Darla since returning from the island, although she suspects her neighbors are not happy with her. The media isn't there to see them, but they've had to wade through the vans at the end of their driveways regardless.

"Yeah, you," Darla says to the reporter, pointing. "You're media?"

The reporter clears his throat. "Yeah. WBAC."

"Right. Well, would you do me a favor and kindly fuck off?"

The reporter raises his eyebrows. If Georgia were in a different situation, she might laugh.

Darla adds, "And that's on the record, if it helps."

For a moment, it seems like he might resist her, although in the end, there's something about Darla he seems to find persuasive. He gives Georgia one last longing look before climbing back into his van.

Georgia, too shaken still to be embarrassed, meets her neighbor's eyes over the shrubs.

"Thank you," she says.

Darla just smiles.

Julie lives in a cute, quiet townhome on a cute, quiet street in Adams Morgan. Georgia has been here only once before, for Julie's baby shower last year.

As she ascends the front stoop now, she thinks back to the day and how much easier life was, even if it didn't feel easy at the time. At the time, Georgia was very pregnant with Ruby, and she was running behind on her billable hour requirement. Also, Clover was dealing with a seemingly never-ending series of ear infections, for which the pediatrician was threatening tubes in her ears. (In the end, they did end up getting the tubes, which was a quick and easy procedure and helped the ear infections immensely.)

She wonders now if there's any possibility that she will look back on *this* time in her life and think it was easier than it seemed at the time. (She seriously doubts this.)

She contemplates ringing the doorbell, but in the end she knocks.

"Thanks for knocking," Julie says when she answers. "I *just* got Heath down."

Georgia smiles and lets Julie usher her into the house, which is just so Julie with all its vintage secondhand furniture and its fabulous ensemble of wallpaper.

"Hi," Julie says, pulling her in for a hug. She smells the way she always does, like soap and citrus. Georgia thinks of Julie mostly as a work friend, although in her home now, she realizes that she has always been more than that.

"How are you doing?" Julie says. "And how's Ruby? Diabetes! I didn't even get to talk to you about that. On top of everything." She shakes her head. "That must've been so scary."

She motions for Georgia to lead the way inside.

"It was scary," Georgia says as they enter the kitchen, as Julie silently instructs her to sit down. "It was actually terrifying."

At the kitchen island, Julie leans on her elbows, her eyes wide with attention.

"I can't imagine," she says.

"Me neither, honestly. It all still kind of feels like a dream."

"But are you guys managing now? Is it getting any easier?"

"Oh yeah, we are. I mean, whole grain pasta is actually atrocious, but other than that, I think we're okay."

Julie gives her a half smile, as though unsure whether they're allowed to joke about this yet.

"Do you want coffee?" she says, standing up. "Or tea? I've got that minty kind you like."

"Oh, I'd love some of that, thanks."

As Julie busies herself with the kettle, Georgia absorbs the room around her, so quaint and cute but interrupted nearly everywhere with baby things: a kitschy plastic high chair, a pile of blocks by the door. By her sink is an arrangement of sippy cups.

"So," Julie says once the kettle is on. She crosses the kitchen and lowers herself into the chair across from Georgia. "You've probably had a hell of a week."

"Not my best," Georgia agrees.

"That's a milder assessment than I was expecting."

"You're right. I've had postpartum hemorrhoids more enjoyable than this."

This time, Julie allows herself to smile fully. It fades quickly though as she looks down to her nails.

"Well, I don't know if this is going to be good news or bad then," she says, speaking to her hands instead of Georgia. "But I wanted to tell you before I did it." She looks up, meeting Georgia's eyes with an unexpected intensity. "I've decided to come forward about everything."

She says this a bit too loudly, so when she's finished talking, the room seems extra quiet. She's still looking at Georgia, although the intensity behind her eyes has faltered. Georgia realizes she's expecting her to say something, although she doesn't know what to say except, "Oh."

Julie flinches at this, and Georgia has the sense that she should correct herself. She doesn't know what else to say, though. She doesn't know how to feel.

"You must be pissed," Julie says at last. "Are you pissed that I'm doing this now? When I said I couldn't before?"

Georgia thinks about this very seriously for a moment. Is she pissed? Has she *ever* been pissed at Julie about this? She doesn't know really. For the most part, she hasn't allowed herself to feel angry, mostly because she didn't feel like she deserved anger. After all, Julie didn't *make* her do what she did. That day in her office, the day that started everything, Julie only told Georgia that she knew a reporter at the *Pacific* who had an "idea for a story." It was a story that would be big, everyone agreed, and Julie wanted to help. She wanted to tell her story "to use what happened to me for some good."

This surprised Georgia, because up until that point, Julie had been too afraid to do *anything* about it. She didn't want to press charges. She didn't even want to report the man who did it. "It'll be my word against his," she would say, "and even if they believe me, what will happen then?" And she was right, of course. Even if people believed her, even if she had the full weight of the truth on her side, there was so much for her to lose just by coming forward. And as a single mother of a new baby, Julie had nothing to spare.

This article, though, seemed to resonate with her. "It would make it *mean* something, you know? Like it wasn't all a waste." She wanted to do it, but she was also scared—scared that someone would eventually connect the dots, and that all the dots would lead back to her (a fear that wasn't totally unfounded, as it would turn out).

And yet, Julie never *asked* Georgia to do it. "I just don't know if I can," she said that day in her office, and due to some ancient instinct or some deep, abiding flaw, Georgia said, "Let me tell it then."

Georgia shakes her head slowly now. On the burner, the teakettle starts to hiss.

"I'm not mad," she says, and it's not a lie. Maybe she should have been angry—with the *Pacific*, or with Julie, or at the very least, with herself—but it was never *anger* she felt. She felt stupid. She felt broken. But she didn't feel mad. "But I don't get it. Why now?"

Julie doesn't answer for a moment. She looks different from the last time Georgia saw her, although it's hard to say exactly how. Her cheeks, maybe, which have a bit more color. This, though, could simply be the natural recuperation after having a child.

"Well, you, I guess," Julie says finally. "You've gone through hell. There were so many times I was like, *She's going to tell them. She's going to say it was me, and then my name will be out there*. And I wouldn't have blamed you. I mean, what you went through . . ."

Her voice trails off, her gaze distant. Georgia suspects she knows what's going through her head: the bras, both of them. The horrible things written underneath in chalk. And Julie doesn't even know the full story, all the things Georgia has gone through: the exact number of messages on her phone, the woman at the airport with the drink.

"But you didn't," Julie says at last, seeming to come back. "You kept my secret and kept me safe. And I just . . ." Her voice breaks. She clears her throat and shakes her head, a silent pep talk. "I just figured, if you were strong enough to do all that, then I can be strong enough to do this."

Behind them on the stove, the teakettle has started to shake. Neither of them looks at it. Georgia stares at Julie, and Julie stares right back.

"I wasn't that strong," Georgia says. "I was a mess."

"They're not mutually exclusive."

But Georgia shakes her head. She's surprised by the feeling rising in her: anger, finally.

"No, Julie. You don't . . ." In her mind, she sees Izzy crouched over Cecilia. Cecilia, the last time they saw her. Her hair had been pulled back into a bun, but during the fall, a chunk around her face had broken loose. She looked so disheveled on the stretcher, her hair an uncharacteristic mess. Somehow, it seemed like Cecilia would be more upset about this than about being dead.

"What I did wasn't some great act of courage," Georgia says finally, fighting to stay in control of the anger, in control of her voice. "What I did, didn't make sense. What I did was stupid. All I did was make a huge, catastrophic mess."

At last, the steam in the kettle hits a breaking point. It starts to scream.

Julie jumps up and moves it from the burner. She waits for a second, and Georgia knows exactly what she's doing: waiting to see if it woke Heath up.

When the cries don't come, Julie comes back to the table without pouring the water into the cups. Georgia can feel the anger leaving her already, seeping through her cracks the way it always does. She doesn't deserve to feel angry about this, about what happened. She has no one to blame for it but herself.

"What you did *didn't* make sense," Julie says, her voice steady. If she feels targeted by Georgia's outburst, she is not upset. "You sacrificed yourself for someone else, so no, that's not really rational, but don't tell me it's not courageous."

Georgia opens her mouth to argue, but Julie talks over her.

"And yeah, you made a huge mess. You ruined that woman's research. She'll never get to—I don't know. *Study* anyone else. She'll never make a motherhood pill, or whatever her plan was. You destroyed that whole program, her entire life's work."

Her entire life's work. It's so sad to think about it that way, that not only did Cecilia the woman die, but so did Cecilia the idea. Maybe she deserved it. Still, it's hard for Georgia not to think of Cecilia as just another victim, if only a victim of her own bad ideas.

Georgia doesn't realize she's crying again until Julie touches her hand, until she looks up and meets her friend's eyes, which are clear.

"You made a mess, Georgia," she whispers. "A huge, catastrophic one. And thank God for that."

~

In the car outside Julie's house later, Georgia sits in the driver's seat, her keys on her lap. She didn't finish her tea before Heath woke up, babbling away in his crib. Georgia held the baby for only a few minutes, admiring how big and happy he was, before saying she had to go. Julie poured the rest of her tea into a cardboard cup and hugged her before she left.

The cup is now in the cupholder beside her. In one hand, she holds her phone, and in the other, a business card. The one she's kept in her purse for over a week now. It's from the FBI investigator in charge of Cecilia's case back in Hawaii, the same one he gave to every employee before they left.

She almost threw the card away in the airport. And later at home, she almost threw it away again, along with the key fob cloner and the cloned fobs. But she didn't. She kept it tucked in the tiny pocket of her shell purse, just in case.

In her mind, she hears Julie. *Don't tell me it's not courageous.* It's not so different from what Izzy said the night of Cecilia's death. How is it that they both said this, and yet Georgia doesn't recognize the woman they're describing as herself?

She takes a deep breath and dials. Will answers after barely one ring.

"Everything all right?" he says instead of a greeting. She wonders how long until he won't have to ask this.

"Yeah. Well, I mean, no, but no less all right than this morning."

"Well," Will says, but he doesn't know what else to say, so the word just hangs. Georgia decides she's better off just telling him. At this point, there's no need to sugarcoat things.

When she's finished, she's surprised by both the speed and the simplicity of his answer.

"If you think it's the right thing to do," is all he says. Somehow, after everything that's happened, he still trusts her. The question, as usual, is whether she trusts herself.

And does she trust herself? It's been two days since her Phase Two prescription ran out, two days since her last pill. She hasn't refilled the prescription, wouldn't know how to even if she wanted to. And in just two days, she can feel herself coming back already. It turns out that using your mom brain is a lot like riding a bike.

The most surprising part is how she feels about this. How the only word she can use to describe it is shockingly, shamefully, *grief*. And yet, that's what it is. She grieves the loss of who she was . . . or, more accurately, who she imagined herself being. She grieves for the future she thought could be hers, even if that future was never real to begin with.

She looks down at the card, turns it over in her hand. She knows what will happen if she calls it. She knows how it feels to be hated by a sea of faceless people. For them to find her at home, find her in public. And because she knows all this, you would think she would know whether it'll be worth it. She might help Izzy clear her name, but will that tip the balance? Will it be worth what she'll inevitably lose?

With Phase Two, she would know the answer. With Phase Two, this math would be clear.

But now?

She looks down to the phone in her hand.

And then she dials.

"This is Georgia Evans," she says to the man who answers. "I'm a former employee at The Program. You asked us to call if we had any information about Cecilia Clements, and I do. I'm calling because I want to tell you the truth about what happened."

And then she tells him. She tells him, but it's not without fear, because the truth is, she doesn't know if she's making the right decision. She can't, not with her mom brain, which doesn't work the way it used to with its complicated tangles of fear and love. It's a messy thing, the head of a mother.

And thank God it is.

ACKNOWLEDGMENTS

I started writing this book in late 2021, shortly after having my daughter. Although it was my second time around, the postpartum experience didn't fail to shock me. Apart from the usual shocks that come with growing and caring for a brand-new human, it was shocking how *changed* I felt, like I was a totally different person from who I was before having kids. It was around this time that I came across the book *Mom Genes* by Abigail Tucker, which details the (arguably scant, definitely late, but nonetheless necessary) research into what happens to a woman's brain once she becomes a mother. That book, along with *Mother Nature* by Sarah Blaffer Hrdy, provided the inspiration for much of the "research" used by The Program in my novel. While my book fictionalizes the real research, I tried to keep the heart of the science intact, so I owe an enormous debt of gratitude to both of these authors and their books. (Of course, any technical errors in *Mom Brain* are completely my own!)

When it comes to shaping the science into a story, I first owe a huge thank-you to Sam Hiyate of The Rights Factory. Sam, I'm forever grateful for the years you were my agent and editor, and for the years ahead with you as my friend. Also a big thanks to Kat Foxx for guiding both me and my book on its journey into the world, and to everyone at The Rights Factory who had a hand in this project, including Claire Cavanagh, Chloe Robinson, and Maria Donati.

Endless gratitude to my editor, Laura Wheeler, for just "getting" both the heart and the humor of my writing, and for helping me say exactly what I meant. *Thank you* doesn't feel like enough! Also a huge thanks to Caitlin Halstead for being a champion of this book from the beginning. And of course, bringing a book into the world is not totally dissimilar from mothering little humans: It takes a village. I am so thankful for my village, the whole Harper Muse team, particularly Matt Baugher, Kimberly Carlton, Hannah Harless, Sicily Lippincott, and Kevin Smith. Thank you, thank you, thank you!

My writing would not be what it is without the help of my critique partner and friend, Jaclyn Goldis. Jaclyn, you continually amaze me with your wisdom in writing and beyond. Also a special thank-you to Amy Nizzere, who has been with NicoleHackettBooks before NicoleHackettBooks was even NicoleHackettBooks. Thank you for sticking with me through all these years and for the many, many words of mine you've read along the way!

I also want to thank Erika, Andrea, and Hannah, who were my best friends long before they became my "mom friends." Thank you, guys, for the years of loving and encouraging me at my lowest points and celebrating with me at my highest (even if it meant traveling across the country to do so). And of course, a book about motherhood could not be written without the "Mom Chat": Abby, Anah, Ashley, Brooke, Jen, Kim, Lindsey, Lisa, Meaghan, Nicole, Rachael, Rebecca, and Santana. This book is a work of fiction, but I'm sure you'll recognize parts of it from very real texts I've sent over the years. Thank you for reminding me that I'm not alone, that I'm not crazy (well, mostly not crazy), and that my mom brain can indeed be a superpower.

When it comes to encouragement, you can't get better than my family. I love all of you very, very much.

In particular, I want to mention Aunt Laurie and Aunt Marcy, probably the two most engaged NicoleHackettBooks Instagram followers on the internet, and Kim Patro, for showing up for me and my books in the most literal way. I am so blessed by each of you!

I also need to thank Sam, aka "Aunt Sam," for being my coolest cheerleader and my children's second favorite person in the world after Uncle Zach's beard. Sam, I don't take for granted how lucky I am to have you as my sister. Also a big shout-out to Zach, owner of the beard among many admirable qualities. Zach, I've considered you family for years now, but the moment you walked up those stairs to DJ Khaled at Wrightsville Beach, I knew you were truly one of us.

I also want to thank my brother, who makes me think about things—including plot points!—in ways I otherwise wouldn't. Thank you for being you, Nathan!

And of course, I could never write a book without thanking my parents. Mom and Dad, whatever I achieve in life is only possible because I have you as my foundation. *Thank you* doesn't come close to what I want to say, but it's a start.

I've dedicated this book to women, but like everything I do, it's also for my kids. Noodles, nothing I've ever done (or will ever do) is more important than being your mom. I love you beyond words.

And finally, forever, my husband. Derrick, I am only the mom I am because of the dad you are, the wife I am because of the husband you are, and the author I am because of the partner you are. I worry I juggle these things much too messily at times, but I never worry about who I'm juggling them with.

DISCUSSION QUESTIONS

1. What connotations come to mind when you hear the term *mom brain*? Where do you think those connotations come from, and do you think they reflect reality?
2. What do you think about the conclusions Cecilia drew from the rat mothers? If you are a mother, do those conclusions ring at all true based on your experience?
3. If the women in the Diamond really did give their consent, was Cecilia's research on them unethical?
4. What do you think Izzy meant when she said that Cecilia's goal is to replace motherhood with a "hollow copy of motherhood that means nothing"?
5. When Cecilia introduced Phase Three to Georgia, she referred to the people who might want the new drug as *mothers* even though they had presumably never had children. Do you think this word choice validates Izzy's understanding of Cecilia's mission, and if so, do you think Izzy's feelings about the mission were justified?
6. Cecilia is portrayed as the villain in this story. However, if Cecilia truly believed that her mission was in women's best interest, do you think that's the correct way to think of her?
7. Do you think Georgia would ever take Phase Two again if she had the opportunity?

From the Publisher

GREAT BOOKS

ARE EVEN BETTER WHEN THEY'RE SHARED!

Help other readers find this one:

- Post a review at your favorite online bookseller
- Post a picture on a social media account and share why you enjoyed it
- Send a note to a friend who would also love it—or better yet, give them a copy

Thanks for reading!

ABOUT THE AUTHOR

Nicole Hackett lives with her husband and two kids in Maryland, where she works as a biochemical patent agent. She is the author of the "cleverly constructed thriller" (*Kirkus Reviews*) *The Perfect Ones* and is one of those annoying people who run on vacation.

Connect with her online at nicolehackettbooks.com
Instagram: @nicolehackettbooks
Facebook: @nicolehackettbooks